A WEB OF DELUSION

BARRY MERCHANT

Spiderwize
Peterborough
2019

IN MEMORY:

Bhante Urgyen Sangharashita
(1936-2018)

Derek Merchant
(1936-2006)

John Merchant
(1940-2015)

CHAPTER ONE

Henrietta Marlow used to walk nonchalantly around Heatherslade as though she owned the wealthy place. When you were slim and attractive, with an oversized ego which scanned all the available men in sight, all was possible. Even some of the old men were rather excited by the appearance of the long-haired youngster. She wore clothes that were so tight that even they fell in love, or rather, were besotted with such crude sexuality for the first time in fifty years.

These occasional morning forays somewhat trimmed her thoughts, if not her physical beauty, allowing her to focus more on her job. Management, computers, basic bookkeeping – it wasn't the sort of employment that the international local jet-set would take seriously. But such work gave her the opportunity to exercise her sexual prowess over unsuspecting male clients; those who were naive enough to throw their employer's money at the services she peddled rather skilfully.

Within a few weeks of walking the same paths in her usual provocative, crotch hugging attire, she became acutely aware of a village stuck in time. Where the bloody hell had her parents brought her to live? she continuously thought. The only people she did notice that gave her a nod or wry smile, were old people with large dilapidated houses. It was an ideal place to latch on to some old rich codger, to look after him the only way she knew how. She might just end up with chattels beyond her wildest dreams. Curtains rustled a few inches when she passed some houses. Could it have been wives sizing up the opposition? Henrietta's ego demanded that it was the old men who were motivated by early morning brandy, drooling at the goddess sent to them by their maker. It was known that men were calling her Aurora, the Goddess of dawn - all hoping to be kidnapped and live under her heavenly spell.

Henrietta rarely ventured into the local pub for an early coffee. Most mornings by 11am it was full of retired men wearing their hand sewn suits and institutional ties. They had plenty of money and lots of stories to tell for anyone insane enough to listen. It usually brought a large scotch too for the latter! After a lifetime of action, those old fuddy-duddies deserved the few congratulations that were begrudgingly bestowed upon them by lesser mortals. Time faded quickly though. Most of them were overweight, short sighted, talked to themselves incessantly and greeted most friendly customers with a melodious loud fart. Only the inner circle, no doubt!

No sooner had Ms Marlow entered the pub than the men would fight to buy her a drink. She always declined alcohol but knew that coffee would flow her way in abundance if she required it. She loved to tease the chaps to the verge of delirium as French scent enveloped every nook and cranny. Obsolete virile sperm came to life once again when Henrietta was around. High blood pressures and potential heart attacks waited impatiently up in the rotten rafters waiting for the call.

'It is my turn to buy coffee for our most precious young woman,' shouted Ian Murray, a regular drinker and an ardent leading fraterniser of the unofficial fan club of the village's most sexy female.

'Other than me Henrietta, what will you have?' asked the tall, mild mannered, former accountant who had resided locally for many years.

'Latte, please,' she replied.

'How are you keeping Ms Marlow?' asked George Biddlecombe, another regular who prayed that she would come into the pub, if only for a short while, to give them all a rare female smile.

'I'm fine thank you,' she said as she sat herself down on an armchair ten feet or so away from the men drinking at the bar.

The barman brought her coffee to the table where she sat. As she sipped the drink slowly, she fantasized that she was drinking vodka, scotch, soda or any other strong beverage. She didn't want local people to know about her private social life.

'You look rather pretty in light green today. I must say your clothes are always.......'

'Now, now Edward, my dear boy, you must not go over the top,' heckled Herbert.

'Only admiring Miss Marlow's attire,' said Edward Sutcliffe, yet another retiree and pub drinker who was fascinated with the new village attraction.

'How is your work Henrietta?' asked Ian Murray, who would no doubt have sold his chattels and goods to have spent just a few hours alone with the beauty in front of him.

'Very well, thank you,' she replied. Her policy had

always been not to tell them anything personal. She kept it straightforward and kept them guessing. She had held this secretive attitude towards most people since she could remember, but was especially careful when talking to the old codgers - as she nick-named them.

'Never see you with any men friends Henrietta,' commented Herbert.

'There are plenty, I can assure you,' she tantalisingly informed the men. One man in particular excited her feelings.

However, unbeknown to all except her immediate family, she was immensely frustrated with her shallow village existence. She was young, gregarious and full of drive and energy that cried for creative expression. One man in particular made her life painful.

Meanwhile, Henrietta stayed away as much as possible from the local roads, unless she had no choice but to drive. The small old village of Heatherslade had been beset with traffic problems for years. Every morning and most evenings, huge continental lorries and road haulage motorway trucks with mountainous heaps of varying unwanted rubbish, coaches and other vehicles pounded the village's feeble infrastructure. Fumes from those terrifying monsters shrouded and choked the place. This once comfortable oasis of peace, which according to the Domesday Book dated back to 1071, urgently needed some sort of bypass to be built a few miles to the south before the whole edifice came tumbling down around its ageing population.

Besides the daily frustration of sitting in a stationary vehicle, there was a much more colourful world to experience only feet away. Depending on the time of year, the verges were usually full of flowers smiling at those willing to look. The divine scents of primrose, daffodil, elder and buddleia, rose above the smell of choking fumes. Singing birds were not going to be drowned by the incessant noise of vehicles either. Blackbirds could be heard most mornings. Moving clouds, accompanied by the whispers of winds, often witnessed drivers with heavy workloads, unpaid bills and other human woes, which for a time could be forgotten. Your days were numbered if you suffered from a long-term lung, respiratory or similar chronic condition. It was the pollution that could harm her body that most frightened Henrietta Marlow. She wrote, phoned, emailed and generally gave the local and parish councils her thoughts on the matter.

The village consisted of sixty or so mansions, detached houses, bungalows and modern assortments of residences. Some of the owners, and they were all owned, had one way or another managed to inherit. No doubt their respective individual well-off estates were increased considerably by personal tax allowances being increased by government in the 1980s! In several cases, it was not known who a particular dwelling had originally belonged to. It was said that even some, if not most, of the local 19th century censuses were rather misleading, which added to the mystery of Heatherslade. But that is best left to history. Local people grappled with their own living problems.

Sundays were the highlight of the week, when gallons of alcohol would be consumed by the old residents who congregated in the only village public house to be found, to the delights of its users, within several miles. Former bank managers, senior civil servants, barristers, sea captains and a menagerie of the great and good would sit on their bulging backsides for hours in The Willow Tree Pub, to wallow, as usual, in their former glory. Their former great deeds, if that is what they were, took second best only to the pictures of the scowling face of Churchill looking down upon them with terrifying scorn. That is, of course, except when most of them drove their dilapidated cars a hundred yards to the local Anglican church of All Angels for two hours to pray for more income and a brief, scandalous word with Reverend Bullchat. By contrast, the ageing spinsters, though reluctantly, placed a few pounds in the church donation box before hurrying their skin and bones back to their homes.

The Parish Council was made up of some of the influential residents, men such as Captain Fox-Rice. Aged 74 and Chairman of the Highways Committee, he claimed to have sailed into every port in the world and left offspring whenever or wherever possible. Such a statement was perfectly plausible for a person known to get just what he wanted, regardless of the consequences. Short, fat and arrogant, he summed up the inept council's lazy, irresponsible and indecisive attitude over not deciding to make the decision to resolve the local vehicle debacle. Seated upon the comfortable well sprung pub armchair, the Captain, with meritocracy in mind, surveyed his immediate surroundings to see who he could give an ear bashing. He was more than keen to spread his worldly wisdom. On such occasions he was no doubt reminded of his hero, Lord Nelson, whose life sized monument adorned the exceptionally attractive rear garden of Fox-Rice's large inherited house.

There was suggestion, though most denied it, that the Captain, and a now deceased villager – one Colonel Mabbutt – had tried unsuccessfully to purchase prime, local farming land with the intention of developing a large private housing estate. One or two old souls still remembered the vociferous attack on landowning gentry, who at the time resided elsewhere. If the application had not been rejected by the council, the pair stood to make millions out of the deal.

'Well hello there my dear boy. How are you Herbert? I've not seen you since the last Parish meeting. What's your poison?' he asked in a well-meaning, yet underhand sort of way. It was the kind of attitude that implied Herbert should be doing something rather more productive like sorting out the Highway's problems.

'Hello Bob, how are you? I've not yet recovered from that grilling you gave all the councillors two weeks ago regarding the local road progress, or rather lack of it. Anyway, I'll have a scotch and soda, and as you are in the boat, a large one for me.'

'Coming up dear boy,' he shouted to his fellow councillor and long-time friend Herbert Tate, who at 73 looked very well and healthy after a life of action at sea himself.

Although a decent chap, Herbert Tate had this pathological desire to tell idiotic jokes parrot fashion. Consequently, many gave him short shrift until they began to understand that he was harmless, although given the chance, like many lurking around the village he had a Lenin like mentality and dreamt of being unleashed. After all, thirty years of action could torment the mind into carrying out revengeful delusional ideas

7

on people yet unheard of. One got the impression that Tate was a fitness fanatic, hence his well-built body and pre-occupation with self-preservation. He gave the impression that he was very capable of looking after himself. In fact, some of the village men, although past their best, had been trained to kill. It was probable that some still owned guns hidden away in home-made fortresses. Outer appearances could be deceptive.

'Tough going sorting out the old pub Tate?' asked Hector Munro, a 78-year-old former barrister who had grafted for months painting, bricklaying and labouring on the local pub.

'Certainly was Hector. Some days I could have fought a bull to the death I was so pumped up. It must have been thoughts of the Marlow girl that so inspired me,' he concluded.

'Now, now Tate, that's enough of that,' replied John Wrightson, a big, burly, bald former senior civil servant, who had served under several prime ministers.

'It was a pity we didn't get old Bob digging a few holes in his hot pants and pink socks. Hey lads?' said Herbert Tate, smiling as he gestured at the parish council Chairman, who was pre-occupied with more important matters.

'Always so busy my dear boy sorting out parish problems,' said Fox-Rice seriously, though his waking life consisted of boozing or gardening. A large variety of spirits - not the heavenly sort - were to be found in his shed discreetly hidden amongst the tools, plants and ubiquitous garden gnomes.

It was a large money saving job that Tate and a few other die-hards had undertaken to complete the renovations of the local 17th century inn from a run down, shabby unused drinking house into a comfortable, modern meeting place now providing an extensive a la carte menu. He had also tried to be active in other useful ways – but wasn't quite able to convince some of the older women of that! He was, nonetheless, as keen as mustard and well worthy of being a representative councillor -as were his fellow colleagues, all had different qualities which would help the bigger picture.

Whether they had Tate in mind was not known, but even the old spinsters would occasionally drift into the upgraded pub, some dressed in their grandmother's clothes. They were conditioned not to waste money, and usually ordered only one glass of Empire sherry. They returned quickly to their twilight world back home, before other less sympathetic eyes thought they were on the lookout for a decrepit 80 year old husband to look after them. How cruel the passing of the years could be.

Due to its sinister and colourful history, the Willow Tree had had many different names and owners. Most of its previous occupants were scoundrels of the highest order. Some did a midnight flit fleecing cash and goods belonging to the brewery, while other unsuspecting companies, or unfortunate managers were left clinging to their only possession: a pair of trousers. Others left varying amounts of debt. Police raids were carried out to apprehend managers for stealing and selling stolen goods, including alcohol, spirits and cigarettes, which were consumed on the premises by unsavoury characters - most of whom didn't live locally. Former police officers, under the influence of alcohol, had unofficially informed local councillors that when the pub was known as The Kings Arms, it was used as a safe house for at least two convicts, who without permission from the Queen, had absconded from Dartmoor Prison. One of those former officers was among a large consignment of armed detectives who raided the pub to apprehend the convicts. It was even mooted locally at the time that the pub was used for prostitution, and some of those paying customers were local landowners and farmers. But of course, no one dared to say anything if they valued their livelihoods a hundred years ago. Such secrets and scandals still existed, at least in the memories of the older generations.

Heatherslade had its fair share of spinsters. Many of these now old, delicate women were sent off to boarding schools by fathers who were otherwise engaged working for foreign governments or serving their country in various armed conflicts. Very few saw their fathers at home, and only irregularly at best. Most of the women, once young isolated girls, used to languish in cold, depressing rooms waiting for their mothers, and siblings if they had any, to visit them for an hour or two in private schools up and down Britain. Hardship was good for young girls, it turned them into good wives and hostesses. This was unquestionably instilled in them. Some fortunate girls were taken for a drive to a local park or their nearest village for tea and cakes, but not having spoken to their mothers or fathers for weeks or months at a time, many found the experience of being with their parents emotionally cold and distant. Most felt that they were unloved and unwanted. Furthermore, these middle/upper class values also applied to young men, but most could at least leave home and join one of the armed services. Young women in those repressed days were totally forbidden from such outlets. Though just as intelligent as their male counterparts, young women developed other skills such as: writing, painting and dressmaking.

Many women displayed maturity beyond their years, writing truly powerful, tragic novels that would today be recognised as skilled prose and poetry. Paintings with such vivid colourful emotions depicted deep soulful joy and despondency. Even the romantic, John Martin, sought to understand their artistic secrets.

Most lived comfortably alone in various inherited village dwellings supported by carers. Many had private incomes handed down from forebears. There was a considerable number who lived off proceeds originating from the times of slavery and plantations, when thousands of British people owned land and humans in various colonial countries. With the abolition of slavery - still a distasteful subject never mentioned by those sensitive souls still in receipt of monies from those tragic times - the government compensated slave owners. The subject was occasionally whispered today, but only to the right people in quiet places, never in public. Not unless, of course, those involved wanted to bring disgrace to their families.

One of the spinsters and oldest villager, a rare gem called Celia Hetherington, lived in the detached Victorian house where she was born 92 years ago, along with her son. She had various employments over the years, which were invariably found for her by her landowner father, whom she never really bonded with. Being unworldly and having lived most of her early years tied to strict parents, she became pregnant by the first man she had sexual relations with. He, however, was married and much older than her. In those harsh moralistic times, girls and women who became pregnant would have had private abortions, before girls were sent away in disgrace from their homes to a boarding school. Those most unfortunate women would be confined to a convent for the rest of their lives. Celia, however, was permitted to stay at home to have her son. Illegitimacy was a terrible stigma against the good name of her father, but the family coped regardless. In fact, Celia's father, unlike most, supported his daughter and grandson. Her son, William, now aged 66, was born mentally handicapped and deaf. As he aged, Celia's father's own strict conditioning changed somewhat, which made way for him to take William out on country walks. Nevertheless, he still faced the stigma of being the grandfather of a disabled child - he always insisted on using the term handicapped - and James Hetherington never really overcame the shame. He probably thought that he himself was deficient, or to blame in some strange way. His Victorian upbringing viewed disability, at least in some quarters, as a sign of weakness, a moral or religious inadequacy.

Celia now thought philosophically about the subject: 'We were children and grandchildren of colonists, shut away from the outside world. God knows why. Perhaps being the children of those men ruling half the world, we were expected to be special and follow in their footsteps,' she said occasionally to her friend, fellow spinster and long-time resident, Anne Woodthorne. 'What a monumental painful price those Victorian children paid.'

Other than her one special friend, she could be seen shuffling around the village on her own talking to herself or picking daffodils, primroses and orchids that grew wild. Short and frail with long white hair, Celia spoke with anyone that gave her the time of day, especially children whom she adored. She would buy them sweets - a treat denied to her generation.

Come rain or shine, William Hetherington was nearly always to be found on weekday mornings directing the traffic in Heatherslade Village. His short, rotund presence, invariably smiling from ear to ear was a familiar sight to most of the drivers that regularly used, and jammed, the village road - eventually driving onto the main A373. William would run up and down the road waving at every driver in sight. Some smiled back, a few even waved to him as they sat in their cars fuming, swearing at being in a traffic jam of their own making to a certain extent. The parish had known about this problem for ages but had failed to act effectively. Although the local parish council had conducted various discussions with local council officials, government officials and contractors, they had dragged their heels over the serious traffic issue. There they sat, the parish committee, in their not so plush council offices, arguing over trivialities while congestion increased.

From time to time, William gestured with his heavily stained fingers that he would like a cigarette. Some of the friendlier tipper drivers occasionally gave him one as they sat in their cabs wasting valuable time and swearing incessantly at no one in particular. One tipper driver gave William the nickname Jesus and used to give him a packet of French cigarettes every two weeks when driving through the village on his way back from delivering haulage equipment on the Continent. William would have smoked pig shit if it was scented.

It was those kind gestures by people who didn't even know her son that gave Celia such deep belief in the human spirit. William had been exposed to much love and support at his local church, All Angels, where he had been anointed with sacred oils. Indeed, Reverend Bullchat had dressed her boy in the purple vestments to act as an assistant for a day to help the ecclesiastical officials with a major Christian ceremony. In front of his mother and friends, all smiling, tearful and proud of their village son, William carried a cross from the lych-gate to the altar. Indeed, he was a creature to behold. He was truly a rare gift from God -thought many of those attending. Though there were a few ungracious locals who called him 'village idiot'. In time gone by, he would have been shut indoors, away from prying eyes and bleating mouths.

Sitting there in the traffic chaos most mornings in his car and observing the wherefores was a relatively new resident to Heatherslade Village. Anthony Marlow had moved into an expensive, detached, five bedroomed Georgian House about three years previously with his wife, son and daughter. Working long hours and running his own business had been made more difficult due to him wasting his invaluable time sitting in a long line of traffic for an hour or so each day. Once he tried to find a short-cut across local farming land but got stuck. It had cost him £200 to be pulled out. It was this growing irritability that made him successfully apply to be an elected councillor, though much to his apprehension. He thought he was now in a position to take on the entrenched parish council shilly-shally nonsense. He knew it would be difficult, in fact the odds were stacked against him. As an outsider most people hadn't been overly friendly to him or his family. Regarding the make-up of the village people, he considered himself from the wrong background. Anthony Marlow was no sea captain, civil servant or Four-Star General.

But he was up for the challenge, very little fazed him if his track record was any guide. Besides, he had successful achievements behind him which would hold him in good stead for turbulent times ahead. However, that confidence would be severely threatened, for little did he know at this moment in time that one of his children would become the victim of such a gruesome and horrendous crime that most local police had not experienced before. That didn't include Superintendent Charles Pearce, a wily, crusty old fox who had witnessed most of humanities' heinous misdeeds during his thirty years of harsh service. He had little faith in human decency. The perpetrator, Pearce, said at the time that he had lived beyond the moral norms of humanity. That an individual should dwell in such a hell realm, baffled the many professionals involved. Only great endeavour, fortitude and love would help the family survive.

As Marlow got out of his new blue Jaguar, well-dressed and confident, he walked slowly across the tarmac car park towards the parish council offices. He anticipated that his first meeting with the highway committee would be rather difficult, and was especially concerned at his inexperience of local politics – he would be the youngest councillor.

As the owner of a construction company, Tony Marlow had negotiated with many different people who represented powerful companies. Those experiences had made him aware of the influence that group dynamics could have on otherwise decent people. Group politics, regardless of good ideas and practical solutions, could destroy the good work one could potentially bring to the table. Many times, he had lost an argument when discussing various, well budgeted, contracts with construction companies and councils, primarily, he thought, due to the intransigence of various tough individuals. Marlow was aware that he also, at times, had an uncompromising attitude to life. Wherever he had been during his 55 years - from a tough infant school and anarchic teen, to architectural college and the now wealthy owner of a flourishing construction company, group politics, led by the self-interested, had nearly always been a considerable burden to him and his company financially. But, undeterred, he would do what he thought ethically sound as the new ward councillor to sort out the traffic and other problems. And not forgetting what he promised those local voters - he would now try to achieve the significant changes his office demanded.

The nine councillors had all been seated for several minutes. As of yet, no one had spoken. Most, including Tony Marlow, had placed various papers and folders onto their desks in preparation for the evenings' agenda. The room felt damp and cold. Rainwater from outside trickled down one of the poorly decorated, brown walls. One could have cut the anticipation with a chainsaw it was so palpable. What did they have up their sleeves for the raw recruit?

Fellow councillors beamed at the Chairman, Captain Fox-Rice. 'I would like to welcome Tony Marlow, a newly elected councillor, to our first parish council meeting,' said the Captain, whose sour bloated face summed up his personal feelings about his new colleague.

There was a half-hearted gesture of welcome from most of his fellow councillors. Councillor David Pringleton didn't even make the effort to move his lips. He acted as though the newly installed councillor didn't even exist. That was characteristic of Pringleton, a former police superintendent who wasn't easily moved due to the many years of experiencing humanity's darker side.

Marlow immediately recognised the signs of things to come, as he cautiously eyed the body language of his colleagues from the decided discomfort of his old shaky chair only feet away. At this precise moment, for the first time ever, he felt like walking out and not returning. His only *raison d'etre* was to represent the local parish, not to make life difficult or play immature mind games, he surmised. But was he being overly anxious about the expectations of his colleagues at his first parish meeting? This was not a meeting with a large multi-national construction company, bank manager or a civil court appearance, he reassured himself. It was only a meeting of councillors trying to sort out, among other problems, the village traffic mix-up. Nothing so serious that one would have to include input from the Prime Minister!

'Well let us proceed with this evening's agenda,'

insisted the Captain. 'As we all know, the most pressing problem that threatens to overwhelm the health and quality of life here is the long-standing history of traffic jams that every week-day morning, and many evenings, thread slowly through our little abode,' he explained.

Before anyone else could contribute he further rambled on about the history, finances, residents' complaints and contractors' plans, until councillor Lizzie Trout made an impassioned gesture to be heard. Her large frame jumped, shook and shivered with excitement.

'Yes of course my dear, please make known what you have to say on this most difficult of subjects,' espoused the ruddy complexioned Captain, who looked most officious in his blue pin-striped suit, with matching waistcoat and black shoes that appeared to have been polished with a high gloss paint.

'Captain, excluding Mr Marlow we have all been trying to grapple with the problems you have just articulated for some considerable amount of time. In fact, you have articulated them so many times that I know them verbatim. My posterior squeaks abundantly every time I hear about it; my eyes start to water when I think of the same old stuff I'm constantly told,' she explained to the captain in no uncertain terms.

She placed a growing file of information collected from numerous parish meetings in front of her. She thought of throwing the whole lot into an incinerator and starting again, or throwing the towel in and resigning from the committee. What was the point of carrying on with this charade, dominated by the ruthless and single-minded Captain who thought he owned the village?

He was born in the village, his family could be traced

back generations, and this was from whom he had inherited his grand mansion. He would do his best, no doubt, to obstruct any modernisation - even if it killed the old bastard, she thought. An escalating thought over the months that had taken on wicked proportions was being devised in Ms Trout's devious mind – How could she do away with the old buffer? She was dreaming, fantasizing of snuffing him out in some inconspicuous manner. But she was made of sterner stuff; she wouldn't allow him to dictate everything. Bringing her awareness back to the meeting, she asked Tony Marlow the first question that evening:

'Welcome, Mr Marlow. Do you have any new suggestions to resolve the village vehicle predicament?' asked Ms Trout.

He stood up to address his fellow councillors: 'Having given this problem before us a considerable amount of time, energy and expense,' he emphasised, 'I would like you to consider the plans I am about to place in front of you. We all agreed that a bypass, or larger road, is desperately needed to take away the traffic problem from our village and surrounding villages. We also agreed that it is futile to ask the authorities to run a local bus service through our village and other adjacent villages, which would of course add to the traffic fiasco.'

All the councillors nodded in agreement. Well that was a welcome gesture, Marlow thought to himself. The knives had not yet been exposed, was his instinctive feeling; he was hopeful to start changing minds that had long been used to a fixed way of thinking about certain political matters. He was jumping in at the deep end, going right to the heart of the matter.

'So, councillors, I propose the following… Sometimes the traffic problem stretches back three miles beyond Cowgate village. Going west through our village, there is usually another mile of jams until the road reaches the A373 T-Junction, which is the essence of the problem'.

So far, so good he surmised from the softening faces of those around him. Even the Captain appeared to be interested, or was he just playing games before he brought out his big guns of surprise by proposing an altogether far different set of ideas? The old bastard kept his eyes averted for now.

'It is notoriously difficult to ease your vehicle onto this busy major bypass. The traffic will not slow down to let you on. It is a very dangerous manoeuvre - I've tried it many times. If you take a chance and move out slowly from the village road, the B3434, and enter the main bypass, you do so at your own peril. That action is a frightening proposition,' he said, as he emphasized his plans in the strongest possible terms. The Chairman rose with a few papers in his ultra-white hairy hand. The potential hand of Damocles awaited the Marlow neck.

'Yes, we know most of that councillor Marlow,' said the Chairman. 'We have all experienced what you have just expounded upon. Please tell us of the new cheaper financial option your plans explained earlier on'. By now the Chairman was becoming increasingly agitated by information he had heard a million times before. He had not, of course, acted on that information - so in a way Tony Marlow was deliberately reminding him and his councillors, in detail, of their ineptitude, if such a ploy were plausible.

'Yes, of course, Chair. A much cheaper, wider road

could be constructed a mile before Cowgate village. It would head two miles north-west across old scrub land which has been unused for many years. It would then continue through a small wood over council-owned pasture land, finishing up at the now deserted Chase farm. A slip road could easily be built here for traffic to join the busy A373 with much reduced danger of accidents. We wouldn't need to buy any expensive private land and the contractor, Conway, is far cheaper than the original financial proposal put forward by the other three contractors. Their expensive proposals for a new road would be directed south-west through private farm land and some of beautiful Slindon Wood at the back of our village,' he concluded after some considerable effort trying to convince his fellow councillors. They spent the next thirty minutes or so reading Marlow's plans.

'Thank you so much for that proposal plan, councillor Marlow,' added sceptical Captain Fox-Rice. He addressed the others present. 'Has any councillor anything to add to what has been put before us this evening?'

All agreed that the new proposals were cheaper for local taxpayers and the council, who ultimately would have to finance a great deal of the construction work.

'Very good ladies and gentlemen. I shall take these written plans that Councillor Marlow has worked on so thoroughly to the council for approval,' he expressed in a carefully reassuring voice. It appeared that the Chair himself was convinced of Marlow's professional expertise and was quietly pleased - although he wouldn't acknowledge to anyone that he was a good acquisition for his team. Though one must understand, the Captain unequivocally concluded, it was his team. After other minor business was discussed, the councillors left after two hours of productive work. No harsh words were exchanged, no voices were raised, or mugs thrown - yet anyway. They agreed to meet in four weeks' time.

Several days later, Peter Barnes-Jowell visited one of his affectionate parishioners – someone he had developed a close bond with from when he first moved into the village.

'You look well Celia. Do you still wander around the streets acknowledging your fellow men?' he humbly enquired. 'Several residents told me they were pleased to see you being so active and regard your smiling face with sincere gratitude. I'm calling briefly about the pot holes'.

'Oh, is that right my dear? Well at this time of the year, I love to pick those beautiful wildflowers. They smile and encourage me to take them home as a present for my dear son William who gives them fresh water every day. Some days William walks with me, he loves waving at everyone, but most of the time, I'm afraid, he prefers to walk around the village where all the action is.'

Celia shuffled from the kitchen holding a small tray of tea, cups and currant cakes she had baked. She placed the contents of the tray upon a small wooden table, poured out two cups of tea and placed two cakes on each of the plates. She enjoyed being independent, although she did have a carer who supported her and William in the mornings and returned to cook their evening meals.

'Would you like another cup of tea?' Celia eagerly asked.

'No thank you my dear. The tea and buns were superb, but detrimental to my waistline I'm afraid. Must be on my way, although I haven't seen William today is he around?' asked the councillor.

'Indeed, he is, Peter. He's out in the back garden sorting out the autumn plants. He loves wallowing in mud, but he also does a lot of digging, pruning and planting. His favourite activity in the garden is throwing worms at the birds, cats and anything else that moves,' she said, with a kindly smile.

Another councillor active in the local community was the youthful Lizzie Trout. In fact, she visited most residents whenever she was able to. She was popular with most people, including Celia, for her commitment to addressing local issues. Everyone knew when she was around because a trail of cigarette smoke followed her every step. Now at the tender age of 77, Lizzie had been smoking since her early 20's when it was considered cool to have a cigarette hanging out the corner of your mouth. The unfortunate legacy of a lifetime's smoking various trendy brands of cigarettes from around the world was a constant cough, wheezing and chest pains. She never complained.

In late November, as bare trees silhouetted the skyline, the parish councillors met for their scheduled meeting at Barnbrook, a small village two miles west of Heatherslade. The old wooden building where the parish council had been meeting for many years had seen better days, and like most of the ageing councillors, needed extensive repair. In actuality, the building should have been burned to the ground and a replacement found, but council funds were in great demand. No doubt the dilapidated old building had not escaped the notice of self-made millionaire Tony Marlow. He had probably already assessed the cost for a new building, and his company could build a new one a lot cheaper than most no doubt. But at this stage, mindful of being a new councillor and resident, he didn't want to undermine his parish colleagues by stirring the proverbial shit too much just yet.

'Well good evening councillors. I hope all is well. I've submitted councillor Marlow's new bypass plans to the head of Sleeford Council highway department, and he will be in contact soon. Try not to be too optimistic,' said the Chair, trying to hide a grin, and aware that the council didn't have a pot to urinate in.

'So other than several minor issues outstanding, what is on the agenda for this evening?' Chairman Fox-Rice eagerly enquired.

Paying little attention to the last question, the most vocal support for Marlow came from Councillor Cyril Brockleby - another councillor who lived locally. A rather decent chap, and similar to the Chair, he had served most of his life in the navy, but according to the Captain was of an inferior rank. His friendly smiling round face, full of freckles, was his most redeeming quality. With two large tufts of hair sticking out from the side of his large head, and ears the size and shape of cabbages, he resembled a scarecrow from the local allotment. Yet due to his gregarious nature, most people liked Cyril Brockleby. With political sensibilities and assiduous performance, he was in fact the ideal parish councillor. Notwithstanding that he had sustained many physical injuries; a scar down the side of his face, shrapnel wounds to his back and both legs, and walked with a pronounced limp from his days of serving his country on the high seas. Brockleby was another tough parish councillor, no doubt they all were in their own unique way - unassuming yet could be relied upon in times of crisis.

'I for one would like to thank my dear councillor Mr Marlow for his unstinting work. Brilliant my dear chap. May there be healthier days ahead for this village, and all the other local villages in the future. We have got to clean our planet up, by god we have, and you Marlow, I hope in time you will make your contribution. Well done old chap,' said Cyril Brockleby as he stood like some Christian martyr, praising his local parish councillor.

But underneath his gargantuan chin, Captain Fox-Rice wasn't at all happy with Marlow receiving such mighty accolades, after all he was a mere rookie attending only his second meeting. Never mind, the Captain thought, there would be such times when he will have to clip his tiny wings and ground himself for a length of time. What goes around comes around, he self-predicted. Was this the nasty sign of things to come to befall the parish council, or Fox-Rice's overblown ego taking a temporary bashing?

Unbeknown to their other colleagues, councillors Lizzie Trout, Tony Marlow and Henry Drummond had been meeting to discuss the possibility of a new community centre for the village. The subject had been mooted around by several councillors for some time, but they thought it inappropriate for Heatherslade. Marlow felt a bit of a fraud for this "behind the counter deceitfulness" because he himself had hammered the other councillors for ganging up on him, or so he thought, at his first parish meeting. The group mentality he had called it. In fact, he had come to the conclusion that it represented a herd mentality, where individuals didn't have to take responsibility. Marlow reprimanded himself for his immature, impulsive behaviour. Owning his own company and employing many personnel, he should have been aware of projecting his own tasteless feelings onto others, who, like him, were elected councillors. Yet along with two colleagues, he had taken the initiative where others feared to tread.

'May I once again bring up the subject of a new community centre for Heatherslade? The Chair will, of course, be familiar with the proposal that I placed before him some time ago,' explained councillor Drummond as his eyelids narrowed, anticipating a verbal bashing from the incredulous Captain Fox-Rice.

'Councillor Drummond, how many times in the past have we sat here, shining the backsides of our burgeoning posteriors, discussing this hopeless case? Surely a community centre would lower the tone of the village. I, for one, do not by any means look forward to the painful prospect of being invaded by loud motorbikes ridden by aggressive, leather-clad young men from our nearest town, Maysbridge, some ten miles in that direction,' he gestured with his hand.

'Besides, why do we need the young inhabitants from such a place of undoubted decadence to undermine our beautiful, charming village? I've lived here all my life, as you all know, of course,' retorted the red-faced Captain, loosening his old school tie. 'And I for one do not want to see it brought down to chaos resembling a Derby Day gypsy fairground or thugs attending a Millwall football match. And besides, we don't have the funds, neither

26

does the council, for this so called community centre,' said the Captain most eloquently.

'But Captain, with respect, we need to modernise our village and make it fit for the 21st century. The village has been and still is a marvellous place to live. I was born here and have lived here all my life. Growing up here, with my dear supportive parents, was undoubtedly an idyllic place for most young people. We could walk and cycle for miles around. The infant school wasn't that far from here in those days, and we had no traffic problems, but modern life has affected our village just like most of the others around the country. Our children and grandchildren are driven by various means to different schools and shop with their parents at the large industrial supermarkets. They rarely meet each other on the streets or in the woods like we did. Most of the local children are glued to their computers like shit to a blanket, I'm afraid to say. The children and their parents need to meet more in a convivial environment. The bottom line is, it's a completely different world captain,' said Councillor Drummond, who was incessantly, rather nervously, touching his gold framed glasses while trying to reassure the assembled group in front of him.

The animated Chair rose to his feet, and sighed audibly to his fellow councillors that he was vehemently opposed to any kind of new hall in his revered village. 'You must all vote in principle with a clear conscience, for or against this proposal,' he assured them.

'Well we shall discuss this proposal in further detail at the next parish meeting in four weeks fellow councillors,' retorted the Chair, as he proceeded to rather unfairly lambaste Tony Marlow about the evenings' business.

'I assume you were behind this evenings' ungracious proposal for the new village hall Marlow, it's about up your ethical street, you moron,' was Fox-Rice's nasty accusation.

'If you weren't such an old man, I would give you a good thrashing for that statement,' said Tony Marlow, as he walked out of the meeting seething over an unwarranted and ill-founded accusation.

Despite a rough upbringing, Marlow was mindful he had moved on with his life, but was still capable of physically handling himself if he needed to. Marlow had been socialised by a father who had been a hard tearaway used to fights, drunkenness and minor crime. When employed he had earned a poor living as a building site navvy, yet somehow always provided for his family regardless of his own needs. Marlow's father went to work without food many times to sustain him for ten gruelling hours of hard slog so that his children could eat. He didn't give a damn about authority; he stole site materials, food from shops and clothes wherever he could to survive. He also encouraged his two sons not to let others push them around, to be tough and to do their best in life. That philosophy had rubbed off onto his offspring's endeavours.

Whether that applied to Marlow's daughter was another matter. When he briefly pondered on the subject it caused him much inner turmoil. Marlow suppressed the strong feelings that he had for his daughter. It was too much to handle. Where had he failed? She appeared to be unhappy and frustrated with her life. The brief personal time he did get he tried to keep for all his family. Living with his wife brought him boundless happiness. And his son, who lived in another part of the country, was apparently making good professional progress. But Henrietta constantly hacked away at his wavering ideas about how he could help and support her. Material needs could only go so far to resolve whatever was causing her much dismay. It made matters worse when she refused to discuss her problems with her parents. He was certainly aware by now, informed by local politics, that the village needed a new vision to inform its future. Many youngsters, like Philip Stark and Daisy Cusack, appeared to have energy and sparkle in abundance, he thought. His daughter, if given the chance, could be a considerable asset to the village. With this in mind, a rare opportunity gave him time to speak with Henrietta on their own.

'How are things for you in Heatherslade sweetheart?' he tentatively asked her.

'All right, I suppose,' she reluctantly answered.

'Is there anything that you find particularly difficult, or something your mother or I can help you with?' Marlow was fishing, delving for answers. At times, he wished he could have dragged it out of her. She was so bloody stubborn, he continually thought.

'What are you on about dad? I'm well enough.' She was, of course, holding back something.

'Well Henny, it appears you are terribly frustrated with your life.'

'Not in the least,' she nonchalantly gestured.

'Don't you like it here in the village?'

'It's OK. Gets me down at times, I suppose. Those silly old village farts I find tedious at times, but it's home, isn't it?' she said, while looking out of the window into another world that presumably existed only in her head.

'Look, Henrietta, don't suffer in silence,' Marlow emphasized.

'I'll be all right. Don't worry about me. Things should work out in the end!'

All the councillors visited residents from time to time, according to their residents' problems and who could best solve them. In time, Tony Marlow became a familiar face to most of the ageing residents. They were more intrigued to meet the father of the sexy young woman who pranced around the village; rather than present a parish problem to him. Most of them just wanted to invite the handsome newcomer in for tea and find out about his life. Anne, Celia and many more were, on the whole, lonely, isolated and welcomed with open arms anyone willing to give them a few minutes of their time. For the first few months Marlow was busy, mainly in the evenings, presenting himself to villagers for rather spurious reasons. This was an integral part of his official office. Besides, being a businessman during the day, evenings gave him the opportunity to hear interesting stories long forgotten by their owners. He drank gallons of tea, ate mountains of various home-made cakes and listened to enough stories to write a volume of memoirs.

However, momentous change was about to hit the village which would impact on lives there forever. One family in particular would experience the threatening upheaval directly, but most residents would be affected by the emotional storm that was about to descend upon the place!

CHAPTER TWO

On April 28th at around 3am, torrential rain lashed down upon Tony Marlow's home in Heatherslade. Two police cars with lights flashing like a village fairground pulled up outside his house. Four police officers, led by a stern looking senior officer, knocked very loudly on Marlow's front door. But it wasn't until minutes later, dressed in his pyjamas and still half asleep, that he realised what was happening.

'Good morning Sir. I'm Inspector Childs from Maysbridge CID. Are you Mr Tony Marlow?' asked the rather tall, slim, middle aged police officer.

'That's right officer. I'm Tony Marlow. What's the problem? How can I help you?' he anxiously enquired.

'It would be helpful, Mr Marlow, if myself and two of my officers could come indoors to explain the problem to you. It's your daughter, Henrietta Marlow, we found her identification in her bag. She was taken to St Peter's hospital near Marble Arch at around midnight, we understand she suffered several knife wounds to various parts of her body. No person or persons, as of yet, have been apprehended for this crime. But beyond that Sir, I'm sorry, at this stage I have no further information, except to say she was in a critical condition but has now been stabilized. I'm so sorry to bring such bad news,' explained the Inspector.

'Don't you know which parts of her body have been wounded? I hope, for God's sake, it's not her face. Oh, for God's sake,' cried Tony.

By this stage he had been joined by his wife, Eleanor. They desperately held each other as they wept profusely upon hearing the tragic news. Who could have perpetrated such an inhuman, violent and despicable act? As the police finalised their departure from Marlow's home, they explained how the family could visit Henrietta, and provided various details about the people that would help and support him and his wife. Both the Marlows, naturally, felt heartbroken and dumbstruck as they sat down in their dining room holding hands, unable to move. Both said nothing, still mortified by the shocking news the police had just given them.

About thirty minutes had passed when Tony Marlow quickly jumped up from the sofa; with his hands shaking he fumbled as he tried to wipe his eyes. He realised that he immediately had to phone St Peter's hospital to enquire about the medical condition of his daughter and, hopefully, drive there to be at her side as soon as possible. Then he must phone his son, Toby, who lived in Essex, to explain what had happened to his sister and ask him to meet him at the hospital.

He must not panic. He needed to try and be professional; his emotions strained as they gripped him on the spot where he stood holding his mobile phone. He tried to reassure himself that years of training would hold him together, especially at this most crucial moment in his life. He had done his utmost to provide for his adored family, he wouldn't let anything shake his confidence when his daughter desperately needed him. He and his wife gave her life and made sure she and their son had a good start in life. What he owned: a thriving business, large house and financial security, would mean nothing without his family around to give his life meaning and purpose. He must hold his emotions in check. He was known by colleagues and friends for his authoritative voice and firm resolve, he always expected commitment from others, regardless of their background. But now his secure world was being undermined by others he didn't know; he now lived in an uncertain world where he was unable to help his daughter as she suffered in a strange environment, with no family near to support her.

'Is that Woodcote Ward? I'm Tony Marlow. Please, please tell me how my daughter is. I'm desperate to know. Can I visit her this morning? Can I talk with a doctor?' he pleaded with the person at the other end of the phone. Whoever she was, he didn't know or care. He was just desperate to find out information concerning his daughter.

'Hello Mr Marlow, my name is Dr Webster. I have been treating your daughter for the last few hours for various injuries sustained late last night. All I can say about her at this moment is that she is stable after responding well to surgery. As you can imagine, after having a strong anaesthetic she is sleeping and will be unconscious for some time. There is no point visiting her until she has fully regained consciousness and has been assessed by the consultant sometime within the next twelve hours. Please leave your contact details and we shall let you know when to visit your daughter,' the carefully measured voice reassured Tony Marlow.

After a long and painful conversation with his son, where he explained the sparse information he had about Henrietta, Tony tentatively placed the phone feet away on the dining room table anxiously awaiting any information. His hands were visibly shaking. Rage vibrated through his body. He couldn't conceive that this trauma had taken over his consciousness. He was impotent in shielding his fearful wife from the unimaginable burden that she must have been suffering.

After receiving many frantic phone calls throughout the next twelve hours enquiring about their daughter, St Peter's hospital eventually phoned the Marlows to explain Henrietta's current medical condition. She was now fully conscious, the doctor was pleased that the surgery had been fully completed and she was able to talk to staff. They could visit their daughter as soon as possible.

Hours later, the Marlows left home with a heavy heart, and full of foreboding, to visit their daughter in St Peter's hospital. They expected the worst, but their lifelong optimism suggested otherwise. They were totally preoccupied with Henrietta's successful recovery. Tony drove out of the village, sped along empty country lanes and dual-carriage ways, before encountering the mayhem of the motorway which was full of reckless sociopaths. The latter drove as though others didn't exist and appeared to view individuals as having little value, Marlow felt strongly. He hated the world right now.

Upon arriving at the hospital, the car park came as a great relief to them both after a car journey full of anxiety. Tony felt his clammy hands fixed against the steering wheel. Tightly holding hands, they walked along brightly coloured, polished corridors, with the smell of disinfectant pervaing the air, until they found Tudor Ward, where their daughter lay in bed receiving treatment after experiencing such a violent ordeal.

'Hello Mr and Mrs Marlow, I'm Dr Gardiner, the surgical registrar. I operated on your daughter's wounds, there are six all told. Most are what we call superficial wounds to her left arm, hand and ear. There are, unfortunately, two deeper wounds to her right shoulder and right hand that required many stitches. We're hopeful that the wounds will heal given time. She will probably require physiotherapy to her right hand. In that respect, only time will tell,' said the quiet, young doctor informing the Marlows that Henrietta was in capable medical hands.

They didn't know what to expect as they entered the single room. Henrietta lay sleeping in bed bandaged with visible stitches on several parts of her otherwise slim, attractive feminine body. Toby, weeping, spontaneously threw his arms around his parents. All three stood together for several minutes, arms locked tight around each other's warm bodies. A young nurse entered the room with tea, encouraged them to take off their jackets and sit on the three comfortable looking armchairs. She then proceeded to take the patients' pulse, check the drip and enter something on a clipboard. The lilac coloured room brightened up an otherwise silent, gloomy atmosphere. No doubt many different and conflicting emotions and feelings had implanted themselves within the Marlow family - all eyes were on Henrietta.

'Other than what you explained to me on the phone, do you know any other information about what happened to Henrietta? Who else was involved, where did the incident take place and why? I realise it is early days, but the police and hospital have been incredibly silent on the matter,' Toby asked his equally exasperated parents. Similarly, he needed vital questions answered with much urgency. Toby knew that the official wheels took time to move into motion.

'Yes, I agree with you Toby. Look, you are a practising barrister, what can we do to find out more information? Is it best to phone the police directly? I have the inspectors' contact number, or should we ask a solicitor to brief us, or make enquiries to the hospital CEO? Whatever we must do, we must do it now Toby,' Tony Marlow responded. Inside he was seething, full of revenge for the bastard who had disfigured his daughter. He wasn't thinking straight, understandably. Thoughts of underworld figures: gangsters and wide boys who carried out violent acts for money, crossed his confused mind.

'As a barrister can you not ask any of your colleagues how we can proceed?' asked Eleanor Marlow, Toby's French born mother. She was 52, well proportioned, with long auburn hair. Her American parents had worked in the US Embassy in Paris where she was born.

'Well I can certainly ask them, but as you understand mum, for obvious reasons, I cannot get directly involved with this case. Besides I'm far too inexperienced. I will contact my dear friend Jeremy Sparks in Middleton Chambers, he is more experienced than I am in such matters, but the police haven't concluded their investigations, don't forget. Besides, they have yet to interview Henrietta,' Toby Marlow explained, trying to reassure his parents that he would do his utmost for them.

Now aged 25, Henrietta had tried for at least a year to commute five days a week from her home in Heatherslade village. It was a very arduous and tiresome journey that she realised, eventually, had to change. Early every morning at around 5am, avoiding the depressing traffic jams, she drove her car 10 miles or so to Maysbridge station. A three hour journey in a packed train took her to London. The same old miserable ageing faces on the train stared at her from behind their Financial Times or Telegraph newspapers; she found this excruciatingly painful. Henrietta knew she couldn't carry on as things were, and her parents realised that something had to be done to support their flagging daughter who would arrive home most evenings after 9pm shattered and despondent. After several quick gin and tonics to calm her ever growing anxiety, she withdrew to her room. There she felt safe; all too aware that a few hours hence she would repeat the same journey.

Other than the occasional foray into parochial Maysbridge, all she could muster up most weekends, with a lot of assertive physical energy and mental will, was a drink and meal with her family in the local pub. Even that place was filled with local, crusty old men, the type she encountered walking around the village and commuting to London. In reality, Henrietta hated the arrogant old bastards, whose contemptible lives she thought were completely different from her own working in cosmopolitan London. She loved her supportive family, but the time had come for her to move on.

'Hello, how is my darling, beautiful young Henrietta bearing up then?' was the usual flannel from Fox-Rice.

A fat old senile sea dog, she used to call him. Although trying to be sociable, the main culprit for trying out his sad, pathetic jokes on Henrietta was fitness fanatic Herbert Tate. It was assumed by the more discerning pub users that he had other, more carnal, ideas in his head for the attractive young woman. There was a part of Henrietta Marlow, especially the unscrupulously daring and risky side of her personality, that occasionally flirted and fantasized about getting her hands on their money. The direct way of doing that, she realised, was sex. But she shuddered at the thought that any of those wrinkled old men would be given the opportunity.

Sometime before her life had taken a sudden turn for the worse, Henrietta had graduated from university. Rather conveniently, her father's friend employed her as a marketing manager not far from Sharpthorne, a small town 20 miles from her home. She travelled the 40-mile round trip in the new car her father had bought her for achieving a first degree after reading English. At first she enjoyed her first paid job, she found it interesting, challenging and thought it an ideal career for the future. Being her father's friend, her employer Gavin Steelbrook was of course more flexible when it came to allocating work and other employee conditions. Steelbrook's company, Tristar, used to run management courses for those young people with the intention of climbing the slippery ladder of success. A notion which was at the forefront of Henrietta's mind for the earlier part of her time during her first job, but that desire soon waned after she realised that other, more lucrative gems were to be had in a world of plenty. She was smart, shrewd and when required, manipulative.

After working for a few months, Henrietta was competent enough to start teaching management courses of her own, even though some of her students were twice her age. Participants, especially young virile men, found her gregarious. Now in a position to plan her own working weeks in advance, she found lots of time to have several sexual affairs with men from different backgrounds that she had met in various pubs and clubs. Many of these promiscuous contacts were tempestuous and exposed her to potentially dangerous individuals, whom she had known, in some cases, for only a few hours. Most of Henrietta's outrageous social behaviour was fuelled by continuing, and progressive, amounts of alcohol. It was during this time that she was introduced to skunk, a particularly strong strain of Cannabis. This powerful illegal drug progressively and detrimentally affected Henrietta's unpredictable behaviour. But this murky world wasn't entirely new to her. Years before university, she had indulged in sex, alcohol and drugs with men she met through websites and other effective mediums.

Off the beaten track, in a small 18th century village inn not three miles from where she worked, Henrietta occasionally met David Martin who she had met in the same place just by chance months previously. She had gone there for a large brandy and a chance to spend an hour away from the anxieties of a job she had started to despise. All sorts of fly-by-nights, mavericks, crooks and others that made up humanities maelstrom, associated there. This, calculated Henrietta, resembled her type of place and was used by the lost souls so prevalent today. One of them, David Martin, approached her.

'Hello, I'm David, may I join you?' asked the middle aged, well dressed, overweight chap in front of her. 'I work as a computer salesman. Work is short, so I thought a few drinks would brighten up my rather depressing day'. She hoped he had money to spend and wasn't some cretin looking for quick oral sex in his car. It was at these times that her conscience led her into a world of depravity. On these occasions she failed, for whatever reason, to see people as individuals. They matched her fantasy life completely.

After the formalities were over - how Henrietta loathed them - they exchanged more intimate information about each other. Both were eager, no doubt from the outset, to enjoy themselves once moral boundaries had been lowered to accept anything approaching near gutter mentality.

'You enjoy illegal drugs, David?' Henrietta at last asked her potential partner in crime. It was such a blatantly crude question to ask anyone known for only a few minutes.

'Oh yes, all manner of them - cocaine, tranquillisers, crystal meth, skunk. I love them all. What about yourself, do you like taking drugs, or is this the first time? I hope I'm not offending you but you look rather young,' he expressed most eagerly to the much younger, attractive woman who he thought was up for it. The man was up for it as well. No doubt, he had inhabited this under-world many times before.

'No, you are not offending me whatsoever. I have experience of taking drugs. Skunk, in particular, interests me. Have you got any? If you have, I wouldn't mind a few smokes,' said Henrietta. She had smoked cannabis many times before at university but had avoided skunk due to its addictive and powerful side effects. She had witnessed students half-wrecked, some failing to complete their studies due to the chemical grip the drug had secured. Hell had overtaken them!

An hour later they were in David Martin's small, cheap, vile smelling apartment on the outskirts of Maysbridge. Influenced by too much alcohol and all inhibition having fallen from her personality, Henrietta smoked skunk, watched pornographic films and had aggressive sex several times with Martin. Before it was too late, she needed to phone the boss about her days' work and give him the spiel about progress. He loved to hear that. Walking confidently back to her car, she concluded that fat David Martin wasn't a bad lover. His mouth reeked a bit, his ass sagged and his so-called apartment was only used for one thing - he certainly didn't live there. But he had good ideas that most people would have thought sick, shit, weird and even abnormal. Yet she was into all that heady stuff. Being thrashed was also on her radar. Why did she dislike herself so much? Anyhow, next time she hoped!

Away from those who thought they knew her personally, Henrietta was a different woman. At times she appeared out of control due to the toxic effects of various chemicals that were impacting on her body. Nonetheless, she continued to present herself professionally, thanks to her positive family upbringing and educational training. She managed her time efficiently enough for her boss to give her a salary increase. Henrietta had tied them all in knots by telling them what they wanted to hear. Feeding their egos, she realised, was the way to get what she wanted from people full of bullshit.

As things stood, Henrietta was mindful that she couldn't continue working in Sharpthorne. Her inexperience, and at times manipulative nature, was becoming more entrenched into a seedy social life that, if she didn't act now, would veer out of complete control. She would lose everything she had worked relatively hard to acquire. Primarily this meant the love and support of her family, to undermine that would leave her life in ruins. And she certainly wasn't going to jeopardise that for anything. She also had to leave Tristar with a good reference so that other foolish, potential employers would know what she had achieved working for her father's good friend. It pained Henrietta to think that if it was known that she had been drinking and taking drugs during her employer's time, her impulsive and immature behaviour could possibly have had a devastating effect on her father's friendship with a man he had known for years. Under no circumstances was she going to allow her irresponsibility to cause great pain and anger to her parents, whose total commitment towards her and Toby she couldn't fault.

The sordid life she had been living, albeit covertly, was now behind her. Fresh, new horizons appeared to open up for Henrietta Marlow as she was appointed marketing manager for a small film company in Soho. After eighteen months of working with country bumpkins – the nickname for her former colleagues – the limelight of central London beckoned, and she was determined to make something of her life. She couldn't fail, she thought. Young, educated, intelligent and sexy with a certain amount of sophistication and devious influence, Henrietta thought herself prepared to join the swinging throng of the metropolis. Besides, she was by now well trained in attracting the attention of young, virile men intent on seeking the delights of the feminine flesh. Giving them what they desired, and lots of it, became her mantra.

'Welcome to Film Glow, honey,' said Davina Marsden, Henrietta's new colleague. 'Hope you enjoy it here sweetheart'. Davina was a black American with a strong southern drawl. She resembled a leftover from a 1960's Hollywood dream goddess cult, who didn't quite make the big-time boom. She had long black plaits, a thickly painted face, tight sexy clothes and wore six-inch heels. With four gold front teeth she was sure sending out all the right messages to whoever might be up for it.

'Thank you, I'm so looking forward to this exciting London job after working miles out in the country. At times, it was so provincial, my only associates were four-legged beasts munching and crapping in the local fields,' she half-heartedly explained to her older, glamorous colleague; though she forgot, conveniently, to mention the decadence. Henrietta probably thought that her loudly dressed colleague had the potential to take the limelight away from her. She would have to keep her distance, especially when cavorting with men in the local bars after work. But Davina was in her thirties, ageing rapidly, her figure held together by miles of reinforced fabric and, oh boy, those sagging tits were obscene. No, she wasn't a threat to Henrietta's sexual street credibility.

In horse racing parlance, the latter had classic form, compared to the selling plate status of the former.

'This is a small, friendly company. We all get on quite well, allowing for human frailties and foibles. Mind you, we do have a small, excellent private club of our own above the Indian restaurant, Curry Cottage, a hundred yards down the road. The Indian boys are sweet. It is so much more refined compared to many of those loose, back street pubs, clubs and other dives that have beset Soho in the last fifty years. Most of the boys sit on the toilet to have a piss, if you know what I mean, ducky,' explained Davina. Secretly though, Henrietta, had already approved of such degraded establishments that were now an integral part of modern shallow culture. In her mind, the dives rough and tumble of life had become her social contacts for insensibilities that knew few norms. But that was not to say things couldn't change when she got to know her colleagues on a more personal level. But she hoped the opposite would prevail.

During the next year or so, she fitted into the company culture - something she was very astute at. She became an integral part of the small, successful team of professionals. Henrietta loved using the word "professional" in relation to herself, it made her feel important and gave her credence among her former college friends. In reality, all it meant in her case was lots of communication to important film people around the world trying to sell various franchises, commercial space and other paraphernalia. She earned a decent salary and did her job competently. Plenty of bullshit drove her forward.

Film Glow, an American subsidiary owned by a multi-national company, had been in Beakers Place - a row of dirty Georgian terraced buildings - Soho for nearly ten years. It had by this time built up a proficient reputation providing large conglomerates with necessary film and commercial requirements. As well as fulfilling company financial targets, Henrietta, along with her two office colleagues Tariq and Isabel, socialised in several local bars and clubs. Various other colleagues joined them to participate in the steady flow, sometimes deluge, of ready alcohol. Other stimulants like cannabis, cocaine, and other unknown drugs of dubious quality, were always available.

'Skin up Tariq,' insisted Isabel, who was drunk, clueless and immature. Several of them made their way out of the small, dingy, Victorian pub onto the hard cobblestones of the narrow street. Opposite was a four-story building. Every floor was occupied by prostitutes, known to punters as goose. The whole road was full of them. Seedy looking old men from varying backgrounds came and went every thirty minutes or so. The occupants must have run a conveyor system. The men, faces hidden, walked down the road full of rubbish left out on pavements by anti-social tenants. Chicken bones, pieces of pizza and empty curry takeaway containers were strewn all over the place. Isabel dragged on the skunk roll-up and nearly coughed up her guts, before passing it on to Tariq. He was an experienced skunk smoker and loved the sensation of inhaling such powerful medicine. He bought and sold all kinds of illegal drugs to anyone who could afford the price. He often boasted that his paid job at the film company was just for pin money - something to do during the day before the evening brought forth the big money from mugs galore, he kept reminding himself.

'Come on you bunch of pricks, we've had two fucking great spliffs and I'm in the mood for something stronger. I hope the three of you are coming to my shack in Pimlico for a rasping night,' shouted Tariq, already drunk and with his mind confused by the effects of skunk.

'Sure Tariq, I'm coming,' giggled Henrietta, already out of her mind on a cocktail of alcohol and drugs. Her stockings were torn, stale beer stuck to her expensive leather coat and lipstick was smeared all over her mouth and chin. She looked like she was on the game or had been sleeping rough in a squat.

'How about you Isabel and Patsy, are you up for it?' asked their male colleague, who was confident he could manipulate the females into having a good binge. Not for the first time, of course. All four debauched themselves on several different drugs. Eventually, they lay prostrate where they fell, completely unconscious.

'I feel fucking rotten,' Henrietta croaked to her colleagues around 10am. Her two female colleagues were nowhere to be seen. But Tariq wasn't concerned about trivial matters as he drank his coffee, totally oblivious.

'You look fucking rough old slag,' he said to her.

'So do you shit-head,' she replied.

'Get out of bed and sort yourself out. You're a disgrace,' Pathan shouted.

'Yea, and fuck you Mr big guy,' she rattled back.

'You want to make money, so get out of that fucking bed and try selling skunk to those young dumb heads in that bar just off Gate Street,' he yelled at Marlow. 'We need the money'.

The two young thrill seekers were seen drinking, taking drugs and shouting at each other in various local bars and clubs. It appeared that they were destined to meet as soul partners. Their karma had locked horns and nothing but inevitable tragedy could release them from self-inflicted torment. Their relationship was cemented by the desire to sell drugs and make money from whoever was available, regardless of the consequences. Travelling a road full of danger, excitement and chronic anxiety. Craving dictated the pace.

That was the abusive nature of their so-called relationship. Physical and verbal violence had dominated since they first met. But Henrietta had gradually spent more time over the past four months at Tariq's flat, or occasionally elsewhere; anywhere rather than making the long journey back by train and car to Heatherslade. The commute was too much for her to handle. Besides, her emotional and physical worlds now belonged in London. She had left the parochial life behind, so she reckoned. She had made up her mind to move to a flat somewhere as near as possible to central London, depending on the expense. Under the influence of drugs, she had even given fleeting thoughts to becoming a high-class prostitute to pay her way among the elites of London. She had the class, sexuality and stamina to make a fortune. Unsurprisingly, her parents had seen their daughter struggling with various problems associated with travel for some time and were in wholehearted agreement to her moving.

'Your mother and I have decided to put down a

substantial deposit on a flat for you, Henny. More than 70%, so that leaves a small mortgage. We are aware how difficult the travelling is for you, and besides, you need to be more independent. We recognise your life is elsewhere in London where you are working and have met new friends. The money shall be withdrawn from a trust that I set up for you and Toby some time ago,' said Toby Marlow, as he and his wife hugged their daughter, pleased that they could support her to move on with life.

Henrietta sat in her parents' plush sitting room pondering the endless possibilities that had just opened up for her now she would have her own apartment. Uppermost in her thoughts were the finances. She knew renting in inner London costs a fortune.   Isabel, for example, forked out over half her monthly salary on a run-down bedsit in Shoreditch. That included sharing a filthy bathroom and kitchen with several others. Henrietta had herself slept there on occasion when she couldn't travel home due to another of their many drug and alcohol binges. She thought the place was a slum. Many times she had woken in a melancholic haze watching bugs walking across the ceiling. And it was not unusual to see male nude strangers walking around the flat, urinating in the sink and stealing food from the fridges. At times it frightened Isabel and Henrietta.

But now that Henrietta was getting her own place she would, compared to colleagues, have minimal outgoings. In her over rampant mind that meant one important factor. She could now over indulge, gorge herself, let fly her proclivities to their fullest. It gave her the golden opportunity to invite others back to her private flat, in a respectable area, where other professionals lived a possibly hedonistic lifestyle but didn't intrude on others. After all, Henrietta had always been used to a cosy, secure middle-class life living with her trusting parents. She didn't mind the squalor of pubs, clubs and other dives, but she also needed her creature comforts.

With all the necessary legal documents sorted out by her always dependable father, Henrietta sat on her new leather sofa thinking how fortunate she was. The two-bedroom 1960s flat had been newly decorated in corn yellow and light oak green. Most of the furniture was new. All that surrounded her had been at the expense of her parents. What could she have done without their predictable support? Brilliant sunshine filtered through the curtains. She sat there for some time basking in the warmth. A reassuring glow spread all over her body. Millions, she realised, would have done anything to have been in her Kings Road high heeled leather boots.

Barry Merchant

CHAPTER 3

'Hello Mr and Mrs Marlow, thank you for coming to the police station. I'm Inspector Childs, you may recall me from when I first visited your home,' he said. How could they forget such a traumatic experience?

'Thank you for inviting us here. We will help all we can,' said Marlow, most anxious all was not well.

'It has been two months since your daughter was wounded and taken to hospital. She is still an inpatient at the same hospital,' said the inspector.

'That's correct. We only recently visited her. She is recovering well,' said Mr Marlow, full of anticipation.

'I'm pleased to hear that. After questioning your daughter about the descriptions of the person or persons that might have attacked her, we have not been able, so far, to interview any suspects – but this is ongoing. I must also let you know that the nursing staff, when legally obliged to check your daughter's personal belongings, found a substantial amount of cocaine in her possession. I have to inform you now that when she is discharged, she will be charged with possessing an illegal drug. Police have questioned your daughter this morning and warned her that criminal charges will be proceeded with. We do not intend to place a 24 hour police guard on her, but at this stage you may need to consult a solicitor,' explained the inspector in a serious and determined voice. Although he had performed these words many times, not unlike an Old Vic actor, he wasn't unsympathetic towards the Marlows. Indeed, the inspector's son was of a similar age.

For a while, the Marlows sat completely quiet, staring with blank, expressionless faces at the light brown wall in front of them. They were dumbfounded. Shattered! Was this really happening to them and Henrietta? She had been attacked by a maniac; now she was about to be charged with drug possession. It couldn't be true, they thought. Who was doing these heinous things to their family? For the first time in many years, Tony Marlow felt impotent to act. In a while he would have to recover, but right now his guts felt like exploding. Mrs Marlow continued to weep over her daughters' terrible predicament.

'I'm sorry to have shocked and upset you both. I wish your daughter a healthy recovery,' Inspector Childs remarked. He added: 'Please be aware that we might need to question your daughter again about the attack'.

After spending one of the most painful hours of their whole lives listening to the unthinkable, they walked slowly, hesitatingly, yet reassuringly holding hands, out of the police station. With only one destination in mind, they drove the ten miles from Maysbridge in complete silence until arriving at their home. Once inside, it felt rather hollow when they thought about their recent painful experiences, although they felt secure.

Tony Marlow's usual confident, authoritative, even arrogant voice had been sapped from him by forces beyond his control. He had his own successful business, was financially comfortable and married to an educated and loving wife and mother, who had supported him all the way. His home was decorated and furnished so that his family could feel loved, secure and free to enjoy themselves in an environment which had been nurtured for comfort. Yet at this traumatic time he had to stop to take it all in, and more importantly, plan for the serious problems ahead.

'Can you imagine what local people will say?' Marlow bitterly asked his wife.

'The local and national press will have a fucking field day with us. They'll try to tear us to shreds no doubt. There will be plenty of people lining up to try and undermine me. Not to mention ridicule from some of the councillors,' he said contemptuously.

'It's going to get tough Tony. We can only do our best for the family. I think most people, after due consideration, will act decently. That's my experience, but human nature is fickle and always subject to change darling,' said Eleanor, whose soft, kind voice reassured Tony.

'Yea, I think you are right sweetheart,' he replied.

'I'm phoning Peter Harvey to explain that I need a few days off work. I'm sure he will understand,' said Eleanor, who had worked as an interior designer for Peter - a master furniture craftsman in Fernswood - for over ten years.

The next day at the crack of dawn, the Marlows drove with great urgency to visit their daughter in hospital. When they opened the door to her room, which was still full of medical paraphernalia, they found her sobbing. She was inconsolable about the grief she had brought upon her innocent family. Henrietta was confused, lost and not really understanding. She was unaware as to how the cocaine ended up in her bag. But she did confess to her parents that she had taken cocaine on several occasions with her colleagues.

'I'm really sorry mum and dad. I've been on this drug, and other drugs since college when I first smoked cannabis. When I'm out of hospital and on my feet again, I'm going to seek therapy. My company are supportive and will hold on to my job until I improve. I haven't got a clue who knifed me. It's all a blur at the moment. I feel useless. I'm a failure. I'm not worthy of good parents like you. Sorry mum and dad for bringing problems to your village home,' she cried helplessly as her parents held her tight.

By this time the inevitable chatter of the brutal attack on Henrietta Marlow had spread like wildfire throughout the village. Of course, the drug charge had not yet been carried out. That was an incendiary device waiting to be ignited once the papers were given full reign. Near mutilation of a village charge was enough to bring support, protection and non-judgement for the time being. Flowers, cards, letters, boxes of chocolates and many other gifts of solidarity were delivered to Henrietta's parents' home. Some of the letters were from strangers. One or two were from the usual cranks. Most people in the village were ignorant of the fact that she had moved back home from London. What would grapevine whispers say about the place where she was attacked? It was the very place she had run to for a new start.

All Tony Marlow's supportive fellow councillors had phoned him immediately. They knew all was not well. Mountains of flowers were sent expressing sincere condolences from the parish. A collective outpouring of kindness and concern followed. Many others who Tony Marlow had met somewhere along life's perilous road, contacted him and the rest of his family to express their deep shock and sadness at the sudden and unprovoked attack upon a defenceless young woman. What monster could inflict so much suffering, and yet still remain at large to strike any unsuspecting soul?

Captain Fox-Rice was welcomed into the Marlow household. Uncharacteristically, the chair of the parish council spontaneously threw his big arms around the suffering parents. Gone was the lifetime adversarial tongue and stiff gait; a more conciliatory, understanding person stood there full of genuine compassion for his village friends. The captain's near blue eyes shone with light, transfixed and feeling the tangible emotional darkness within.

'Hello my dear friends. From the bottom of my heart I sympathise with the great emotional burden you carry,' Rice-Fox muttered apologetically as he handed them a large envelope for their daughter.

'Thank you so much for visiting, Robert, and for your kind regards. Our daughter is doing well in hospital and expects to be discharged in a few days. She will need physiotherapy afterwards,' Marlow explained.

'I wish her well dear Tony and Eleanor. If I can help, you know of course that I'm there for you both'.

The captain was pleased that he had tried to help and support his village kind, if only temporarily What lay ahead could become potentially explosive.

This was followed up a few days later by the inevitable presence of Reverend Bullchat seeking comfort for one of his strayed sheep. No doubt in his public school, theologically conditioned mind, Henrietta needed God's blessing and the Almighty's comfort. Many at that most strained time would not have disagreed with him. It was characteristic of Bullchat who was a good person, had a compassionate heart and always meant so well. His calling to his Almighty was total commitment. Besides, after many years of education and training, it couldn't be anything else - his stipend would not have covered what most villagers payed their gardeners. Whatever the day, time or consequence, the vicar was there with unwavering love, support and purpose.

'On Sunday we shall pray for Henrietta to become healthy again. We shall also pray for all the Marlow family, that they find inner peace once more,' said Bullchat with a humble smile.

Although not asked directly by Bullchat himself, the Marlows thought they had no choice but to attend a service at their local church. Otherwise, Marlow surmised, word no doubt would surface sooner or later that they weren't committed to village life. And in part, that at least meant the occasional church service. Marlow thought it all to be hogwash. This opinion originated from his experience at school and college, where some old white haired man - usually from a former colonial background - used to forgive all their sins. Whatever they were, Marlow never found out. Besides, his father's own Catholic upbringing brought him only anger, resentment and constant hoping for the dissolution of all churches.

Nonetheless, he would take his whole family to church services in the foreseeable future, with a view to meeting familiar faces in an altogether different place. Instead of drinking scotch in the local, he would share water with them in the house of the Lord. Marlow had come to realise that for the lonely elders, the local church provided a vital social, if not spiritual, support and reassurance. It showed them that others cared about their well-being. None other than Bullchat himself started the informal caring service several years ago, when an elderly male parishioner had died alone, and was eventually found emaciated some time later.

Three weeks later, Henrietta Marlow, aged 26, stood in the elevated wooden dock of Branster Magistrate Court, West London. The court was built in the early Victorian period, when many men and women were sentenced to death or transported across the world for petty crimes. Miss Marlow had become another prisoner, joining many thousands, but unlike her, most would never see their loved ones again. She was instructed to sit on the same spot where notorious mass murderers, rapists and spies had once been represented by legal people who had pleaded, nearly always in vain, for their lives to be spared. The large building, dominated by a mahogany bench where the legal enforcers sat, sent cold shivers throughout Henrietta's underweight body. Hospital confinement and the inability to eat regularly meant she looked frail and vulnerable. Her anxious family sat immediately behind her. Two female colleagues sat further back. Her QC, in a black pin-striped suit, sat nearest the stipendiary magistrate. All was set, the courtroom resembled a thriller ready to be performed at the Garrick, the actors were about to proceed with their case.

The prosecution had delivered their case to the court.

In addition to the examination of police evidence, they put forward a small amount of cocaine which had been found in the defendant's bag while undergoing treatment in hospital. Straightforward, all delivered within thirty minutes. It was then incumbent on the defence to argue their case.

'Sir, I represent the defendant. She has pleaded guilty to possessing an illegal substance: namely cocaine for her own use. She has no prior convictions, is of previously exemplary character, is currently employed as a manager for a film company and comes from a supportive home. The defendant's parents are here Sir. Sir, with all respect, could you deal with this case, instead of wasting time and money by taking it to the Crown Court?' pleaded Jonathan Sedges, a most striking looking, battled hardened chap who was around 60 years of age. He was short and fat with a purplish veined face, most likely as a result of swilling scotch in various back street bars of London with colleagues after successful cases.

'Yes, I agree Mr Sedges. I shall retire to read medical and probationary reports to guide my judgement,' the spectacled stipendiary magistrate, Peter Fenwick, responded.

The magistrate returned to the court within an hour. In anticipation, a quiet courtroom sat speculating. The Marlows, rather understandably, were terrified of the forthcoming judgement. Henrietta's mind was in a turbulent state of affairs, unconvinced of her destiny. Whatever the legal outcome of her case today, could she, or rather would she, stop using drugs? Or did she already know the answer to those entrenched and unanswerable question? Besides, what else lay ahead of her in a world that she quite honestly thought rather mundane in every way. Seeing through the superficial glitz and glamour of Soho and its unintended consequences - drugs and alcohol - added some inner spice, vision, fantasy if you like. Fuck it all, she thought, I'll keep on the same tracks until an almighty buffer hits me square in the face.

'Will the defendant please stand?' requested the court usher, as Henrietta Marlow's whole body trembled uncontrollably.

'Miss Marlow you have acted irresponsibly for one so educated, and from a secure and supportive home. I have taken account of the brutal attack upon you, which must have been traumatic. I have also taken account of the findings your counsel has submitted on your behalf. It is the judgement of this court that you will pay a fine of £500. You will also pay a further £300 towards the prosecution costs. Furthermore, with regards to your drug taking, you will attend a drug awareness course which will be designated by a probation officer. Go from this courthouse and succeed in your life,' the ageing, stern faced magistrate concluded.

In the so-called enlightened era, one may have legitimately asked why this abused young woman, with no previous convictions and alleged good character, was exposed to the brutal court apparatus. The court procedure and police heavy handedness appeared not to have changed that much since before Victorian times. Why now then did they expose her to personal humiliation for such a relatively minor offence? Surely it would have been more productive for all concerned to have dealt with Henrietta Marlow's drug taking using wise council and common sense. The court costs must have been considered - police time could have been more judiciously employed elsewhere. More importantly, this young woman now had a criminal record which could be detrimental to future employment. It was of course still maintained that the state knew best how to deal with its wayward citizens. Nearly all British institutions were overcrowded with people, who for the most part, would not benefit from being incarcerated. Public safety was of course paramount, but the above indictment, surely, didn't warrant such draconian measures?

Within a week the news had spread, like some growing germ, all over Heatherslade village. The local newspapers carried the sensational headline: 'Local woman fined for taking cocaine'. This was used as an opening gambit to whet the appetites of those determined to make a big story out of it. Many were sympathetic to one of their own being attacked - but other, more important information had been deliberately withheld by journalists for financial reasons. According to a few indignant and outraged people, the die had been cast. Some stories lasted for a few hours, others went on for life. Fact or fiction: that was the short sighted, unpredictable verdict of what many locals thought of the Marlows at the time. Mind you, Henrietta Marlow hadn't killed someone, or robbed a bank, or even stolen a car. In the so-called modern age, she had only been caught with a small amount of an illegal drug, which wasn't a hanging offence. Meanwhile, Miss Marlow was more than comfortable to live by bourgeois standards. She was used to being pampered, not only by her parents but her extended family too.

But unlike on the last occasion, when Henrietta had

been attacked by a person or persons unknown, very few people, not surprisingly, contacted the Marlows this time. Sympathy did, however, come from Tony's brother and good friend Cecil, aged 52 - an optician somewhere in South Wales - and other family members that he rarely saw. Genuine, long standing friends also phoned to reassure him that it wasn't the end of the world. Hard-nosed Marlow, on reflection, thought the same. Fuck em, he thought, after years of working hard to develop his business - sometimes amid bruising negotiations with unscrupulous gangsters called businessmen - he wasn't prepared to allow a few hollow noises to detract him. Besides, now that his daughter was back home for a while recuperating, his main priority was her recovery until such time as she returned to her own flat.

With that in mind, Marlow certainly wasn't going to miss the next parish meeting, which had been cancelled several times due to his absence. Representing his local villagers still motivated him. Re-energised and with his head held high, he made his way to meet his parish council colleagues.

'Good evening fellow councillors,' smiled chair Fox-Rice, 'I hope all is well. I would like to jump straight into the historical problem of the village vehicle issue and our recent funding application to Sleeford Council. I'm sorry to say that I've not yet heard from them. They are as cash strapped as Ebenezer Scrooge. That leads us on to the proposed new community centre, although I wish the idea could be dumped and forgotten,' the chair muttered to himself.

It was at this moment that the councillors remembered that at the last parish meeting the chair and Tony Marlow nearly came to undignified blows over the subject. It ended with the latter directing a few harsh, ripe and justified words at Rice-Fox, before walking out of the meeting.

'Fellow councillors, could we please discuss this proposal in a reasonable manner which befits our parish duties? Unlike on the last occasion when things got rather heated. Could I also remind you that there were seven councillors at the last meeting who supported the motion,' remarked Peter Barnes-Jowell, whose Quaker practise, since his early college days, tried to inform quiet reflection.

Everyone nodded, smiled or gestured in some way to indicate that they agreed with Barnes-Jowell. Two disagreed with the proposal, it was their right of course, but it was also important for councillors to share the views of local people. Even hearing the word made the chair cringe, Rice-Fox's strong feelings of the village being overrun by young, long-haired hoodlums about to burn the place to the ground was probably baseless. But it did project deep insecurity for a village he loved. Regardless of his previous life, where everyone jumped at his stern voice, he was now retired, and virtually powerless like most people in the village. Being chair of the parish council, however, did afford him a minor position of merit. Many villagers, especially the elders, supported Rice-Fox, regardless of the pros and cons of the argument. His views still carried much political weight due to his previous life as a sea captain, his conspicuous grand house, and a long line of family influence.

'Like the chair, I still oppose a new community centre,' confirmed councillor Pringleton. All the other councillors confirmed, in principle, that they supported a new community centre, even though there wasn't currently enough money available to even install a village seat. But the final and most vociferous councillor to speak appeared to echo the general consensus on this difficult issue.

'Colleagues, I have had several residents contact me over the past two years feeling irritated by our bloody ineptitude to act. We are here to represent local people, and generally try to enhance village infrastructure. Please could we at least agree in principle to build the centre, and when, or if, the finances become available, we can then inform local people. We all realise, for God's sake, that most of the monies would have to be found by the council,' retorted councillor Drummond, who had long been an ardent supporter of community cohesion.

Henrietta had been recuperating at her parents' home for nearly a month. After all the traumatic upheaval, she marvelled at the peace, quiet and support she experienced living in Heatherslade once again. During the long days, as her parents worked elsewhere, she sat alone in the sitting room that backed onto the large garden and marvelled at the number of birds she had not seen before. She had probably seen them flying into the garden to eat food from the bird boxes; yet her mind and her feelings had been so pre-occupied with other things that she hadn't registered them. Whether in rain, wind or sun, the birds always turned up for their daily rations. She started to recognise, with the help of one of her mother's many books, the names of various birds. They looked so small, frail and vulnerable, echoing Henrietta's own emotions. She was intrigued by the speed of the small birds, the finches and tits in particular, especially when they nosed-dived to drink water, eat nuts and make their getaway. They were constantly vigilant, which reminded Henrietta of openly smoking skunk in Soho - she was always on the lookout, thinking that the police were ready to pounce. These feelings made her shudder at the madness that had become her life.

Tony Marlow had paid privately for the services of a physiotherapist - a young vivacious woman who lived north of the village - to visit his daughter twice weekly. Not unlike her client, she projected those female qualities now essential for the modern woman. Her new, fast, red car attracted the discerning eye. In his financial position, only the best was good enough for Tony Marlow's family. The injuries Henrietta had sustained to her right shoulder and the tendons of her right hand, were deep and severe. It was the latter that required regular exercise, otherwise her hand might have become atrophied. She made a considerable physical effort at every session, acutely aware that she needed two functioning hands to earn money. At times she became morbid, usually after her physiotherapist had left, with feelings of a futile, sad life of disability, dependence and drudgery. If that happened, she constantly thought of various methods of committing suicide. Overdosing with drugs, alcohol, slashing her wrists and many other desperate measures could be employed to end it all. Nonetheless, she needed to remain positive and calm when she recalled the actions of her former life.

Phone calls from various colleagues at Film Glow certainly helped Henrietta to remain focused. One person she really didn't want to hear from, Tariq Pathan, constantly bombarded her with offensive calls regarding buying and selling drugs. She kept her mobile phone and computer switched off most days. But there were always frightening messages waiting for her. What could she do about them? Had the time come to be candid with her parents about the last few years and to explain all the sordid, casual, abusive sexual affairs? Should she be honest about the many illegal drugs she had sold for money? She had delved into nearly all the drugs that were available on the underground crime scene. She wasn't proud of her recent past but if she came clean to her parents she was confident she could still make things work out. She wasn't perfect, she concluded, but who was? So many powerful people did one thing in front of the public, yet another behind the scenes. She would have to accept what was coming her way, painful as that may be.

On sudden impulse she phoned Tariq. She wasn't going to take his anger and aggression anymore. She was going to confront her past, and that included Pathan. Her whole body was shaking as she phoned his mobile.

'Leave me alone you bastard. Fucking leave me alone. I don't do drugs. That's final. If you contact me again, I shall go straight to the police and tell them the truth. You bastard you knifed me several times,' she angrily shouted. Now it had been stated clearly to Pathan for the first time since the attack. She wasn't that frightened of him anymore. He wasn't some sort of big gangster or successful businessman, he wasn't even a competent management consultant. He was a coward of the highest order. He made money by selling illegal drugs to weak and damaged people whose lives were being wrecked - once ably assisted by Miss Marlow!

'After a few weeks of rest and physiotherapy darling, do you think you are making progress?' Eleanor Marlow asked her daughter, who had gained weight.

'Sure mum. It's another world here from the one in London where everybody hasn't time to think, feel or smile. I'm more relaxed and confident. I've been out walking today for a mile or two around the village. Saw a few old creatures; they looked so old, bless them, they resembled scrawny chickens. They acknowledged my presence,' she explained as her dad walked into the sitting room holding a tray of drinks.

Sitting opposite her parents, she thought how well dressed and attractive they both looked. Henrietta felt anxious and tense, but she knew the time was right to explain her sordid past to them - regardless of how painful it would be.

'Mum and dad, I have something very important that I should, I mean, I want to explain to you,' she muttered hesitantly. Henrietta took a large gulp of white wine and continued to address her parents. 'I have been taking illegal drugs, hard drugs, class A drugs, since my days before Tristar. I took cocaine, skunk, methamphetamine, ketamine, poppers, GBH, virtually anything that was placed in front of me. I'm so sorry to tell you all this. My body craved the bloody stuff. I was addicted and probably, to a certain extent, still am,' she said, as torrents of tears and years of repression rolled down her soft cheeks. She was only temporarily relieved of an inner burden that cried for expression and redemption.

'I'm so shocked to hear that, sweetheart,' said Mrs Marlow, whose sad eyes were fixed on her daughter's tense body language. She wished she could protect her daughter from a world that was harming her, but realised she was a mature woman who had to make her own decisions from now on. That vulnerable little girl she had once protected with all her inner strength would now need to move at her own pace. Henrietta's road ahead was unknown; long, murky and potentially perilous.

Rather impulsively, and totally out of character, Tony Marlow shouted at the young frightened woman in front of him.

'For fuck sake Henrietta what has been going on? What have you been doing to yourself?' he said angrily, demanding answers.

'I can't really explain dad. Things just happened. I sort of let them happen, I suppose,' she said vaguely.

'What does that fucking mean Henrietta? Things just happened. What do you mean? You don't just take drugs. You made a conscious decision to take them for the pleasure you thought you would experience. It's pure reckless behaviour,' her father shouted.

She was free to do what she liked, she thought, searching herself. But like others in a similarly precarious position, she felt alone and vulnerable. Drugs, she had thought, provided a sort of smash and grab on reality that induced in her something that had hitherto been missing. Notwithstanding the love her parents had given her all her short life, there was an impoverishment that desperately needed fulfilment. Her identity, such as it was, had been conditioned by others. She needed to grasp the chance to break free of that while it pervaded her consciousness.

There couldn't be any going back. It was out of the question. She had to be brave, imaginative, creative, and above all else, she needed to focus on a pragmatic, yet unknown future. Freedom beckoned. She had, after all, craved for it.

'Well I suppose in one way it was reckless,' she reluctantly agreed with her father. 'But in another way it is my life and I was trying to live it. Well in a way, I think I still am,' she said rather confusingly to her wounded parents.

'Live your life Henrietta, but look at the problems you are causing to innocent people such as me and your mother for God's sake,' he said. 'Besides, you are fortunate that we are in a position to provide for you during your rehabilitation. Are you not?' he asked as he continued to express his downright disgust with the daughter that had received the best that he and his wife could have offered her.

'Mum and dad, I not only took all those illegal drugs as I've explained, but my then boyfriend, Tariq Pathan, and I used to sell them to friends, colleagues and anyone else, and there were many who needed them in the dives we used. We didn't make a fortune. What we did make we used to buy more drugs, and sometimes clothes,' Henrietta reluctantly explained to her frozen faced parents.

'Sweetheart, I'm so saddened by what I have just heard that it makes my heart bleed for you,' her mother said, crying into her shaking hands. Where had the vivacious Mrs Marlow, University educated in Paris, failed in her duty towards her daughter? she pondered. It was as though another person had possessed the body of Henrietta Marlow: having stolen her personality, character and whole way of life.

'I'm lost for words,' said Tony Marlow, his anger finally getting the better of him as he threw the wine glass he was holding against the wall. As the blue crystal wine glass scattered all over the floor, red parallel lines ran down the attractive yellow wallpaper. Pain personified the Marlow household. No one spoke until Henrietta, voice trembling, stood and addressed her parents.

'I'm so sorry mummy and daddy. Please forgive me for being so selfish,' she sobbed uncontrollably in front of her suffering parents. Was she as free as she had thought, or was it all a dream, a delusion that would somehow work its way, given time, through her immature emotions? The next revelation would surely stretch the unbearable to its limits.

'Mummy and daddy, I'm four months pregnant,' Henrietta hesitatingly told her parents, who were silenced for several long minutes. They both sat there staring at the wall, not knowing how to respond to the devastating information their daughter had just revealed. Suddenly, without any words being spoken, the parents spontaneously jumped to their feet and wrapped their arms round their daughter. Considering all that had happened to Henrietta in such a relatively short time, the parents were confronted with the most pressing problem to be inflicted on her.

'Who is the father?' asked Tony Marlow.

'Tariq Pathan, a colleague at Film Glow,' she told her father, whose anxiety levels were difficult to contain.

'Is this the same cretin you took and sold drugs with?' he asked. His eyes looked past her, beyond the garden and up into the woods, where at times he had wandered on his own seeking solace from the world of construction. He had found a small, comfortable hollow, just big enough for his tallish, slim body to think out intractable problems. If only he could be there now among the dark undergrowth, where the quiet animals gave him space and always listened, even though they didn't provide solutions.

Right now, all Marlow wanted was retribution for his traumatised daughter. He had a strong impulse to kill the bastard who made his daughter pregnant, gave her illegal drugs and, no doubt, encouraged her to sell them too. If he saw him right now, he would have slain the wretch to pieces without any compunction. But somehow he had to quell the raging fires, hoping that Pathan would, at some stage, suffer in Dante's fires of hell.

Henrietta still held guilt within her. She had not confided in her parents, or anyone else, including the police, that it was Tariq Pathan who had knifed her - just like a butcher cutting a side of meat fresh in a slaughterhouse. When, if at all, would she open up about the perpetrator? Why didn't she inform the police, or at least explain what had happened to her parents? Fear had entrenched itself within Henrietta's whole being. If she spoke out, Pathan would kill her. It preoccupied her every day to think that he was still at large, dangerous and deranged enough to end her life before she could find the inner confidence to let the world know of him. He had probably been dealing drugs for years if his expensive apartment in Pimlico was any guide. Besides, she now wondered what some of his older customers had referred to when they were visiting his home buying drugs. Comments like 'you were cheaper years ago' and 'prison hasn't changed you' now began to make sense. He clearly had a criminal background. When he was smoking crack and reckless with words, she realised what he meant by 'earning lots of illegal money' and 'his day job being a pretence for his drug dealings'. What a naive fool she had been; she lambasted herself.

Regarding his daughter's pregnancy, Marlow thought of at least three possibilities that he could suggest that could give her some sort of personal choice. None of them would be an easy solution, for he didn't want to exacerbate an already painful predicament, but he would do his utmost for the person in front of him.

'Would you like to have the baby Henrietta? I mean your mum and I will support you, of course. What are your feelings about it?' Marlow quietly asked her.

'I don't know dad. My feelings are confused and troubled at the moment,' she explained.

'Sweetheart,' her mother said, 'there are several options that I can suggest, but please don't feel you have to follow any of them. There is an abortion. Sorry to mention that. You could have the child adopted or care for your child yourself, perhaps in the early days with the support of a private carer. Of course, your father and I would also look after it, and also the financial side of things. I don't know how your father feels about it, but you could live here for...'

'Of course, she can,' Marlow eagerly interrupted. Now over 55 years of age and with a longish life of hard work behind him, albeit still full of energy, Tony Marlow had for some time felt the biological pull of helping to nurture and teach offspring within his family. Besides, given that his son was unlikely to have children of his own, Marlow knew that his opportunity of being a doting grandfather was diminishing in front of his eyes. Instinct warned him that if his daughter had an abortion, she would move back to London and continue with her life – and with it, yet more hedonism.

If it came to it, he was even prepared to fall to his knees and beg his daughter to have her child, so desperate he was for another meaningful role in life. He would love the golden opportunity to socialise with another young, vulnerable human being, dependant on him for sustenance and development. He knew in his heart that he could provide a stimulating environment whereby the youngster would have controlled freedom to play, express itself and grow into a strong individual. These were massive projections on his part, Marlow conceded. Nonetheless, experience and fortitude were on his side.

He walked upstairs to his office for a moment of reflection. As he watched the torrential rain falling, he recalled with some lucidity his daughter's younger socialisation. Her selfish and attention seeking behaviour as a child had been at times disruptive in an otherwise happy home. Her behaviour was in contrast with that of her older brother Toby, who was kind, friendly and for the most part contented. Henrietta, he realised, had always had a strong gregarious streak to her extroverted and flashy personality. She always needed to be the centre of attention. If that didn't materialise, Henrietta used to scream, shout, swear and throw outrageous hysterics until the spotlight fell on her beautiful face. Her behaviour, however, did improve after puberty. But it appeared that she had instead become secretive, cunning, and manipulative. She didn't take anyone or anything seriously enough, Marlow surmised. At times, her anger was very destructive for one so young. She indulged her pleasures by burning worms, pulling wings off butterflies, dropping the cat from the top of the garden apple tree, and most sadistically of all - she stuck pins in Toby's body. Toby never used to complain very much about the aggressive inflictions, but as he grew up and went to university, he became less involved with his sister. Nowadays, due to the nature of his legal work and his residence in Essex, he rarely spoke with her. Marlow was beginning to realise that he could have repressed his daughter's uncontrolled and immature behaviour. During his years spent developing a successful business, he didn't have the time to try and understand the reasons behind his daughter's self-destructive attitude. Because of his own poverty-stricken upbringing, he blamed himself for spoiling his own daughter: he over-indulged her grandiose behaviour to the extent that she, at times, emotionally ruled the household.

'I'm so fucked up. If I kept my child, regardless of whether I lived here or in London, I couldn't keep working full-time. And that means my company would sack me. You are both so very good to me but I don't deserve it. In time, I want to move back to London and continue with my life. Of course, many things have to change, I am aware of that, like addressing my drug problem,' said Henrietta. She had also realised, in a momentary flash, that Tariq Pathan - the father of her child - did not know she was pregnant. She intended that this status quo would remain indefinitely. It gave her power and control which she could use against him at any time, she thought contemptuously of the wretch who deserved to experience his own suffering.

But was that statement to her parents about sorting out her drug addiction habit sincerely felt or genuinely conveyed?? They probably had their doubts; and Henrietta knew it would be improbable to escape the chemical clutches of the snakes that poisoned her mind of hidden pleasures and painful tremors. Her old way of life was waiting for her if she returned to London. If she didn't inform on Tariq Pathan now, and of course she had no witnesses to support her claims against him, he would continue to supply her and many others with stronger and more dangerous drugs from South America - until she hit the proverbial brick wall.

CHAPTER FOUR

The sun shone brightly on Heatherslade Village. It appeared to be a special place at that moment in time. Was it preparing itself to be ordained for higher, unknown qualities to be bestowed upon it when conditions approved? Bright golden daffodils, along with other blooming flowers, were to be seen everywhere. Bees, butterflies and various insects quenched their thirst. Seasonal birds, intermixing with native ones, flew as if a procession was about to commence - the celebration of something personal and important.

After two weeks of recuperation, Henrietta was discharged from a private London clinic. The guilt and indignity of an abortion remained intensely painful for her. But she nonetheless continued to smile with her relaxed family alongside her as they all walked slowly and deliberately towards All Angels church. They were there to celebrate their good fortune: Henrietta was well. The family appeared united after months of strife, and summer had arrived which meant long warm sunny days together enjoying the smiles, kisses and hugs that had been in short supply recently. Even Toby who was usually emotionally restrained seemed happy to be with his family after months of imposed isolation. He was particularly pleased that his sister was now living with their parents after the experience of the clinical and impersonal torment of the plush London hospital that had sucked the life out of her.

Another reason to rejoice was the opportunity for Eleanor Marlow to sing in the church choir once again. Due to work and family commitments she had been available only on certain occasions to sing church music - her great passion in life - with local friends she had made over the last few years. While studying for an economics degree at the Sorbonne University, she sang in some of the great 18th century churches and cathedrals in Paris. Her accomplished voice raised itself to the heavens wherever she sang. Praised by clergy and laity alike; her Christian conviction was to sing the praises of the God she had worshipped since her early days when she attended the American church with her devoted parents in Paris. In her youth, her mother had also been a notable soprano singer for many years, performing in and around New York. What made this occasion very special for Eleanor was being invited to sing by Reverend Bullchat himself. She viewed this as a great honour, bestowed upon her by God's representative on earth.

Bullchat took his commitment to God very seriously. He told people at every opportunity that he had been chosen by the almighty to carry out his earthly work for the betterment of mankind. Tony Marlow himself scoffed at such comments as trite and delusional, but kept his personal feelings close to his chest, aware that such heretical ideas could alienate him from his village neighbours. Besides, Bullchat had visited the Marlow family when their daughter was in crisis, and Tony respected his concern. Marlow had been informed on more than one occasion that Bullchat, although from a privileged background, had spent many years helping the poor, forgotten, downtrodden and sick in the slums of Indian villages. Now that was worthy of the highest praises, thought Marlow. The latter's friend, Billy Blumley, had himself worked for many years as a Christian volunteer in various Indian slum villages with the lower castes. He was aware, as he informed Marlow, what the local vicar, and other unselfish people like him had given to help others. 'A great quality,' he concluded.

'If the almighty exists, and I certainly think he does,' enthused Blumley, 'Bullchat, and others sharing his spiritual aspirations, shall sit at the feet of him in heaven.'

As the Marlow family walked through the old, wooden lychgate covered in perennial moss and into the church, it was as though another world had opened up for them. The old organ sounded deep, sombre and sublime. Spiritual life – something that was so often missing in the material world - seemed to take over. The old hammer styled beams appeared to shake with delight. Wooden pews full of parishioners turned to welcome them as multi-coloured glass from the windows threw shards of lighted rays into the well of the old dark church. If one listened intently enough, the steel boots of field labourers could be heard walking into the church a century or more ago after sixteen hours of graft. That metal sound became louder as brown faced men, caps in hand, filed out quicker than they entered, anticipating a few pints of locally brewed ale. According to a few older villagers, occasional whispered voices of people long departed from this earth could still be heard among the cracks, crevices and cobwebbed corners of the church.

Eleanor took her position within the assembled choir of men and women, young and old. Each had blood connections to the village. Eleanor looked divine, adorned in a brilliant white smock with mauve trimming. Long attractive hair and shining green eyes emboldened her sharp features resembling the Greek goddess of love. Her family sat nearby not far from the 18th century rood screen depicting biblical iconography, which was painted by a village descendent. Sweet smelling incense pervaded the air. Bullchat rose mindfully to the top of the pulpit to oversee his flock.

'Welcome everyone, to this house of God. May his presence fill your everyday life with love, goodness and compassion for world peace. I also welcome into our religious presence the Marlow family, who, amongst many others, have had their own personal problems recently. May they all find love here today,' smiled the Reverend. Tony Marlow found these words humbling. They filled him - for the first time in his life - with a much deeper understanding of human fallibility: especially his own.

The choir sang with all its might. The sweet words echoed around the little old church that had long been a refuge for the great, good and working villagers of Heatherslade. Many military men had married, prayed, sang, broken bread and drank wine in this hallowed place. But many never returned to their village from various conflicts around the world. They were remembered at every opportunity by the clergy and locals. Indeed, Councillors Robert Rice-Fox and Brockleby both lost several family members in different wars. All Angels was a place, above all else, where one could find inner peace to focus on those heroes and loved ones who sacrificed all. Wall plaques adorned with Angels echoed the past with austere silence.

All Angels' congregation emerged once again back into the brilliant early afternoon sun. It appeared that the local wildlife had congregated to welcome them with songs and chat worthy of much merit. People shared their understanding and kindness for one another. William Hetherington sat on the grass feeding the birds with big, fat, wriggling worms to offer his kind nourishment.

It appeared that all was well with the world of Heatherslade village. However, the conditions that besieged Henrietta and her family had not disappeared. If Henrietta was honest, the shadow of Tariq Pathan still presented its ugly vision of fear whenever she was unaware of its power to insult and degrade. She either had to live with it or go straight to the police and explain everything. They would protect her until Pathan had been apprehended. Failing her inner voices meant indefinite self-loathing. As she had already grappled with the insane idea of running away from her parents' security, there were very little options available to her but to face the inevitable facts.

Lizzie Trout, Herbert Tate and Percy Cusack were already drinking merrily, discussing local gossip, hearsay and so on. They were ensconced in their usual cosy armchairs when the Marlow family entered the Willow Tree pub. They had not been in their local watering hole for some considerable time. Very little had changed during that period, especially the same old faces who were propped up by the bar in case they fell, drinking their Sunday lunchtime tipple.

'Well hello Tony, Eleanor and Henrietta you are looking most attractive my dear! And Toby, I do believe. I've not seen you for some considerable time my dear. How are you?' asked Herbert. Due to his legal work, Toby had visited his parents infrequently. He missed the warm company of his parents - but like his sister, he wasn't overly keen on the village pub. Tony knew of course that most of the people were from a different generation, with altogether different views and values from his own. For such a reserved man, one might have thought that being a barrister and articulating legal merits with considerable presence in packed courts was an unlikely profession. But Toby did, nonetheless, like Tate, Percy Cusack and few others. He was respectful of their past professions and what they had achieved for humanity.

Central to his life at present, however, was developing a successful legal career at the bar which required commitment, hard work and a thick skin. Outside of court they were gentlemen, and most were sensitive and helpful, yet inside that lions' den his peers were ruthless and single minded. These were qualities he needed to develop if he were to thrive and take the lead over other aspiring lawyers. He appeared to be up for the challenge.

'I'm well, thank you, Mr Tate,' he replied with a sensitive smile. 'And how about your good self? Are you still a councillor on the local parish council?'

'Oh yes, I'm well. Thanks to other councillors like your dad and local residents complaining, quite rightly of various things, I'm kept busy and focused on village life, just in case I go astray,' he winked at Toby.

The other two councillors acknowledged the Marlows' presence. Other locals nodded their approval. Though not a word had past the lips of any of the family, they all wondered if the notorious local news gossipers had already found out about the further revelations of Henrietta Marlow's lifestyle. It was inevitable that sooner or later the village film goddess's wicked ways would enter the public arena for discussion, judgement and condemnation. Henrietta, due to guilt and intense anxiety, thought a million faces were intensely looking at her in the pub. Particularly the older women, whose moralistic codes of behaviour had already labelled her a loose woman, and one not fit to walk brashly into their pub without showing repentance. She could only imagine the outcry once they became aware of her drug dealing and the indecency of having an abortion with no known father around for support. But what did she expect after flaunting herself, without compunction, around the village like some wild alley cat dressed in high heels? Although the sun continued to shine through the pub windows, her lofty dream of a new beginning began to wane.

The noise of the pub merriment grew as Percy Cusack approached the bar for another round of drinks. He loved nothing more than a few pints of ale on a Sunday morning to give him a lift for the week ahead. Though his wife was today visiting her grandchildren, she and Percy were renowned for their regular beer quaffing. In fact, they made their own, gallons of the stuff - so much that gossip suggested they could have started their own micro-brewery in the shed at the back of their large detached house. It was the standing village joke that Mrs Cusack fell over, or through, so many hedges due to the evil grog! The fact that she used to be an optician didn't help matters. With three grown up daughters and six grandchildren, the eccentric Percy - a former airline pilot - was game for most things given the opportunity. Neither Cusack nor his wife were ideal candidates for front row membership of the temperance movement. They were, however, decent and hard-working people whose enthusiasm for the local community was infectious.

'Another pint Percy?' asked Herbert Tate, not that either man, including Lizzie Trout, needed any strong persuasion when it came to much needed and maligned degenerative wallop.

'Not another old boy,' was the mild sarcasm from the captain, who was sitting on a rather flimsy stool for his spreading backside at the end of the bar. Sundays were Robert Fox-Rice's special day, just like the other six days when he spruced himself up in one of his many pin-striped three-piece suits and yellow bow tie. He looked dapper, minus the slim build. The captain wasn't averse, with sufficient whisky consumed, to singing a few lines of old sea shanties he had picked up during his long travels. But he had made a sizeable contribution towards the good of Heatherslade village ever since he could waddle down the old, local flinty tracks that were the norm when he was a child.

It was due to the diligent, cunning and conniving work of Herbert Tate that the council chose to tarmac and concrete the roads, making safety a priority. He cajoled and badgered the local Tory MP at the time - almost single handedly - into visiting the village. Eventually, browbeaten by relentless pressure, he added his political strength behind Tate's successful application.

Tony Marlow brought a small tray of drinks back to

where his family were sitting in the new extension of the pub. This end of the pub was furthest from bar; it was quiet, with a only few other families eating. No one said a word for several minutes. They all appeared pre-occupied with inner thoughts or were too self-conscious of their surroundings. Whatever the cause, Mrs Marlow broke the ice on a day that had so far been enjoyable. The sun still shone. Various birds congregated on the feeders outside the window. All the family were together again. It was a joyous occasion.

'It's important, I think, to visit our local pub sometimes if only just to say hallo to various villagers,' pondered Mrs Marlow. She had been in the place no more than a handful of times since moving to the village. She had always found British pubs rather boring, nondescript places. Warm ale, tasteless food and uncomfortable furniture appeared to be the norm. That was her brief experience of London, compared to bars in Paris.

'I agree mum. But there are very good restaurants in London, and elsewhere,' said Tony.

'This place is crap if you ask me,' said a vociferous Henrietta.

'How do you feel since leaving the clinic Henny?' asked Tony.

'I don't want to talk about that subject in here dad, if you don't mind,' she replied.

'Of course not, sweetheart,' he said reassuringly.

'Shall we eat here today gang or go home and roast that large piece of lamb mum bought yesterday?' suggested Tony who was trying his damned hardest to give his family an enjoyable time.

'Fuck this place dad,' said Henrietta.

'Yea, let's go home to eat. What do you think mum?' asked Toby.

'Yes, I fancy going home,' she said.

It was only when Percy Cusack had departed from the Willow Tree – no doubt to continue drinking homemade beer with his wife - that the other two were prepared to start to discuss the new Henrietta Marlow revelations.

'I've heard, unwittingly, all manner of unfounded chatter about the young woman's alleged illegal drug taking and abortion. Soon it will be said that she's shagging the King of Siam. That's if there is one,' Lizzie Trout reluctantly informed her fellow councillor and lover. It was inevitable that the nature of such tittle-tattle would emerge sooner rather than later in a small village. They were living off the air which was made thicker and rancid by those whose shallow lives revolved around condemnation.

'Indeed, so have I sweetheart,' responded a rather depressed looking Herbert Tate, whose usual demeanour suggested forgiveness. 'What can one say, other than let things unfold. The Marlows have had a pretty tough time of it recently,' he said. 'The guillotine awaits,' Tate said, in jest. In their official positions, they had heard it all before. Vindictiveness knew no bounds.

The inevitable chattering knives were wielding their dangerous cutting edges, and had for some time been pointing at the two councillors. Trout and Tate didn't wish or intend to shred their long-standing sexual affair to pieces. Oh, what depraved comforts! But the two councillors carried out their public duties with the best ethical intentions. What they did in their own personal time, morally, legally or otherwise, was for their consciences to appraise. Both were single and had no children. That was the way it had always been for the both of them. Neither had ever needed or wanted a family, but both responded to the call of duty when it came to supporting local villagers.

Tate had told nearly everyone that he was so fortunate to have inherited his parents' early Victorian detached house. Along with the French designed gardens came a stream full of fish and full-sized tennis court; it had been owned by several generations of Tates. His father had worked as a career served civil servant in the admiralty. It wasn't surprising, therefore, that his son was sent way, as they said in those days, to private schools, Cambridge and Dartmouth Naval College.

Due to everything being attributed to dear old Tate, his compatibility with Lizzie Trout was unsurprisingly enterprising. Both were bold, unafraid and fearless when looking into the penetrating eyes of fortitude. The unknown didn't frighten them at all. Trout was born in Dorset, but her parents moved to Heatherslade Village when she was ten years old where they were offered local teaching jobs. Lizzie herself had worked in hospital management in Maysbridge. She was first attracted to Tate not because of his so called virile appearance, but as the domineering leader of the local walking group they both regularly attended. He was soon attracted by her bulging frame.

CHAPTER FIVE

As late Autumn fell, Tariq Pathan's window of opportunity to carry out his scheme of perverted revenge presented itself. He felt almost ecstatic. His seething anger, which knew no bounds, again dredged itself up from dangerous depths. Why? He had been informed by colleagues that Henrietta Marlow had been made redundant. She had rented out her flat to an agency and was residing with her parents. He gloated at the prospect of knowing she was unemployed, but of course her parents had money, lots of it, and she would never have to worry about anything. She also had an income from her posh middle-class apartment - a gold mine in central London. Pathan also knew that she and her brother Toby were both included in her parents' substantial Trust-Fund which was set up for them when they were both children. Both stood to inherit a fortune. Pathan's anger grew alarmingly at the thought of her living a bourgeois lifestyle, sitting on her fat backside doing nothing with security all around her. Meanwhile, he would have to keep working at Film Glow. He needed the money, so he claimed, but selling illegal drugs was a lucrative market attracting a growing number of mugs compelled to keep taking their poisons.

His warped mind knew he had to take full revenge of Henrietta Marlow's unimaginable and disastrous behaviour, which could lead to his undoing. He knew it was only a matter of time before she would decide to have him arrested for brutally attacking her - though she had very little evidence against him. She had been as culpable as he had when it came to illegally selling drugs, sometimes to vulnerable young children, and grabbing her share of the money. Hate money! Henrietta Marlow was devious, selfish and only concerned by her own well-being. But then so was he. He thought all women were promiscuous, immoral and not worthy of respect. Pathan knew on some level that he couldn't dominate her any more. She was free of his constant rage, jealousy and intimidation. No free person should have to experience what she had for the past two years. At the bleakest of times she had resorted to phoning the Samaritans for help and support. They helped her, were sympathetic and encouraged her to immediately inform the police. She was so frightened of his violent and wild unpredictability that even the thought of police involvement compelled her to indulge in more mind-numbing drugs to escape.

The only way out of his predicament, Pathan concluded, was to kill her. He was going to carry it out at the earliest opportunity. He was now committed and nothing was going to stop him. All he had to do was work out a full proof plan: cunning, conniving and audacious. Most importantly, he would ensure that her days on this earth were numbered. With this now at the forefront of his demented mind, he phoned Henrietta Marlow several times. He knew that by phoning early in the afternoon her parents would be at work. Henrietta had told him this many times in the past when they were on friendly terms and in regular phone contact. As there had been a considerable change in their once amicable relationship, she had now come clean to her family, but she still had no idea what her former psychopathic lover was planning.

'Why don't you leave me alone you bastard? We are finished Tariq,' shouted Henrietta. She wished, she hadn't answered her mobile phone and had instead just left him to leave his usual rants, raves and bullshit on her voicemail. 'What the fuck do you want?' she asked. He was a contemptuous person who hadn't given a damn about her over the years. If she was honest, she really couldn't have valued herself by taking a multitude of drugs. After all, he didn't physically thrust those drugs down her throat. She couldn't gulp them down quick enough when seeking mind expanding experiences that, inevitably, tore her inner life to shreds. The bastard couldn't hurt her anymore, she concluded. She must this very night come clean, wholeheartedly, with her parents about the violent nature of her previous relationship with Pathan. She must bite the exploding bullet and tell them that Pathan tried to kill her, even though she knew there was very little evidence to present to the authorities. But the abuse must end, she concluded.

'You are worthless, a louse of the lowest order. Stay away from me or else. I shall give you big trouble Pathan,' she shouted.

'Look Henny, I know our relationship is finished. But I just wanted a chat with you while I drink my coffee during my break in this Greek Street bistro. You know, the one you particularly enjoyed for its Italian breads and salami. Eddie, the dishy, sexy waiter asks how you are by the way?' he said quietly and kindly, yet all the time manipulating Henrietta into a false sense of security.

'Are you on your own sweetheart in that large, beautiful house of yours?' he spoke softly, but with a voice seeking revenge.

'I am. My parents are both working hard as usual, unlike you louse, and won't be home until around 6pm,' she foolishly told Pathan. Of course, she didn't realise how she was being manipulated. Her security had been torn to pieces. She was in mortal danger but unaware that Pathan was preparing to invade her home, her personal space, her whole life. He wasn't in Greek Street at all, he was sitting in a country car park listening to his car radio not two miles from Heatherslade village. He had got the bitch right where he wanted her.

Pathan sat in his parked car breathing heavily, anticipating reaching the one person who he most hated as his plans became more focused. Hoping his number plate wasn't noticed by some nosy bastard and reported to the police or council, he tentatively got out of his black Mercedes - which he had bought using the proceeds of his illegal drugs sales. After hours of driving and aimlessly waiting around the fresh air immediately hit his senses. He took in a few deep breaths to orientate himself before setting out in Slindon Woods on paths he had planned beforehand from an Ordnance Survey map of the area. Pathan thought himself a clever operator, like a modern spy, studying maps which were strewn across his apartment floor. He had found various paths that led to Heatherslade village, and more importantly, in case of an emergency he had taken it upon himself to find other ways out for when he needed to collect his car from the clearing in the wood. It was crucial that he had detailed knowledge of the woods and surrounding areas, just in case he was chased by some would-be hero who knew the place better than he. Many obsessional thoughts preoccupied his anxious mind.

He set out on the path he had fastidiously planned, convinced that large tall conifer trees acted as a screen in most of the wood. Attractive brown and golden leaves were falling as he continued walking. Slindon Woods was full of deciduous beech, oak, elm and birch, which made it popular with the public. The sky above was darkening as dusk approached. Further along the muddy track, more conifers exacerbated the impending gloom. The undergrowth was dark green, approaching blackness in parts, and all around appeared to stare and speak. 'Don't do it', was echoed. Pathan stopped and took a large swig from a brandy bottle he pulled from his pocket to settle his tightening muscles. Another mouthful hit his brain with force, pulled him together and reduced the beats of his thumping heart. Did he know what he was actually doing? Pathan sat down on a fallen tree to make sure he was heading in the right direction. He felt confused. Thousands of wild animals appeared to be laughing at him from all around: 'You stupid bastard,' they screamed. 'Who do you think you are ending a perfectly healthy life?' Pathan felt extremely anxious. He took several more mouthfuls of brandy to steady his taught nerves. The alcohol was working; his brain was once again focused on its intended depravity - to kill Henrietta Marlow. That was what the voices demanded, and that was what needed to be achieved.

Henrietta Marlow was now only half a mile away, a twenty minute walk from the large house where the most heinous crime was about to be perpetrated. He could do it, he must do it, the threatening voices demanded. Failure at this stage was inconceivable, especially for someone as special and demented as King Tariq Pathan. He knew he was unique. The multiplicity of drugs he had ingested confirmed this without question, he was a narcissist. But another fellow drug traveller, Henrietta Marlow, was one of the most depraved of them all. He knew that, of course, from his experience of her drug crazed behaviour. Her insane, bizarre behaviour had caused incalculable damage to innocent youngsters when peddling their drugs amongst some of Soho's grime, filth and degraded shit. The dregs that others neither wanted nor needed. He was now out to set the record straight, to give a voice to those who didn't make it past their early teens. The woman not two hundred yards from his clutches was responsible for shaming human existence, Pathan convinced himself.

On the verge of dusk as he mentally prepared himself, Pathan descended the final four hundred feet down through brambles and bracken when he was suddenly frightened out of his skin by several hissing feral cats that ran across his path. That made his nerves jangle and stopped him in his tracks. He breathed rather heavily. He was sweating profusely, his long expensive overcoat was covered in moss and thorns, with other detritus accumulating around him as he walked through the woods. Focused once again, he thought his map directions would take him between two tall privet hedges - which was a public thoroughfare, with houses either side - and into Blackbird Rise. Incidentally, those privet hedges he had just passed belonged to Celia Hetherington and Anne Woodhouse who had witnessed many things, some most pernicious, during their long reign in the village. But even they, with varied tales of personal histories behind them, could not have imagined the terror that was about to befall one so young.

His nerves were as taut as violin strings. As no one was around, he took two more large swigs of brandy. He threw the empty bottle under a verge side bush. A rather short sighted, rash action indeed. Pathan walked slowly for several minutes and eventually found Henrietta Marlow's home. There it stood in all its grandiosity. Large, detached, clean, posh and with all the trimmings of affluence. It seemed as though the drug selling bitch had been ensconced for some time, lapping up a privileged lifestyle denied to many other decent people. According to Pathan, her time had come to pay the ultimate price for being inhuman to so many innocent kids, for choking them to death with poisons not even fit for warfare. He now had to carry out the act before her parents arrived back. From across the road he noticed that the only lights came from the lounge at the back of the house. Pathan had detailed information about her family, home and village. He had cunningly written everything down; he had detailed information even though he had never been to the village before. She couldn't deceive him anymore. The game was up!

His dark clothes blended in with the dimly lit road. Breathing even deeper than before, his body muscles stiffening, he quietly walked around the side of the house until he found the small kitchen door. It was open; he was in luck. Nerves next to breaking point, he prepared himself for her final demise. He heard a faint voice coming from the back room next to the kitchen. Henrietta was speaking to someone on the phone. Fuck my luck, Pathan thought - this was the last thing he needed. Sweat pouring down his face, gloves on and a gruesome long bladed knife in his pocket, he quietly entered the kitchen. She was still speaking to one of her cronies on the phone. Perhaps she was even setting up a drug deal. Henrietta Marlow thought she was the centre of the world.

With the black handled blade raised in his clenched fist, he charged into the room and plunged the knife straight into her neck. He repeated the act several times until she lay there slumped on the armchair, dead. Blood poured from the many wounds to her neck, shoulder and chest. Her beautiful slim body was limp, still and lifeless. A gruesome sight. Her smooth face, drained of blood, grew white and hollow. Where had she gone? No one deserved such a terrible, disgusting, brutal end to life. Not one of her family was there to comfort her in those last desperate moments of suffering. There would be only utter disdain for Pathan.

He stood staring at her body like a frozen statue, trying to dissociate himself from his actions. The two of them were together for the final time. He had witnessed her die in agony. Painful silence penetrated his being. What now? he thought, after he had eventually achieved his sordid goal. He had crossed the line of no return. Hereafter, Pathan's inner thoughts would undoubtedly persecute, torment and ultimately drag him into a hell without mercy.

He didn't know whether the person Henrietta had been phoning had overheard anything, but he immediately removed the sim card from the mobile and put both in his coat pocket. Clinically, resembling a butcher or laboratory worker, he scrupulously washed the knife under hot water in the kitchen - at all time keeping his gloves on. After sponging down his jacket, he put all the used cleaning materials in his pocket, turned out the lights, closed the kitchen door and stood in the fresh air. He stood motionless as he swallowed deep mouthfuls of cool air, trying to grasp, to comprehend, the enormity of his actions.

Sensing once again where he was, Pathan briskly walked past the two privet hedges, found the track and walked back up the hill, slipping over muddy ground twice, before entering Slindon Woods. He felt safe now that he had the cover of trees and dusk to protect him. He pulled out a small torch and map from his pocket which contained written directions to lead him safely back to his car. He momentarily thought of Henrietta's lifeless body, but the urgency to continue walking through the wood in pitch black darkness took all his concentration. His brisk walk turned to a slow running pace as he began to panic about his whereabouts. Pathan had lost the path he marked out for himself. Once again, he pulled out the torch and map to reassure himself that he was heading in the right direction. Then he thought of his car. What if some nosy bastard had informed the police and had it towed away, or it had been vandalised by children, or opportunist criminals had stopped to steal parts of it? His anxiety levels began to rise again. Fuck it, he thought, I'm lost and in danger of getting caught by the police. 'Take a minute or two and think rationally about your position on the path and how it relates to the map,' he said to himself. 'You're Pathan, the great one, don't forget.' It was so dark that he couldn't see two inches in front of him. He was frightened, anxious and petrified. Various sounds that he had not heard before started to deafen him. He imagined that he could hear people laughing at him. The laughter became louder and closer to him. 'Get yourself together Pathan, for fuck sake,' he tried to reassure himself that all was well, and that he wasn't in any imminent danger of being apprehended.

After several more glimpses at the map for guidance, he eventually found the path that led him to his parked car, hidden in a small clearing some fifty yards from a small lane. All appeared to be well. No one, as far as he could ascertain, had tampered with it. Standing there in the dark clearing, sweating profusely, he felt a million miles from humanity. This was hardly surprising due to the nature of his inhuman actions not an hour previously. He could run, hide, pray, take drugs or whatever. But he couldn't escape that inner voice reminding him that harsh consequences awaited those who deliberately, coldly and brutally took the life of another person. What had he done to deserve such persecution? Pathan protested. It was her, Henrietta Marlow, who was the culprit by poisoning so many young, innocent people. He tried to rationalise the terrible, self-inflicted predicament he was now in right up to his scrawny neck. Once he had explained the whole sordid story to the police, her parents and the mass media, then all would be revealed to the world, Pathan's delusions kept yelling at him. Meanwhile, he would have to play it rather cagey and keep hidden away from everyday life. This would mean finding an alternate home. This intense burden on Pathan from now on would intensify without precedent. He was the architect of his own downfall!

Pathan shook the dirt off his wet and torn coat, brushed himself down and cleaned his muddy shoes with rags in the boot of the car. He now looked less anxious; he was relatively clean and well-dressed if the police stopped him for some routine enquiry. Being Tariq Pathan, he could deal competently with any problem, no matter what it was. His confidence slowly returning, he got into his car, started it and drove out of the clearing and onto the dark unlit lane. Ten minutes later he was driving on the busy A373, not heading for London - but where to? No one knew.

Barry Merchant

CHAPTER SIX

Driving their new Daimler, the Marlows had returned to Heatherslade after another long, gruelling yet enjoyable day's work. It was around 7pm, the usual time they managed to sit down to a thoroughly deserved drink. Everything they owned represented a startling success based on many years of hard work. The grand icing on the rich, layered cake was two young, beautiful and intelligent children. What more could any parents wish for? All was well with their self-filled dream.

On the evening of 16th November, the Marlows' world fell apart and shattered into a million pieces when they found their daughter lying slumped over an armchair, mutilated, bloodied and dead. They were witnesses to an outrageous carnage. Only a deranged, psychopathic killer could have inflicted such depravity. Trying to keep her love warm and cherished, their arms encircled Henrietta's lifeless body. All three were now one. They couldn't let go until they had kissed her beautiful body goodbye. What the Marlows actually experienced and felt at that precise moment was, understandably, incomprehension.

Within minutes, three police cars sped into the quiet unprepared village, lights flashing and sirens wailing. The older inhabitants were totally shocked by the noise and action of people in uniforms running around sectioning off taped areas around the family home. Apart from the wagging gossip and occasional illicit sexual liaison, life was mostly quiet, predictable and staid in the village. Nerves started to jangle; those of a nervous disposition took a few more pills to calm themselves down. An ambulance was quickly followed by a forensic team of investigators, though most residents were unable to see anything due to the evening having descended into darkness. Uniformed and civilian official personnel walked briskly into the house with the intention of questioning the traumatised parents about the terrible crime brought upon their family. At that point in time, one could only guess at the atmosphere that surrounded the embattled household. The suffering within must have been unbearable, for even the most hardened police officer could hardly understand that a human being could bring such incalculable devastation to an innocent young woman.

Uniformed officers commenced a detailed search on their hands and knees of the front and rear gardens for evidence. The middle-aged forensic doctor inspected Henrietta's body for various signs, marks and other distinguishing evidence to assist the potentially arduous investigation. Ambulance staff stood nearby ready to assist; later they pushed her sealed body on a trolley to their flashing vehicle and drove to Maysbridge hospital mortuary. Later, a more detailed medical assessment would be carried out by a pathologist, possibly followed at a later stage by an inquest.

Such harrowing moments were so palpable that the tension soon spread around the village from neighbour to neighbour. Its effect was just like a wildfire, burning rapidly out of control through acres of dry bush. As time went on, some people began to panic. By this time it appeared that half of the village had now congregated around the Marlow home. They were soon followed by most of the pub customers. Those too old, infirm or drunk to walk, drove to the crime scene. They wanted to add their faces to the swelling crowd of onlookers who appeared intent on adding something - most didn't know what - to the ugly proceedings being played out in front of their noses. It was theatrical, nauseous, even intimidating, yet such was the nature of suffering that it attracted those whose usual everyday lives barely existed. No doubt, of course, there were friends and colleagues in the crowd who genuinely, desperately felt the need to support a village resident. In reality, most were confused and bewildered by the pandemonium. Not even the police conducting the in-depth enquires would offer any official information. It was much too early for that. Their mere presence was reassuring enough. But already leaking out to the public was the news that a life had been cruelly and inexplicably extinguished. Only painstaking work by the authorities could in time shed information on what actually happened on that fatal night. People held their breath, anticipating that many lives would never be the same again.

Added pressure on the family was exacerbated by the appearance of local cowboy journalists seeking sensational headlines for the next weeks' muck spreading newspaper. News based on evidence was a secondary consideration for those journalists, as long as it sounded right to readers and was supported - by misleading or subjective interviews with local people and distorted photographs of worried neighbours - nothing else mattered. Journalists knew they could extract most things from the everyday person who would sell their soul for a quote in the local Evening Argos. Ethical boundaries didn't matter, according to Michael Tribe, an old local hack whose only idea of a scoop was that it must be cheap and sell newspapers.

'Was she always like this Madam, the young Marlow girl?' Tribe asked an ageing neighbour who was gawking at the mass in front of her. 'I mean did she have lots of boyfriends? It's well known she had been on illegal drugs for years,' he tried to press home his obvious intentions of manipulating her into submitting something, anything.

'I'm afraid I don't know my dear. I don't know the family at all. They haven't been living here that long... several years I suppose. They say the father, Tony Marlow, is a millionaire from humble beginnings, but I'm not that sure,' she responded, smiling at Tribe's weather beaten, rather ugly face.

'Made good has he, Tony Marlow you say? Well that's interesting. I wonder if he ever kept his eye on his wandering daughter?' Tribe spelt out his cynicism.

'Don't know, I'm sure,' the lady responded. She began to edge away from the nosy and inquisitive journalist.

The local Evening Argos cohort expected the modern well-to-do local savages not to throw the traditional spears at people like the Marlows. Instead, they would use a more sophisticated, underhanded means of undermining the lower classes, after all - they lived in a privileged village with a great and memorable history. They, of course, were those gallant individuals, diminishing in numbers, who lived off the sweat and brow of slavery.

Biologically superior, they thought of outsiders as modern money grabbers whose only intention was to wreck their secure way of life. Sadly, this was the attitude of the older generation.

Some of the usually reserved villagers pressed forward, attracted by the police lights that flooded the front and rear gardens of the house. Most expected the worst. However, those like Celia Hetherington, Anne Woodthorne and other sincere supporters were more optimistic. Regardless of their background they were full of hope. What that hope was they weren't quite sure. Their personal backgrounds made them aware of how misleading quick judgements could be.

Charles Pearce, who led the team of local detectives, had the unenviable task of interviewing the Marlow family. He was an experienced police officer, not unaccustomed to human suffering, with many years of service. Murder to him wasn't unusual. But why had this particular crime happened in middle-class Heatherslade village, where the last recorded crime was about five years previously for drunk and disorderly behaviour? It wasn't exactly heavy duty, illegal activity, he thought.

'My deep condolences from all the police, Mr and Mrs Marlow. At this time of unspeakable tragedy for you both, I apologise, but it is my duty to interview you both. As the crime took place only hours previously, there may well be vital evidence left by the guilty that could further help us with our enquiries. I have assigned a female police liaison officer to support you through this most terrible ordeal. Also, a police guard will be stationed outside your house tonight and for the next few days if you need the security. Please forgive the bright lights in your gardens. Officers are carrying out a minute search of the grounds for a short while. But they will be back tomorrow to continue. I'm sure you understand,' said Pearce in a carefully reassuring yet apologetic voice.

'Of course, we understand superintendent, thank you,' replied a sad, shocked Tony Marlow.

Keeping questions intentionally to a minimum, Pearce arduously yet methodically went through Henrietta's life from a young age. His questions were painful, intrusive, penetrating, cold even, but nonetheless provided invaluable information to the mind of an experienced investigator. Any piece of evidence, regardless of how insignificant, was to the superintendent a potential gem - another possible piece of the jigsaw fitting nicely into place. Pearce had a thoroughbred instinct, which had developed over many years of hunting down nasty, brutal, insane killers. He could act like a polecat, weasel, stoat or any other similar animal when sniffing out the unusual, abnormal, low life wretches around. Very little escaped his attention. That's the way he was trained, tough and uncompromising since he first joined the police force at the age of eighteen. Kicked up the arse, knocked into shape and shouted at by his superiors; it was the best training any young police officer could have. If he had known the murderer's name at the time, Pearce would have shouted: 'Look out I'm not far behind you bastard'.

The most vital piece of evidence so far came from the lips of Tony Marlow himself, after he was questioned for an hour by Pearce. He explained that his daughter's drug taking had got out of hand. She had pleaded guilty in court to illegal drug possession. The police, of course, were well aware of that little hiccup. But the police didn't know anything about the existence of Tariq Pathan, which would have given a new and different dimension to the case. What the Marlows didn't know, much like the police, was that it was in fact Pathan that had cold-bloodedly knifed Henrietta. Unfortunately, that evidence would elude the two parties for some time. But the puzzle was beginning to take shape.

As the questioning of the Marlows continued, Inspector Tamworth – Pearce's assistant - along with two colleagues and forensics, went through the house with a fine toothcomb. They used modern sophisticated equipment to search for any minute pieces of evidence that the naked eye couldn't detect. They were looking for something so small that only a microscope could explain a rare piece of detritus vital for the puzzle. Even a small piece of grit might infinitely open up proceedings. Numerous finger prints were found in these kinds of investigations. Only one print was most vital. Human hair was to be analysed, phones to be inspected and much hard detective work to go ahead before any sort of coherent picture could be assembled. It wasn't work for the squeamish or shirkers. Not in Pearce's team anyway!

Throughout late evening, uniformed police officers continued to interview local people, house by house. This continued the following day and they were hopeful that someone might have seen or heard something that they thought unusual or different from that encountered in everyday life in the village. Most residents were dilatory, ageing, and not an insignificant number were hard of hearing. This meant that if a television or radio was blaring away, most couldn't even hear their front door bells ringing - yet alone noises outside the house or further afield. Nonetheless, nearly all co-operated with the young officers. Most ageing residents invited the officers indoors, encouraged them to take their jackets off and to sit around the autumn fire for tea and scones - just like they did when they were young with their parents. With superb police sensitivity the residents were told of the nature of their presence and the importance of any information they might have. Details of the murder began to spread throughout the village. This was encouraged by Pearce, who wanted to reassure local people that the police were there to help and support. He had posters hurriedly printed and distributed to each house informing locals of various phone numbers to ring with any new evidence or concerns. The governor made sure he stamped his authority on proceedings. Pearce found time to visit a few of the more vulnerable residents. They appeared to love his brusque manner. Most hadn't met someone like him before.

Celia Hetherington was most adamant that the young officers needed nourishment in the cold autumn air. She had valuable evidence that she thought might be helpful to the police enquiries. Tea and cake would help them as they walked around the village, talking endlessly to different people. The investigations would take up a lot of energy, vitality and staying power, she concluded.

'Look, young man, what's your name by the way? David, that's good. You can sit there, in aunty Sybil's old armchair, and I shall proceed to explain what I saw, or thought I saw, earlier on in Slindon Woods. Early evening, I think it was, I was looking out of the back windows. I have enjoyed looking out into the darkness ever since I was a young girl. I have a certain fondness of ghosts, gorgons, goons and other silly things. Anyway, I saw a light flash several times,' said Celia.

'Was that a continuous flash Mrs Hetherington, or intermittent?' asked the constable, who wrote in his little book at the same time.

'Yes it was intermittent young man,' Celia explained.

'Very helpful. Thank you,' he replied as he made his way, accompanied by William offering toffees, out through Celia's dilapidated old front door. This information was interesting. The police officer at once communicated it to his superior officer who acted as the nerve centre for operations in the village. He collated anything he deemed useful. The cogs seemed to be in action. Wherever he was, Pathan was being hunted down.

The sun shone through low grey skies over Heatherslade village. The few ash and elm trees had shed their warm golden leaves but stood tall, strong and proud, thankful to be in a village that nurtured them. Raucous rooks, crows and jackdaws dominated Slindon woods. It was their home. Migrating birds had departed for warmer climes. Local farms were already preparing for winter. It was time to batten down the hatches, store the food and collect wood for the hearth. Local rituals that had been practised through the centuries across Britain had once again sprung to life. But the village was understandably rather subdued, still traumatised as the police continued their investigation again early next morning.

Tony and Eleanor Marlow, accompanied by Toby, had driven down early that morning from London. Naturally they had been unable to sleep. They closed their eyes for the odd hour or so but were preoccupied with their painful loss. Two male police officers had been stationed outside the house all night. Sadly, journalists would stop at nothing for the opportunity to get more intimate photographs. But the liaison officer, an experienced female in family bereavement, supported the family. The family GP had visited to check on their wellbeing, but they had declined his sedative medication. Dr Sterland would call again soon. Reverend Bullchat, sensitive to the situation, had called at around 10am to offer his condolences and to reassure the family that in church today and for the rest of the week, the congregation would pray for them. The Marlows were moved by such kindness and compassion. At this early stage, flowers and cards were being delivered by post and by hand from local people. Many had phoned the Marlow home in tears. Tears of such depth that they appeared to manifest throughout the village.

Several hours later, a whole entourage of national and international journalists converged on Heatherslade. Their loud, colourful presence threatened to take over a village not used to modern circus-like paraphernalia. Some had cameras the size of small cannons. So big and heavy were they that several straps were needed to carry them. Fortunately for the Marlows and their neighbours, the security tapes had been lengthened by the police to keep control of the growing number of people congregating outside. Strict orders by the governor, superintendent Pearce, made sure that journalists, locals or whoever, did not encroach on the Marlows' home.

Important information materialised a while later as police continued interviewing local people. Mr Popple, an elderly resident of many years, had observantly found the empty brandy bottle that had been discarded by

Pathan. He was out walking his boxer dog in the early morning when he saw it by chance, covered in frost, laying under a yew bush in Sparrow Hawk Way - not a hundred yards from the deceased home.

'This is a vital piece of evidence. Send it off to the laboratory at once,' demanded Inspector Tamworth, another experienced, middle aged police officer who had worked his way through the hardened ranks. Tall, big and brash, with a noticeable squint in his right eye, Tamworth was liked by his underlings. They had no other choice!

Another vital piece of evidence emerged from an interviewing officer in Jackdaw Close. Doris Wagham had been a widower for some time after being married for nearly fifty years to Henry, who worked as a scientist. He did secret work for the government apparently. Not even Doris knew. She was anorexic and surly, with eagle like eyes. She didn't miss a trick. Her only sibling, a brother, lived with her occasionally, but he mainly lived in small, squalid bedsits. The most he ever did to earn a living was to assist in a bookshop somewhere in the seedy streets of London. He was a lost soul among the swirling masses of the metropolis, she informed her friends.

'Sometime yesterday, early evening officer, I was sitting in the back lounge watching television like I usually am, and I saw this light flashing on and off a few times in the woods,' she explained clearly.

'How many times did it flash Mrs Wagham? Were they long flashes or shorter intermittent flashes?' asked the young female officer, who was writing down notes as they spoke.

'Intermittent flashes about a few minutes apart I think,' she eagerly told the officer. With that information, which confirmed yesterday's other sighting, the officer immediately contacted the sergeant in charge of operations.

'Do you live locally, young lady?' Mrs Wagham tentatively asked the officer.

'In Ashburton village. I grew up there. Lovely little place Mrs Wagham,' the short, plump, softly spoken officer replied.

'Your job must be interesting darling. Dealing with all that crime and whatnot. In my day us women didn't get the opportunity to do something really exciting like young women today. Only men could do those things,' she commented sadly.

'Yes, the job has its moments I can assure you,' the officer confirmed Mrs Wagham's hidden frustrations.

Acting upon the newly received information, a small team of officers accompanied by forensics were selected to inspect Slindon Woods. Like soldiers marching off to war, the group of young constables strode out towards the bottom of the hill, just beyond the privet hedges that Pathan had walked past. In the daylight it was noticeable that the path through the woods was worn, used by locals walking to and from the woods. Slowly making their way up the hill several feet apart, they looked for anything unusual that might give them a tiny lead. At this stage they had little concrete evidence as to who, or what, they could expect to find.

They knew Pathan's name and where he had worked. That information was being checked out at this very moment. If they could question him, he could either be held for further questioning, released on police bail or totally eliminated from police enquiries. But he wasn't yet considered a major suspect. He was one of many being considered for further investigation. There were, of course, pathology examination reports to be considered, and forensic reports and other consuming enquiries to be conducted. Tamworth kept reminding his young inexperienced staff of this - just in case they had other ideas of boozing or watching soccer matches.

Nothing out of the ordinary was found combing the hill. Just the usual muddy foot prints, bracken, mounds of grass, old bicycles and all manner of human waste littered throughout the place. The search through the woods wasn't that productive either. There were only muddy paths used by dog walkers, hikers and runners, along with the occasional illicit lover or two hoping for some carnal pleasure away from prying eyes. Whether Tate and Trout had exercised their sexual monolithic bulks in front of the perplexed birds was not known, it had now passed into faded history. The forest consisted of broken branches, empty bird's nests and lots of moss and lichen hanging from trees – there was nothing else for the officers to observe. No doubt all the young men wanted was a bacon sandwich and hot cup of tea back at their mobile café, instead of fucking around in a dirty, damp wood full of dog and human faeces. The police were actually trying to follow the vague directions that Celia Hetherington and Doris Wagham had given them. But a few flashing lights in a dense wood at night was a different kettle of fish when trying to locate something similar in daylight. Could two old hags be relied upon for accurate information? A fool's errand perhaps, but to keep on searching was the endless rallying cry.

Both women reported that the flashing lights may have

originated from a nearby lane which was now a former farm track, so the police and two forensic scientists eventually made their way to the suspected place. Their own maps indicated that the track could have been used by the person or persons involved in the Henrietta Marlow murder. A recently used receipt was found on the ground. The young male forensic worker, attached to Maysbridge Hospital laboratory but seconded to the police, took tyre and several feet imprints for analysis and further evidence. He beavered away looking at that and prodding this while his older female colleague took notes and photographs of the clearing and car park and drew sketches of various small items. Science was now such a powerful evidential tool for the police when it came to producing court evidence. It was the objective, usually impartial view of science that could persuade juries to convict or not. Many of the old coppers, the trilby type like Pearce, had in the past seen many old lags released from court scot-free. They were obviously guilty, but the courts just didn't have the necessary evidence to convict them.

Tamworth was the protégé of superintendent Pearce. He indulged and exposed the inspector to all he knew. That came from what he was taught by his superior under a strict tutelage only the police institutional regime could deliver. From a young aspiring cop in nappies, Tamworth was conditioned under a strict method of detection: believe no one or nothing, he was unceremoniously instructed. Evidence based on fact and knowledge was all he would need to succeed. But with experience also came the importance of instinct or intuition, he constantly reminded his irritated colleagues.

'Remember,' Pearce incessantly reminded Tamworth, 'human sincerity does not exist. People say and do all manner of heinous acts to escape detection. From young boys' denial of stealing apples to the murderer pleading mercy on his way to the gallows. And people carry out misdeeds in great numbers,' was his mantra to young CID officers. 'Humans are the worst sort of animal,' he carried this thought in the forefront of his mind.

Pearce and cynicism were close bedfellows. For him, a wife and family reflected a life of drudgery and dependence based on a carrot and stick style sexuality. He viewed it all as a millstone or a penance, he could see himself with a huge harness around his neck, trudging aimlessly up and down a field all day. He wasn't a committed romantic.

The modern world of equality that superintendent Pearce now lived in didn't exactly square with his contentious views of female officers. All of them were self-sufficient, under worked and spoilt - just like most of the hoity-toity villagers in Heatherslade. His views hadn't gone down well with most of his colleagues, especially not with the chief constable. Political correctness was the most pernicious tendency of our time, he told the bosses. He was viewed as an embarrassment, even though he was an effective copper. It all came to a blistering row when a female officer, below him in rank, was promoted. Soured by police politics, in time he would retire to live a quiet country life in his newly built bungalow a few miles from Kingscot. But the public hadn't heard the last of the Governor.

Whatever the future had in store, the Henrietta Marlow case continued to be Maysbridge police's number one priority. Acting upon information received from a local farmer about the Pathan car, Pearce and assistant sergeant Thomas decided they would walk through Slindon Woods to meet up with the farmer himself. It was a unusual step given their rank. Had the team missed anything important while they were in the woods? Pearce didn't trust anyone.

The two walked briskly down the road, past the now infamous hedges, climbed up the muddy hill and into the woods – they saw nothing beyond the ordinary so far. They both looked around the undergrowth for potential evidence, but there was only the usual Autumn rubbish and discarded human detritus. They poked around here and there hoping to find anything useful. Further along the path they turned right. The deadly silence was broken occasionally by sounds of various birds fighting in the trees above for nesting rights. Thomas checked the notes previously written down by the police officers who had walked through the woods.

'Well, did those useless buffoons miss anything Thomas?' asked the superintendent, who was sweating profusely after the exertion of walking up the hill clothed in a suit, overcoat and trilby dressed like some posh banker. 'Phew. I'm out of fucking shape my son. Too much beef and red wine, that's my problem,' Pearce smiled at his colleague who didn't know whether to laugh or cry.

'So far Sir, it appears that the few notes they did make are accurate,' the other replied.

'Thank fuck for that,' retorted Pearce.

The two police officers kept walking until they eventually came upon a small clearing where a meeting had been pre-arranged with Bill Turton. He was short, fat and chronically shy. His family had been farming Bagshot farm for about twenty years. They had taken over the tenancy of the fifty-acre pig farm from the late Bill Partridge, his uncle. On the night in question, Turton had been cleaning his mud-stained tractor after ploughing. Through the darkness of the evening he noticed lights flashing on and off in the clearing, made originally for farm vehicles to allow others to pass in the narrow lane. Though his farm was three hundred yards away, he could clearly remember the occasion. The car incident aroused his suspicions and he wondered if this might have been linked to the murder.

'I know the area well officer. It's unusual for vehicles to be up here in the evening. This is an isolated place. It attracts the occasional day time traffic where men stop for a piss or fag or even a shag, but that's about all,' he recalled to superintendent Pearce, whose sharp look at the middle-aged man in front of him carried with it some scepticism - just as it did with most people.

'What sort of car do you think it was Sir?' enquired Pearce.

'Impossible to tell in the dark and from several hundred feet away,' he said.

'That's understandable Mr Turton,' remarked Sargent Thomas.

The governor was aware that photographs and casts of several different car tyres found there were at this very moment being scrutinised by scientists. Another possible piece of the jigsaw was, he thought, sliding into position. With a police car waiting for the two officers, they thanked the farmer and gave him a phone number for future reference. They were then driven back to Heatherslade - more important business awaited.

Local, national and international journalists had now been camped outside the Marlow home for several days. They had been moved back fifty feet on three occasions but continued to move forward to their original position. The chief constable had received many phone calls from villagers complaining of being harassed for stories and photographs by journalists. Some had been offered money inducements to tell their innermost secrets about the Marlow family. A few had even received explicit letters alluding to payments digging up the most sordid and unedifying gossip about Henrietta Marlow's short life.

All this outside intrusion had not fallen short of Pearce's radar transmission. After being read the riot act by Chief Constable Adrian Bean, the superintendent had been instructed to move the media circus. For Pearce and his senior colleagues, this was nothing new. The one gruesome responsibility he most detested was dealing with the media. Police were constantly being trained to deal with a more sophisticated news media whose sole intention was to manipulate various individuals, especially the police. If they didn't have their wits about them, personal and official information could be unwittingly leaked to the world within seconds, with potentially devastating consequences. Many a decent copper had been brought down by devious means employed by some of the foulest journalists alive.

Armed with twenty young, burly, male constables with Pearce at the helm, the officers descended on the growing number of journalists. The blue uniforms had marched the two hundred yards to demonstrate who was really in charge. Pearce instructed his colleagues what to do, and when and how it should be carried out if the mangy group of so-called professionals failed to listen. He called together a group of journalists who appeared to represent most of their cohort. Riff-raff he called them. He wasn't going to mess around with people who had so far shown little respect for a family deep in grief. Besides, most of the villagers were in deep sympathy with the family and the last thing on their minds was colluding with outsiders. Personal differences aside, Heatherslade residents were undeniably skilful when it came to looking after their own. Villagers closed ranks to outsiders who threatened the stability of their way of life. They were led by the incorrigible Captain Fox-Rice. With the world's cameras on him, the governor stood forward like a modern day Julius Caesar.

'Right you lot. I'm superintendent Pearce and I'm leading this investigation into the murder of Henrietta Marlow. Most of you have been camped here or nearby waiting for information. The chief constable has ordered me to move you on now. Your days are numbered. We have found a place on the outskirts of the village where you can set up your caravan of tricks. No negotiations. You have heard what I have just told you. Any questions regarding this investigation?' the superintendent smiled scornfully at the assembled baggage in front of him as the strong biting wind swirled about him.

'Sir, could you please give the country their first update with regards to the possible identity of the murderer or murderers of this innocent young woman?' asked a young black woman representing the Daily Mail.

By this stage Pearce was well informed with forensic

and personal information into the known identity of Tariq Pathan. Now was the appropriate time to mention names and facts, and if challenged, he was more than capable of standing his ground. He had to get this right, he kept reminding himself, otherwise his colleagues, the press, politicians and anyone so inclined would have him over a barrel.

'The police are looking for a 30 year old male named Tariq Pathan. He was employed by Film Glow, the same company as the deceased Henrietta Marlow. Since her murder, Pathan has not attended work. As he is a suspect, we need to interview him. We have issued a photograph and personal details to all police forces in order to apprehend him. Let me emphasize that he is only a suspect at this stage,' said Pearce gravely, narrowing his eyes.

'Sir. Brian Gravestone for the BBC. How was she murdered and what is known about the suspect's nationality and race?' enquired Brian.

'No comment to the second question. But to the first question, a large knife or something very similar severed her large carotid artery. She died within a very short time. There were also multiple cuts, slashes, rips and bruises to her neck, shoulders and arms,' came the police superintendent's emotionally charged answer. 'One more question,' he said.

'Superintendent. Polkington for Maysbridge Gazette. Is Pathan implicated in the wounding of the deceased several months ago? Were they lovers?'

'I don't have any information about Pathan's involvement in Miss Marlow's wounding. It is thought, however, that they were lovers, or at least spent time together socially,' was the superintendent's politically correct reply.

'Ladies and gentlemen,' he gave a rare smile at the assembled, 'we need your co-operation in bringing Tariq Pathan into police questioning as soon as possible. Newspaper photographs of Pathan, radio commentary, television coverage and other medium is a vital tool in finding this man. We believe he is dangerous, so the public must not approach him. Inform the police immediately of any sightings. Now, I'm afraid you all have to move from this position as your presence, as I have said, is causing problems for the family of the deceased and their neighbours. If you care to take all your paraphernalia, including accumulated rubbish, and follow sergeant Thomas he will walk you the half mile to a place where you can stay for a while. But remember - you can camp on the waste ground, eat, drink and even shit yourselves, but don't interfere with any local people or I shall throw your baggage out quicker than you arrived. I hope that that's clear,' Pearce spoke in no uncertain terms. Failure to comply wasn't a part of the governors' repertoire.

Thomas marched them all off to waste ground adjacent to the village. The motley crew resembled a group of new age travellers being evicted from private land into police custody. Old and young, black and white, tall, thin, fat and unclassifiable; they walked slowly behind their master to the promised land full of saplings, thistle, bramble, human and animal excrement and piles of various rubbish dumped over time. No doubt some of it had been dumped by irate drivers waiting impatiently in long traffic queues. If it was the police's intention to get rid of them altogether, if this ugly, desolate place didn't work, then nothing would. But the journalists were well equipped and seemingly prepared for all eventualities by their employers, whose sole intention was obtaining news - any kind of news that could sell papers to the masses. Whether it was based on fact, fiction or other means was irrelevant to the masters of spin. Within an hour they had skilfully parked their mobile cafe, caravans and toilets. They were back in business.

Old hands with many years' experience of reporting human tragedy around the world were amongst the crew. Hard, tough and durable like military tanks, many of the journalists weren't discouraged by the marching orders imposed by superintendent Pearce. Many of the old jockstraps, as the police called them, had known him for years ever since he was an over-enthusiastic bombastic rising young star within the police force. Even in his twenties he would act as though he was a general in charge of an army of soldiers, shouting at young, frightened colleagues who must have thought they had joined the wrong institution.

'He was a right bastard of a creature,' commented Jake Shap to some of his fellow reporters and veterans of the news media circus as they supped tea seated on canvas in their new home. A journalist for over thirty years, Jake had worked for many different newspapers and magazines and had had many a verbal tirade with the infamous Pearce.

'Never a kind word for anyone was his motto. On the wrong day he had the power to make life fucking hell,' smiled the old hack, now employed by London based News Chronicle. 'He was only sociable when you bought him a large scotch, preferably two'.

Later that evening, Tony Marlow's sibling Cecil was seen walking into the house. He had travelled from South Wales to support his family. Because of their different professional careers, the brothers had not spent a great deal of time together throughout the years. Although single, Cecil was a busy man running his own private lucrative dental practise which he bought ten years ago in a suburb of Cardiff. He was also an ardent golfer, ran the local amateur dramatics company with unparalleled zeal and was an irregular church attendee - despite his father's catholic conditioning and his brothers' agnosticism. Heaven and hell aside, sibling affection was unmistakably close and sincere.

Heatherslade village had tried its utmost to prepare itself for a painful day: the funeral of Henrietta Marlow. But the sombre atmosphere was inevitable. The village came to a standstill as the residents waited, anticipated and breathed deeply to witness one of their own going to her final resting place. During the night before and in the early morning, many more flowers had been placed outside the Marlow home in condolence. The family were in shock and consumed by grief. The many different coloured flowers glittered and sparkled in the winter sun as the large black hearse pulled up outside. Six black suited men carried the mahogany coffin, bedecked with a light blue satin cover and beautiful white roses, to the waiting car. The Marlows held hands and walked gracefully behind their daughter. People with heads bowed in respect lined the streets. Silence fell over the village – even the birds were quiet.

The hearse slowly made its way to All Angels church. Those who were able walked behind. Some sobbed, many held hands in a defiant gesture of solidarity against the evils that would take over if given the opportunity. Reverend Bullchat was waiting at the door to lead the coffin into the flower scented church, followed by the family. The coffin was placed under the wooden figure of Jesus Christ. The sun shone through the multi-coloured stained glass window onto the coffin. The heavens had spoken it seemed.

The celebration of Henrietta Marlow's life was attended by family, former colleagues, friends and acquaintances. Some of them recited poetry, read biblical stories and told of personal experiences. All were elegies for a young woman cruelly taken from those who loved her. Moved to tears, Tony Marlow delivered a moving testimony to his daughter's short but worthwhile life.

'She wasn't perfect, but she was our darling daughter. She was a precious gem that will forever shine radiantly over all those that knew her. Her mother and I gave her life, put air into those lungs so that she might grow and fulfil her potential. That, sadly, was not to be. She is now at peace,' he concluded as he sobbed, unrestrained in front of the assembled congregation.

'Stop. Be still. Listen to your breath,' Tony said to himself. 'Silence the noise running you senseless. Feel the breath coming in and out of your nose Tony. What is it saying to you? Feel the feelings. Painful. Breath, breath and breath. That's all there is right now. Stop punishing yourself. You are a good father Tony'.

Finally, Reverend Bullchat sang a litany in praise of Henrietta. All Angels church resounded to an overwhelming, joyous singing that shook the old building as the coffin was taken out to the cemetery for a private family burial. Alongside Bullchat, the four lonely Marlow figures said a final goodbye. Henrietta was the first Marlow to be buried in the red, rich soil of Heatherslade.

CHAPTER SEVEN

It subsequently transpired that on the fatal night of the murder of Henrietta Marlow, Pathan had driven to a prearranged destination. He didn't drive anywhere near his London home on that night and hadn't any time since. He was astute enough to realise that he would soon be hunted. Two weeks later, the police broke into his Pimlico apartment. There they found vitally important forensic evidence that considerably informed the ongoing investigation. Bank details, drug dealer's details and phone numbers of different people - some known to police - placed another large piece of the jigsaw into the right place. As a consequence, his current employer, former employers and colleagues and friends were all interviewed. Some of the latter were re-interviewed. Pearce and his London colleagues weren't satisfied with their original statements. Believe no one - was the superintendent's mantra. The governor played games with those who he suspected knew more than first thought. He would tantalise and threaten them if they didn't cooperate, he would raid their properties for drugs. He would inform employers about their bent employees and contact parents, siblings and friends to ask about their whereabouts, thereby planting seeds of doubt or confusion. This was all highly suspect policing for a senior ranked officer. Not that it worried or concerned Pearce. After much pressure, they all claimed not to have assisted or to have even seen Pathan since the Heatherslade killing. If they were lying, only big problems awaited them, warned the metropolitan police officer.

Pathan hadn't contacted any of his family either, including his two siblings, with whom he once had a close relationship. His mother had been so worried by her son's disappearance that she had been prescribed medication by her GP. Pathan's parents were mortified when they saw a photograph of their son on the front page of their evening newspaper. After that terrible experience they refused to read newspapers, watch television or listen to the radio. They both spent more time in their local mosque where the local Imam gave considerable support, as did neighbours up and down the street. Although quiet and reserved people, the Pathans were liked by their community. Mr Pathan informed police that he had many family ties still in Pakistan. This was hardly surprising as the family could be traced back generations. However, the police had acted a few days before by cancelling Pathan's passport and issuing arrest warrants to all airports, seaports and any other likely place of exit. Pathan was being increasingly hemmed in. He was running out of places to hide. Sooner or later he would be unearthed like some dangerous vermin trying desperately to cling onto freedom. But by this time, he had flown out of the country. On this occasion, Pearce had been slow off the starting block!

Important information filtered through concerning the sordid life Pathan had lived. Violent relationships with women appeared to be cherished by the murderer from Pimlico. He treated women with complete disdain, according to his former wife. Having been married to him for five years, they had raised two children, but he beat her regularly whenever he felt like it. His viciousness knew no bounds. When taking illegal drugs he received great pleasure from caning his two children. The more they screamed in pain the more excited he became and continued to inflict further suffering. Naturally his wife tried to intervene by placing herself in front of her terrified and brutalised youngsters. At such times, he would continue beating his wife until she begged for mercy. By now a vivid picture had emerged of a psychopathic man who would stop at nothing to satisfy his own perverted desires.

When the local police raided several of his friends' houses in Bradford, the gruesome picture of Pathan was further confirmed. From a young boy at primary school he had been known for his violent behaviour against anyone who dared confront him. He was sent to a detention centre and twice to prison for assault, wounding and larceny. Eventually he left Bradford, aged 23, for London, telling everyone they were losers by wasting their time hanging around where nothing good or important ever happened. Who needed ten kids, a lousy job and a religious ear bashing from the Imam? he warned them. Now aged 35, he had returned on numerous occasions to visit his family, but had not made any contact with others. None of his previous friends wanted to be associated with scum like Pathan. Local men labelled him with that name. Most gave him a wide birth. The men weren't frightened of him anymore. They thought him a coward, donkey, ghost: all names that carried a pejorative label from his background.

The prearranged destination organised by Pathan was in a small car park off the A371, near Cheddar, not far from Bath. On arrival he got into the car of his accomplice. The latter asked no questions. Neither did he wish to. This was around midnight on the same day of the murder. Pathan felt extremely anxious about his safety, not knowing if the police were already onto him. The other person had already made necessary arrangements for Pathan's car to be dumped and set on fire near Flitsbury forest, two miles from human habitation. It wouldn't be found for many months.

In the small hours Pathan was driven to a small nondescript bedsit in a mainly socially deprived part of Bath city, where cash was paid up front and no questions were asked. However, it wouldn't be long before the wealthy, unscrupulous owner of many houses found out the identity of his infamous tenant. Preparing for his evil intention, Pathan had his head shaven and now sported a thick beard. To a certain extent, he was becoming unrecognisable from the photographs that would be circulated. But at this stage, his name wasn't on the police radar, or any other significant radar. Most of the time he laid low in the crummy bedsit reading. Other times he watched television, listened to radio and shook, like trees in a storm, thinking of the future. His conscience, however, wouldn't leave him alone. It badgered, baited and bullied him. Just as he had done to others, he was now on the receiving end. Judgement was not fair! He was living the life of a ghost.

However, he was far ahead of the police and had

booked a single air flight weeks before the murder. He would fly to Pakistan. That shrewd mind had thought of nearly everything. Deep, devious and destructive; Pathan knew how to outwit other similar minded souls, or so he thought. This was what he meant when preaching to friends years ago about empty everyday lives full of drudgery. He was sharp, always on the move and thinking ahead. Most of his assertions were based not on intelligence, but on physical violence. When people disagreed with him, he used force to make them conform.

Nonetheless, Pathan had had his inspirational moments which had allowed him to earn a living, of sorts, prior to Film Glow. He designed and sold his own cheap clothes - but didn't do well. He sold double glazing, ice cream, insurance and near enough anything else that could be sold. After working long hours for a few years, he realised going straight didn't pay. It was for mugs, he had told his friends. So he dabbled in stolen goods before progressing to stolen cars and eventually drugs. He realised that desperate people bought drugs that took them to another planet.

Pathan occasionally made the few short strides to the toilet on the second floor where he resided. If there had been a sink in his room, he would have urinated in it, but all personal hygiene was carried out in the communal bathroom. There were three others, two males and one female, with whom he had to share. Pathan hated using it. It was always filthy and smelled abominably. He always listened intently for others using the bathroom, or leaving the house, or receiving visitors before venturing out himself. Fortunately, his accomplice brought him food, clothes and other personal items. In his position, it was a life of luxury. But of course, it was costing Pathan money, not unsubstantial amounts, to be waited on like near royalty. He could afford it. The one large withdrawal from his bank had set him up for the foreseeable future, he had informed his accomplice. Most people had their price, and his accomplice was no different when it came to making money from a person with few choices.

On the fifth day of his self-imposed incarceration, he quietly opened his bedsit door and most unexpectedly came face to face with an unknown male. They briefly shook hands. Pathan was alarmed by his presence. He hadn't heard him leave a room or ascend the steep, worn out stairs of the Edwardian terraced house.

'Hallo. I'm Terry Sharpe. I live at number 2 across the landing. How do you do?' his smiling face asked. He was tall, thin, with a hippy hair style and an imminently affable attitude.

'Hi there. Nice to meet you. Been here long?' Tariq hesitatingly asked, anxious to know why he hadn't heard this bloke on the landing after all the intense preparation beforehand. He wasn't a police informer, was he? Was he working for the landlord? Pathan took an instant disliking to the gangly, scruffy bloke in front of him. Be aware Tariq, he told himself, he might well be concealing a hidden tape or camera. One thing was for sure, he wasn't going to give this moron any names whatsoever. Paranoia was rearing its ugly head again.

'Been here about a year. I'm a student at the nearby college. I'm studying the theatre industry. Wanna be a designer or something like that,' he remarked.

'Good luck to you,' he said, as Tariq headed for the toilet. He needed to be extra cautious next time, he kept muttering to himself. He would never know what scum like that Sharpe bloke might tell others at the college. Besides he might just bring some of his mates back to the house for booze and drugs – that was the last thing Pathan needed right now. He told himself that he must keep a lower profile from now on, though he kept reassuring himself that he was safe. He realised that the occasional Indie rock music he had overheard must have been coming from Sharpe's bedsit.

Four days later, in the early hours of the 25th November, Pathan and his accomplice tiptoed downstairs carrying his few personal belongings in a suitcase to a waiting car. The night before, they had thoroughly cleaned the bedsit of all evidence in his hide-away. The mobile phone he had used before the murder had been destroyed a few hours prior to the heinous act. Since then he had used several phones bought by his accomplice. They had now also been disposed of. However, he was convinced that sooner or later someone would start singing about him being holed up there. For fame, fortune or ignorance, an individual would tell all!

His flight from Heathrow to Lahore was in five hours. They had no time to waste. His anxiety levels began to rise considerably once again. Pathan wondered whether the police would be waiting for him at the airport. It hadn't been long since the murder, so it was highly unlikely that the police had made any connection with him and Henrietta Marlow. Besides, they didn't have any evidence that he had wounded her. Furthermore, Pathan didn't know whether Henrietta had even told her parents about him stabbing her. Although out of guilt she had told them everything else that went on in her roguish mind. Yes, they were partners in crime. Nevertheless, he was irrationally concerned, petrified even, that by now police forensics would have connected him to the Heatherslade crime scene.

With the roads dark, deserted and cold, his accomplice drove at considerable speed. They had the open road to themselves. Inside the car, all was silent. The faceless accomplice was preoccupied with thoughts of getting rid of his passenger as soon as possible. He had had enough now. He had been faithful to Pathan throughout the whole ordeal. He hadn't complained, although at times he had felt like throwing the towel in. He wanted to get on with his own life and forget all about crime. He couldn't wait to leave Pathan permanently in the past. What if he was caught himself? No doubt he would be facing a long prison sentence. Fuck Pathan. He thought about everything he stood to lose. He could potentially lose everything. The bastard next to him should hang, he thought. Pathan's accomplice was close to breaking point. He couldn't drive to the airport quickly enough.

Pathan wasn't exactly helping himself by wearing dark glasses at 3am. Two young men in a fast, nearly new colourful car could attract the attention of motorway police at such an early time in the morning when few cars were around. They had to get wise.

'Take the shades off bro,' said the driver, you'll get us nicked this time in the morning. 'You stand out like some gangster bro. For fuck sake, shape up.'

'Yea, you're right. Sorry man wasn't thinking straight,' he half apologised to his suffering driver. Pathan thought the young man next to him had been a really supportive bloke. He hadn't known him that long, yet he had stuck his neck out for a person who had defiled humanity's most sacred spiritual boundary: thou shall not kill. He was more than supportive! He had potentially forfeited his freedom, good name, his job, family, friends and colleagues. If caught, there would be no turning back for a young man just starting out on his own road in life. The enormity of it all hit Pathan between the eyes. He didn't deserve to have such a noble person - though some might say stupid, immature and naive - to help him escape to freedom. There would never be freedom for Pathan. Wherever he travelled, whatever he did, whomever he lived with, his conscience would be staring at him. The inner stare would tighten its grip: relentless and unforgiving.

Nothing more was said between the two men until a mile or so before Heathrow airport. It was already busy, bustling with passengers carrying and pulling cases of different sizes and colours. Others were pushing trolleys full of worldly goods. Some of those goods were, of course, stolen. These passengers were hoping they wouldn't be caught by the airport authorities; just like Pathan. Fumes from parked coaches choked people standing around the entrance to the main terminal building. Everyone looked lost, as was usually the case in these huge monolithic cities called airports. There were aimless lines of people everywhere. Where they were going, neither they, nor their tour managers knew. Mayhem reigned supreme!

'Pull in over there in that car park bro,' Pathan told his driver. Here at last, he thought. But his paranoia began to increase again when he realised what lay ahead before the flight departure. He imagined a million eyes staring at him. There was no turning back now; he needed to go into that building brave and confident. If the police were onto him, they would surely have arrested him by now. He withdrew a large jiffy bag from inside his suitcase on the back seat of the car.

'We made it bro, thanks mainly to you,' Pathan said to his accomplice, handing him the jiffy bag. 'There's £2000 in £50 notes for you bro. Thank you so much for what you have done for me. You are a brave person. Thank you. By the way, the notes are all used ones, they are not new. They can't be traced, but don't bung it all in the bank at once. The few grand in my pocket and that suitcase behind is all I have in the world now bro. By now the police must surely have broken into my flat and seized all my gear. Fuck em, they can keep it. It's no good to me where I'm going,' he said confidently.

'Thanks for the cash bro,' said the accomplice. He appeared delighted by the colour of the notes; but thought to himself that he had earned every damn dime of it. He could now pay off his debts and recede into the background. He didn't say another word after thanking Pathan. Within an hour the car would be crushed of all identity. Airport CCTV would no doubt pick up on the false number plate of the car. That wasn't relevant any more. And Pathan, with shaven head, beard and dark glasses should be in Pakistan by the time they realised his identity. The accomplice himself had taken what he thought were fool proof measures to hide his own identity. But very little was fool proof. Pathan hesitatingly got out of the car. Holding his large blue suitcase, he headed towards the check-in desk. The car drove off, and the driver was never seen again.

Pathan stopped abruptly just inside the main entrance to make sense of the sensory overload he was experiencing. It nearly overwhelmed him. The noise of intermittent announcements, powerful lights shining on him like a soccer stadium at night, and various airport staff walking around with different coloured uniforms on made him more confused. What a human jungle; all these people were earning a living in chaotic conditions, he concluded. The imposing police figures holding machine guns really frightened him. Was there a war going on? As his eyes met the ceiling, he was confronted by CCTV cameras - hundreds of them. Not even a fly could move around undetected. What had happened to this insane world? He walked back out of the building to get some much- needed fresh air. It was all too much for him. What had humanity done to itself? What had it done to Pathan? What was he doing to himself? Was all this interconnected?

After a few minutes of gulping down fresh air mixed with toxic fumes from vehicles, Pathan returned to the check-in building. He quickly headed for the toilet where he splashed cold water over his face. His thick black beard was now showing a few stands of grey hair. The mirror stared back at him. It wasn't a pretty sight to behold. His face had grown thin, there were premature bags under his eyes and they cried at him to give himself up to the police. He rejected that inner plea, pulled himself together and walked out of the toilet feeling confident again. He had to find the airline he was flying with and check-in - time was now of the essence. There were only

90 minutes left before take-off, he reminded himself. He would then be heading for another world where he would change his life. He hoped to live in a small village, find a young illiterate girl to marry and have children. Become anonymous!

He had several thousand pounds, a small fortune in a squalid village in Pakistan. In a country where land was so cheap to buy, his potential family would be self-sufficient and secure. People would look up to him due to his western educated accent, money and acquisitions. That is what Pathan had deviously planned. Already his manipulating mind had focused on how to use some innocent girl, aged about thirteen - which wasn't an unusual age to marry in Pakistan - to fulfil his maturing delusions.

Thinking all eyes were on him, he was ever vigilant as he approached the airline check-in desk. Several passengers were in front of him with loads of luggage. Gifts for the poor back home. Many families were going to Pakistan. He recognised the dialect; it was spoken in the same area where his parents came from. It was also the same dialect spoken by many in his neighbourhood in Bradford. Indeed, his parents, although now fluent English speakers, still conversed in their mother tongue. The families were all well-dressed, most of the women wore expensive silk saris, they were courteous and friendly. No doubt, Pathan concluded, most of the fathers had a profession of some description. Sorting out the passports with the assistance from female staff, they spoke impeccable English. Lucky bastards, thought Pathan, they had everything you could wish for. Attractive, well-dressed wives, handsome educated children and money.

Money, that's all anyone needed in life to be happy. He had tried to save all his twenty working years yet had fuck all to show for it. He was an abject failure and he knew it. His final chance to redeem himself would be in Pakistan. Once there he would assume a new identity and hang around with those with land, people who could open the right doors to make money.

'Please put your luggage on the scales. Your passport and travel documents too please Sir,' said the young Oriental check-in staff member. In fact, they were all young, oriental and dressed in garish red uniforms looking like would-be film stars. Thick lipstick, layered rouge on their tiny babyish faces and shining white teeth. They were a feast to the male eye. Pathan was immediately drawn to their aura. He would have given anything at that precise moment to make love with the young beauty in front of him. She knew, of course, what he wanted. She smiled, was very friendly and professional, aware of her boundaries, and like most women took him only so far into her world of sensuality.

'Hello. Yes, here we are. When is the flight, and what is the number of the departure gate please?' he enquired rather anxiously. He wiped the sweat from his brow. He needed to relax; there were no police in the near vicinity as far as he could make out. The nearest one was the older bloke he saw some time ago holding a machine gun. Minus the uniform, Pathan thought he resembled a New York gangster from the 1930s. As soon as this irritating process was over and he was safely through security, he headed straight for the bar. He needed a couple of large brandies to put himself straight. His nerves were jangling and twittering.

'Thank you, Sir. Your luggage has been labelled. Here are your passport and travel documents, Sir. Your flight departs from gate 25 in approximately one hour. Please go to security,' the smiling check-in hostess informed Pathan. Her almond shaped eyes penetrated the depths of his being. He was hooked. Addicted by untamed lust for sex, he realised how some of the girls looked spiteful, over indulged and sought maximum attention. They reminded him of the oriental prostitutes in Pimlico who drove expensive flashy cars and dressed in clothes bought in Harrods. If only he was going home with them tonight and not travelling thousands of miles to escape capture, his life would be complete. He would do anything for them so long as they were happy. What was he thinking? Quick for fuck sake, he needed to get to security. Then he'd have a drink to sort out his tense irritation.

Still preoccupied with various eyes looking at him and CCTV surveillance above, he walked to security check-in. Other than a few personal items in his luggage, all he owned was what he stood up in - he was acutely mindful of the £5,000 he was carrying. He had to have a plausible explanation to convince security why he was carrying so much cash. Failure would mean the end of the road.

'Please place your jacket, shoes, loose change, belt, phone and anything else onto the conveyor belt Sir,' said a young, white, pale looking man wearing a dark blue uniform. Along with two colleagues, he scrutinised Pathan's personal items through the x-ray machine. He successfully walked through the security screen. No alarm sounded. He knew that he had nothing illegal on him.

'Please could you dress and come with me, Sir,' said an older security man, who looked to have a higher rank than those previously. Keep your cool - Pathan kept repeating to himself - you're nearly on the flight. This was just a formality. He hadn't concealed the money, it was inside his jacket pocket. He needed to keep cool.

'Hello Mr Pathan. I'm Mr Chandler, the security supervisor. My colleagues have informed me of the large amount of cash you are carrying with you on board your flight to Pakistan. Could you explain why this is the case?' asked the lanky, rather stern officer.

'Of course I can. I have a dual British-Pakistan citizenship. I am going to Pakistan on a single ticket for an arranged marriage sorted out by my parents. Before flying I found out how much you are legally allowed to take out of the country,' Pathan responded, lying through his teeth.

'Why so much cash? I thought it would have been safer and cheaper to have had your money sent directly to a bank there?' Mr Chandler quite rightly asked.

Keep your cool Pathan, he thought to himself. Keep your fucking cool. This bloke is trying to trick you. You've done nothing wrong, besides the police aren't onto you yet. They still haven't made the connection between you and Henrietta Marlow. But soon they will! Keep your cool.

'As I intend to stay and have a family in Pakistan, I was going to open a bank account there. I need most of the money as a dowry to give my new parents-in-law,' said Pathan, making up a story on the spot to pacify the officer. 'Then I have to pay for the marriage arrangements, rent a home and many other expenses. I just thought it would make things easier over there. In Pakistan, they are not as modern and efficient as in England,' was Pathan's silky, plausible story. He was doing well. No problems.

'Fair enough Mr Pathan. Take your cash and make your way to the departure lounge'.

Pathan walked slowly and purposefully out of the office. He showed who was in control. Inside he felt immense tension that only a large alcoholic drink could sort out. The departure call had not yet been announced. He quickly dived into one of the bars. His brain desperately needed to feel the full force of a large brandy or any other kind of spirit. With a little ice, he drank it in one large gulp. Two minutes later he felt elation rushing through his head, neck, shoulders and his whole body. It resembled the experience of taking cocaine. He was alive again. The intense anxiety fell away. He wasn't fearful of the CCTV cameras in the bar. Fuck the cameras – he thought, now taking on an arrogant attitude. He walked coolly up to the bar and ordered another large brandy. Within three minutes another had been sunk. He felt on top of the world, but before he could swallow another dose of mind-numbing booze, the announcement came for the departure of his flight. He hurried to the lounge and lined up alongside the other passengers. Not yet boarded, he had a cursory look around at the faces. No one was there that he immediately recognised. That relieved him of the possible explanations he might have had to fabricate.

Within touching distance of the airline personnel checking identification, Pathan burst out crying. In front of passengers and staff he fell uncontrollably to his knees begging to Allah for mercy.

'Please forgive me. Please forgive me. I am not worthy

of uttering your great name,' he repeated over and over again, sobbing until people came to his aid. Two older men put their arms around him, trying to console his distress. Others standing around were prepared to help. All activity appeared to have temporarily ceased as two male airline security workers rushed to enquire about one of their customers prostrate on the carpeted floor.

'How can we help you Sir? What has happened?' asked the younger of the two workers. Pathan was helped to his feet and placed on a chair. 'Can I get you water Sir, or anything else?' the same chap asked politely, not really knowing what to do as Pathan continued to sob. His shaking outstretched hands grasped the worker by the arms - hands that were seeking forgiveness for the evil actions wrought upon another. Was he going to confess everything here and now, end the pretence and give himself up to the police? Or would he carry on as before, even though his conscience wouldn't allow any respite?

Pathan dried his eyes and composed himself as another staff member arrived to assist. He was middle aged, and the senior security officer for the airline. Instructing his two colleagues to return to the check-in desk, he encouraged the passengers to continue with their own affairs and sat down next to Pathan.

'I am worried about you Sir. Is there anything I can immediately help you with? Do you still want to fly or would you like us to put you on a later flight to Lahore? The choice is yours,' explained the concerned officer.

Pathan couldn't take his mind off the mental image of Henrietta Marlow being knifed to death by his own foul deeds. The immense, intolerable suffering caused to her family would be with them throughout their lives. For the first time, he accepted that he was worthless.

'Please forgive me. I'm upset to be leaving my parents in England and to start a new life in Pakistan,' was the pathetic lie Pathan gave for his outburst of grief. With that assurance, the officer led Pathan to have his final security check before boarding the large 757 Jet. Just before entering the aeroplane he stopped to take one final intense look at the soil of England. His eyes wandered to the tarmac of the runway, the numerous planes, people that resembled ants running around in the driving rain, working at various tasks. He experienced intense thoughts of his loving old parents and how they had worked so hard all their lives to provide him with a decent life. And this was how their son had repaid them! When they found out about his heinous crime, the suffering would inflict untold emotional damage upon them. As he stood there with the rain lashing onto the windows with great force, he wished he was dead. Although he knew he must enter this plane, he realised that he would soon be hunted like a wild dog. He would be shown no mercy; just as he had showed no mercy to others.

Within forty minutes the jet was flying through space hurtling towards Lahore - the second largest city in Pakistan with over four million inhabitants. Surely the birthplace of Pathan's parents would show him some mercy and a chance to redeem himself. He wanted to show people what he was really made of. Tough, resilient, flexible and able to adapt to a culture that he knew very little about. Other than the information his parents and extended family had given him about their home country, he was heading for an alien landscape. His extended family knew very little about him, other than the few visits to England and photographs of the kids growing up. None of them knew of his imminent arrival. What could Pathan expect of them? There would be many questions from whatever family member he first visited before they allowed him to stay for a while. Depending on where he went, they could well phone his parents asking the nature of his visit without prior notice. That could lead to innumerable problems for his ageing parents who might be persuaded to contact the British police. He didn't want his parents to get in trouble. Pathan hadn't given much thought as to where he would go when he first arrived in Lahore. He had thought about the probability that the British police may have contacted the Pakistani authorities to request his extradition. Interpol might also have been involved. If the police were onto him, and by now that was highly likely, his mug shots would be in every air and seaport, police stations and other official places across the globe.

Near to exhaustion after several days of hiding, making plans for his escape and outsmarting the airport staff, Pathan slept soundly for the next two hours. The one dream he could recall during that time was a blissful state of happiness with his family somewhere in Pakistan. His wife and children were all well fed and clothed. Pathan himself worked for a senior civil servant in the high court as advocate general. His reverie only came to an end when a young female stewardess awakened him.

'Sir, would you like a meal and a drink?' she politely asked him. She spoke impeccable English. Her raven coloured hair, slim athletic build, dark cavernous eyes and sensuous mouth suggested her genes had come from those travelling desert merchants long ago. There was an air of mysticism about her that was beyond the understanding of the sage's mind. She didn't seek attention, nor did she require it.

'Yes please young lady,' was Pathan's brief response. He was still tired and slightly confused by his new surroundings. No sooner had he sat down in the plane than he had fallen asleep. Now waking up to a sea of different faces, he had to re-orientate himself.

'What would that be Sir?' she asked.

'The vegetarian dish with rice and chapati please. And I would like a large scotch with ice. Thank you,' said Pathan. He had already noticed the delightful stewardess serving him, she was dressed in a light blue uniform. Her staff security badge named her as Unsa. She would make a wonderful wife, he thought. But this woman was educated, westernised and could make up her own mind as to what she wanted to do. Unlike the illiterate, poverty-stricken type of young village woman – or girl - that Pathan was hoping to marry.

After dining and drinking another scotch, he struck up a conversation with an older Pakistani man sitting next to him. He was wearing traditional clothes, had a small beard and constantly, yet quietly, recited something that Pathan had not heard before. He assumed it was learned text from the Koran, but he certainly wasn't going to ask. Throughout his early life in Bradford his parents had practised in a similar way. At work, evening meal or any other appropriate situation, they whispered as they recited regular verses they had been taught as children growing up in the Punjab.

'Hello Sir. My name is Tariq. Are you travelling to Lahore?' he asked the gentleman sitting to his right.

'Hello. I'm Zahid. I'm a Punjabi. Yes, I am travelling to Lahore. It's been my home for fifty years. After visiting my brother in Rotherham for six weeks, I am very much looking forward to seeing my wife and family once again,' he explained. The man spoke very good English. He and Pathan started an interesting and enjoyable conversation about their families, employment and various other topics, including religion. They conversed as though they had known each other for many years. Pathan thought of how he could use the old man as a valuable contact in Lahore. He said he had lived there a long time which meant he knew many people that could possibly help him. Pathan was thinking of how he could use the older man to his advantage. Money was the direct way to a human heart, he concluded.

Restless, Pathan walked to the toilet to get some much-needed exercise. He noticed the large jet was full of Pakistanis. He hadn't noticed in the departure lounge that some of the older men were wearing the traditional Baloch, a long robe which looked like a smock-frock hanging down to the floor. As the older passengers slept, most of the younger people and children either watched the on-board film or played different games on the various technologies they had. They laughed, smiled, shouted and ate sweets. He wished, he craved to be a part of what was going on in front of his eyes.

After another brief sleep he awoke, still thinking about visiting an Imam in Lahore to confess what he had done. He thought that would be an essential first step if he wished to start anew. But that could lead to his arrest if the Imam thought he deserved to be punished. Perhaps, he hoped, there would be a sympathetic religious leader in one of the village slums who would be prepared to show him compassion if he agreed to regularly attend and donate money to his Mosque. The one powerful tool he had was money. In various parts of Pakistan, he knew money could buy you anything. Mindful of street robbers and crooks in the capital, as soon as he landed, he needed to open a bank account in a different name. But he had no new identification to verify who he was. He would have to buy a new identity from local gangsters. As poverty was rife, people would jump at the idea of selling their deceased fathers' or brothers' personal details. Once his cash was secure he could start to make enquiries and attempt to contact the uncle who he hadn't seen for some time. That could lead to Pathan being unable to answer many unanswerable and embarrassing questions. He was dubious about the idea ever working.

With many ideas still buzzing and burning in his overloaded mind, flight L2277 from Heathrow landed on time at Lahore Airport. It had taken over seven and half hours. Tariq Pathan was relieved he had arrived, very tired and really terrified that the police would be waiting to arrest him. He was sure that his good run of luck would soon have to end.

He finally emerged from the plane into the intense heat. Feelings of being overwhelmed by events beyond his control made him shake with fear. He was alone in the world, alienated from his home and any familiar face tortured his soul. Feeling the large amount of money inside his jacket pocket once again reassured him somewhat. This was his only security in a city whose inhabitants would think nothing of stealing his money, the clothes on his back and dumping his naked body alongside the dead feral dogs on the local rubbish heap. Of course, Lahore was also a city of affluence. Lots of wealthy people from around the world lived there in splendour. Many owned large mansions with swimming pools and new expensive cars - all maintained by an army of cheap labour that lived nearby in squalor.

His first few tentative steps down from the plane found him on the scorching surface of the runway concrete: he had touched the hallowed land of his forefathers. This was the land that they fought for and won in many battles to develop modern Pakistan today. Tears fell down his cheeks as he thought about his parents, worrying and so desperate to hear from him back in England. It was their brave decision to leave Pakistan all those years ago to seek a better life in Britain. He knew he was a terrible son: a loser and wastrel. Later on, he thought, he needed to try and get a message to them posted in India, which was only forty miles from Lahore. The police couldn't trace him from an anonymous post office address.

With his case in hand, Pathan walked out of the large bustling airport. The noise and heat overwhelmed him. He hailed a modern yellow cab and directed the driver to take him into the city centre to find a bank and accommodation. He found sanctuary lying on the back of the cab rear seat. The air-conditioning cooled him down somewhat from the intense oven that engulfed him outside. With dark glasses, shaven head and a thick black beard growing longer by the minute, he thought himself a desperate man. On arrival in the city, he kept reminding himself he must buy Pakistani clothes like loose trousers and shirts like those most men wore. Being able to converse in the native language, something his father had taught him, he would fit in perfectly as a local everyday resident. Nobody would take any notice of him.

The cab dropped him in a busy road, full of shops and banks resembling any London commercial district. New parked cars occupied every available inch of space. Many people wore westernised clothes. Banks, bars, fast food, sexy women; what more could he want? This Lahore world was his oyster. No one would ever find him here, as long as he played his cards correctly. Though he did need to keep a sharp mind on what he said and to who, to make sure he wasn't arrogant or stupid with his money.

He gave the taxi driver a £5 note as he didn't have rupees. With his case in hand, he walked slowly down the road taking in the various services available to him. People would soon be serving him like royalty. They would address him as Sir and beg for his western money. He might even give the shabbier dressed workers a tip. His delusions kept shouting at him. After walking a hundred yards, a large blue building loomed within his sight. It was the bank he had been looking for to deposit his cash: Western United Bank.

He stood outside the bank trying to focus on how he might explain the large amount of cash once inside. He had to get it right, otherwise the bank may just contact the police, alarmed by an unusual transaction. Not wanting to attract any undue attention, he removed his dark glasses.

Once inside the cool, marble floored bank he slowly walked up to one of the cashiers. His eyes were captured by the large wall murals of young turbaned, bearded warriors sitting astride wild stallions holding red hot spears. Standing in front of a young female, who was wearing a multi-coloured sari, he pulled out a bag containing a bundle of £50 notes from inside his jacket pocket.

'Hello, I would like to open an account and deposit my cash please,' Pathan confidently addressed the woman. Of course, most of that money was the proceeds from selling illegal drugs, but some of it belonged to Henrietta Marlow.

'Yes, of course, Sir. I will require two personal identity documents such as a passport and place of residency,' she replied.

'I have a passport but not the other. I've just arrived today and haven't had time to find accommodation, but hope to sometime later today,' he explained. 'As I don't want to walk round with all this cash on my person, as I'm sure you understand, is there any other service that is available?' he asked, now becoming a little irritated.

'Yes Sir. We have deposit boxes that one can rent for a minimum of one month,' she said with a reassuring smile.

'Great. I will rent a deposit box until I have found accommodation,' Pathan willingly responded.

He produced his valid passport, completed the relevant forms, paid the monthly fee and was taken downstairs by the young cashier. She handed him a key, opened the security door and let him in. Once inside he placed all his cash, except £200 which he would need later, into the deposit box and locked it. The key allowed him to exit the strong room. The key would allow him to use the service any time during opening hours. His money was now secure. He was mightily relieved. It was approaching late afternoon and he urgently needed to find local accommodation.

'Thank you for your help. Do you know of any inexpensive accommodation agencies or places where I could rent a small apartment?' he asked.

'Thank you for your custom Sir. Yes, there is Zahid Barr's agency just a few minutes from here. They should have something for you to rent. Some of my friends have used his service before,' she replied, 'I will write the address for you'.

Feeling relaxed and more confident, Pathan walked down the noisy, busy street with his only companion - the cheap case he bought years ago in Bradford market. Every few yards he was accosted by young poor street children; they could smell a new face in town from five hundred yards. He gave them a few rupees, which was rather short sighted of him. Within a few minutes fifty street urchins were following him like the pied piper. To his great relief, he eventually found the agency in a rather seedy looking nondescript court. Outside every building were people of varying ages, dressed in rags and holding a tin begging. His heart felt for the suffering in front of his eyes. He couldn't pass by without donating a rupee to several of them. He realised that rich and poor lived cheek by-jowl in Lahore. Animals too wandered about as if owned by no one. Although he had money, he was rootless like the wretches who he had seen after leaving the airport. Perhaps the Gods had sent him here to save the homeless. What utter nonsense – Pathan thought to himself –he was a fugitive, and he mustn't forget it! Those kids might have been going to heaven, or somewhere similar, but he was on his way to hell - his tormented voices kept recalling.

Barr's agency was at the end of a gruesome court. He climbed twenty or so concrete steps to the front door. After ringing a bell several times, a man speaking Punjabi told him to go to the fourth floor and to walk into an office. In torrid, putrid heat he walked very slowly up the half rotten wooden stairs carrying his case. He stopped to catch his breath several times before finding the office in question. He knocked on the fading yellow door, wearing his dark glasses once again as he wanted to feel anonymous.

'Come in Sir. Come in. My name is Barr. Good to meet you. You must be looking for accommodation Sir? Have you been in Lahore very long Sir? I've lots of good apartments Sir,' he spoke like a machine gun being fired from behind the desk. His office reminded Pathan of a squat he once used for a few nights when he first arrived in London. It was fit to be condemned. Barr himself wore a long robe with a loose scarf draped around his scrawny, hairy neck. He was thin, had a long bony nose and devious little eyes, suggesting he was out to steal money if at all possible.

From an earlier feeling of elation, a sudden huge wave of panic passed over Pathan. It had just dawned on him that he could well have put the noose firmly around his own neck in his recent dealings at the bank. What a fucking short-sighted idiot he was to have given the bank his passport information!

There was no going back on that contract. It was a perilous decision going into that bank. Pathan had fucked-up big time. He decided there and then that he

151

wouldn't stay any longer than two weeks. He would move on to another province.

'Hello Mr Barr. Yes, I'm looking for a small, clean, short let apartment. I want to keep all this business informal Mr Barr. What I mean is I will give you very little information about me and I will give you cash. No receipts or questions,' Pathan explained, now rather apprehensive.

'I understand absolutely Sir. Where do you want to live for a short while?' he asked

'Johar Town or nearby,' he said in a clear, no nonsense manner.

'Of course, I have just the place in Johar Sir. It is a small, self-contained apartment with bath and toilet. It's less than ten miles from here,' Mr Barr replied, money written all over his grinning face.

'That's fine. Would you prefer pounds or rupees?' he asked rather hurriedly. He was keen to settle the deal and get out of the city. He had, unnecessarily, put himself in a dangerous position. Yet again he was full of anxiety. The men, nonetheless, came to an amicable financial agreement. All Pathan required was the front door key to the apartment.

As Pathan was his last customer of the day, Mr Barr agreed to drive him to his temporary home. He was mightily relieved to get back into the hot but fresh air. The agency smelled of sour sweat - most of which was coming from Mr Barr's body. Pathan felt he would suffocate if he stayed any longer. He wondered how people like Barr still operated from premises not fit for animals, in a modern city like Lahore. But, of course,

London was no different when it came to slum landlords and bent money.

They passed many begging bodies before reaching Mr Barr's car. Minutes later they joined the long queues of vehicles heading out of the packed city.

'Lahore's rush hour, just like London or New York,' the driver explained. 'It is getting worse. I experience this shit six days a week,' he sighed.

Eventually the cars thinned out onto a dual carriageway. The relief was palpable amongst the many men driving home to their families after twelve hours shifts. Pathan felt uncomfortable in the car. Barr's car was old and dilapidated; it had no air conditioning and smelt like a sewer. It was so old that he didn't even recognise the manufacturer, it was most likely some sort of Russian or Iranian pile of metal sold cheaply on the black market, Pathan thought.

His immediate concern was that Mr Barr kept his mouth closed about their personal dealings. If he mentioned the police, in relation to needing more money to keep quiet, he would have no choice but to pay. He had that nasty look about him which Pathan had instinctively picked up on from the outset. He would sell your guts for a pig's ear, Pathan reckoned. Already, trust in the old bastard didn't exist, but in his precarious position what could be done? He needed to get to the apartment and figure out what his next move would be. One thing was for sure, he needed to move to another province like Karachi soon - within days even.

They passed many wheat fields on both sides of the road, Pathan saw men and women working in the blazing sun. How fortunate, he thought, that he didn't have to slave away in such harsh conditions for a meagre income. Many other workers were walking along the highway, carrying various tools, presumably having finished work. Some carried small, round metal containers which contained their daily sustenance. Their faces were almost black and severely lined from years of exposure to the harsh natural elements. No doubt his forebears would have walked the same route home after their daily grind. His parents might also have done so when they were young. Nearly all of the female workers, especially the mature ones, wore cheap rough clothes that completely covered the whole of their bodies. His mother had explained to him and his siblings about the ancient Muslim and Hindu practise of Purdah. It was a custom still being used when his mother was a young woman working in Lahore. The custom was keeping women in seclusion with clothing that concealed them completely, which his mother hated conforming to herself. The practise, however, was confined mainly to indoor places of worship.

In Bradford, both of his parents and their Pakistani family and friends continued to speak out against oppressive attitudes towards women. It was at this time that Pathan thought of his own negative attitude towards women in general - and Henrietta in particular. He wondered whether his dislike of women had been unconsciously conditioned by his exposure to mature Pakistani men in the local Mosque. But they were good men, he assumed, and most of them were still living in the same area. He went to school with their children and had grown up with them. Besides, these married men were still good friends with his own parents. He was hoping he could find a scapegoat to blame for his behaviour, without taking full responsibility for his own actions. So many times his mind had deluded him into thinking he wasn't fully aware at the time of the murder. A plea of insanity was his only defence.

Mr Barr parked his car outside the apartments on the outskirts of Johar Town. It was the middle of the evening and the intense heat was beginning to reduce in temperature. His apartment was next door to a boys' hostel. Pathan hoped he wouldn't be constantly irritated by noise, like singing, music and shouting, coming from next door. He realised the gregarious nature of young Pakistani boys.

'Well here we are Sir. This is the small apartment block to your left. Your number is 6, which is on the first floor. I've written down my address and phone number for you on this slip of paper in case of emergencies. You have the key to the apartment. Thank you for the cash. Is there anything else Sir?' asked the smirking Mr Barr, who had done well financially from this illegal deal. No tax would need to be declared from this client, thought the excited, manipulating schemer. Mr Barr knew the young man sitting next to him, hiding his identity, was up to something - but what that was he couldn't make out. Anyway, he didn't want any trouble himself. He wasn't young any more, though he had a younger wife and children and grandchildren to provide for. He was going to leave it at that.

'No that's all Mr Barr,' said Pathan, who was pleased to get out of the car and desired to lay down for a brief sleep. He was now tired and hungry. He would venture out later for food and drink.

Pathan walked slowly up the concrete stairs dragging his case behind him. He found his apartment at the end of the short corridor. All the walls of the four floors were painted a dirty light brown. Bulbs were spaced out about every ten feet, hanging down from a white flaking ceiling. It was similar, he noted, to pubs and clubs in Soho. He wasn't impressed, but there were no other options. He would make the best of it for a few days, then move on. At least the garden appeared clean and was full of various blooming flowers he had not seen before. There were no takeaway boxes or beer cans on the green lawn, unlike in Pimlico. That much pleased him at least.

The rusty key Barr gave him opened the front door. He walked into an environment reminiscent of a factory furnace. He immediately opened all the six windows of the living room. Cool, fresh evening air flooded the place. He took off most of his clothes and turned on the ceiling fan in the centre of the room. Pathan threw himself on the settee; he was desperate for some peace and quiet after many difficult hours of travelling from Bath to Johar Town. Understandably, air travel from one continent to another, security worries, banking his money and finding this hideout - for in essence that's what this was - had all severely affected his mental state. After being on the run since November, he had found himself in this rotten old dive of a place. Not a lot of progress had been made, he reckoned. Depressed, confused and ready to quit, he felt defeated. One could keep running but, ultimately, no one could hide forever. Although he had thought about it many times before, but with no serious intention, he now realised that handing himself in to the police was the only realistic option. After all the money had been spent, or stolen, where else could he go? He was gradually becoming more unpredictable.

The cool air felt cold on Pathan's nude body. He had opened his eyes to see the sun rising for yet another burning hot day in Pakistan. How long he could withstand the incessant heat he didn't know. He had fallen asleep last night out of sheer fatigue. Even though he had left the fan on for seven hours, it was now 6am by his watch and he still felt sticky and in desperate need of a shower. He sat up on the settee to regain his composure and orientation. The last thirty-six hours had been horrendous. At this stage most of it was just a vague recollection. With eyes still sleepy and sore, he looked at his immediate surroundings. The walls were painted various shades of green, with blue and brown parallel lines. The painter must have been on some sort of dope, he reckoned. There was one large table, four chairs, one settee, blue curtains, a wooden floor and a picture of some old stern looking British army officer on the wall. That was the sum of the furniture in the large room, most of it was clearly worth very little. He dared not think what the other rooms must have looked like.

Pathan took his pants off and had a shower. The warm water felt heavenly on his aching bones. For ten minutes he stood like a statue under the cascading water. Eventually, feeling like a rejuvenated man, he got out of the shower and dried himself with the only towel he had brought with him. That miserly old sod, Mr Barr, had not even included one in the month's cash he had given him. Not only had he failed to provide any towels, but there were no tea towels, toilet paper, soap or any other household goods. What a mean old shifty bastard he was;

Pathan's instincts about him were correct before they had even spoken a word. He was cheap and nasty, and there was not a thing Pathan could do about it.

The bedroom was no different to the other rooms. It was small and painted yellow with matching dirty curtains. His bed for the duration reminded him of the one he had slept in when in Borstal. It was a typical bed found in most British institutions. It had a large iron frame. The hard mattress, which felt like wood, was supported by sagging steel springs underneath. Dirty sheets and blankets covered the bed. This hell hole was the sum total of his life. He kicked the bed, then the wall. If he had possessed a gun at that precise moment, he would have shot himself. But he had to be strong, determined and committed to finding a different identity, somewhere - anywhere.

Pathan was ravenously hungry. Other than two meals on the plane and cheap roadside kebabs in Lahore, he hadn't had anything else to eat. He quickly dressed in clean clothes, trimmed his thick beard and walked down the stairs out onto the pavement. It was 7am. The heat was very humid; Pathan felt he was going to fry if he remained for too long in this temperature. After making enquiries from two teenagers staying in the hostel next door, he was directed to shops and restaurants not half a mile down the dusty, litter strewn road. He eventually walked into a small cafe. Several people, including two families, sat eating. After all the deafening noise elsewhere, Pathan couldn't believe how quiet the place was. The only sound came from the purring fan on the ceiling.

'Good morning sir, how can I help you?' asked the

young, smiling, attractive female behind the counter. She was overly eager to serve him.

He was surprised to hear a local girl speaking such fluent English. Although it dawned on him that Pakistanis preferred to learn English than any other language.

'Although you look no different to any local man, there's something about you that tells me you aren't from this area. Are you from England sir?' she politely enquired.

'I left England years ago to live with my parents in Quetta,' he informed her.

'Ah yes. I've read about that place. I've never been there, but one day I intend to go there. What would you like to order sir?' she asked the lean, hungry man who was looking so intensively into her black coloured eyes that it made her blush.

'What is your first name?' Pathan asked her.

'My name is Mahnoor,' she coyly replied.

'That's a lovely name. I'll have a large lassi, chicken biryani, rice and three naans please Mahnoor. I'm so hungry my stomach is craving your delicious food,' he winked at her. He needed to be more mindful. Pakistani culture was unlike British culture in many ways. His attitude to women may have offended local people. He needed to remember where he was.

She was inwardly overjoyed that an older man appeared to be attracted to her. But she reminded herself that her Muslim religion frowned upon fraternising. Her mother kept reminding her that the mind could quickly deteriorate by looking at an unknown man for too long.

Pathan ate his food like a hungry wolf devouring its prey. The food coursed through his body. He ordered more food: fish, fruit and another large lassi drink. His energy levels had to be replenished as he didn't know when conditions might change, forcing him to escape without notice. Today he was going to buy Pakistani clothes so that he could blend in with the locals. Just basic clothes, nothing too fancy. He'd pick up some loose trousers, kameez shirts, a scarf, long robe and some sort of hat. He was hoping to buy them in a local shop for poor people. He would ask young Mahnoor about these things when she cleared his table.

'Mahnoor, where can I buy some cheap local clothes?' he asked. 'Cheap clothes that local men wear,' he emphasized, noticing for the first time that her clothes; trousers and shirt, appeared to be made from rather cheap material.

'You can buy cheap clothes in a small shop called Passi, just ten minutes from here,' she reassured the would be Pakistani, who at the moment looked, thought and spoke English - but he was fooling no one when it came to the matter of his identity.

'Where do you live?' he asked.

'Oh, I live in a poor area of town with my mother and two young brothers – it's not far from Bahria Housing Estate. My mother washes for professional people. My father died of an illness years ago,' she sighed and looked down at the floor rather sadly. Her thoughts of Pathan's attraction to her had diminished considerably.

With a belly full of delicious hot food, Pathan headed for the Passi shop recommended by the young female worker in the eatery he had just left. Walking along the road he noticed there were very few cars parked outside the cheap yet brightly painted terraced houses and bungalows. Most of them sporting large yellow flowering bushes he had not seen before in Britain. The scent was divine.

He didn't even know what day it was and cared little about such trivial things in his precarious position. Life would go on, with or without him – this was Pathan's new philosophy. After a few more minutes the shop in question appeared. Small, painted in fading blue paint, and with various clothes hanging in the dirty cobwebbed windows, it didn't look the sort of place one would visit out of personal choice. But with little money, poor people had no choice. They were paid low wages, so begging or stealing was the only way to survive for most people. Even though there were pockets of wealth in Johar, most lived by desperate means.

He entered the musty smelling shop. It was dark, shabbily painted and cluttered from floor to ceiling with bundles of clothes. An old hunchback man came shuffling out to greet him. He had long grey hair, no teeth, wore local clothes that stank of urine and wore nothing on his calloused dirty feet. It wasn't exactly an auspicious sight, but Pathan needed these rags to wear when he was not in cities or communicating with professional people. As he looked around him, he gave the whole idea about changing his attire another long hard thought. But the old clothes, he surmised, would at least hide his identity somewhat and give him the confidence to openly talk with people in Punjabi.

'You want clothes sir?' asked the old man in a subservient manner.

'Do you have kameez, trousers and shirts in my size?' he asked.

'Yes sir. Over there, plenty of them,' he pointed to a small dark room at the back of the shop.

Pathan rifled through the bundle of clothes. He tried on various shapes, sizes and colours. Not many of them appealed to his taste, but due to the claustrophobic and foul atmosphere he bought three pairs of each and hurriedly left the shop. Even the hot sticky air outside was refreshing after that place, which reminded him of Barr's human pigsty.

After regaining his composure, he walked back along the hot pavements to his small block of flats. Other than a few scruffy children playing with a ball in the road and several dogs lying panting in the shade, no one was around. Hoping he wouldn't encounter any other residents, he quickly yet quietly walked up the stairs to his flat. Without hesitation, he opened the front door and entered the stifling hot room. Now the time had come to take off his western clothes and replace them with the pathetic specimens he had just bought. Not a pretty sight, he thought as he looked into the mirror to try and make sense of it all. What a terrible state of affairs. He was thousands of miles from home and didn't have a friend in the world who could or would comfort him. He was wanted by the police who were probably searching for him this very minute. If they caught him, only many years of prison lay ahead for the outrageous crime he had committed. The one certainty Pathan carried around with him was that his parents still loved him no matter what he had done, even though he had bought eternal shame on the family.

Pathan sat staring at the sad looking wall trying to sort out his thoughts and feelings. What was he to do?

Should he stay here for a few days, a week or more, or move on now before people became used to him being there? He knew what people were like. They would have nothing better to do than endless, empty talk. He expected a lot of local people had already seen him walking about. Two hours had passed as he continued to think of his miserable existence, sitting there wearing the national Pakistani dress of salwar and kameez: loose trousers and shirt. His shaven head, thick growing beard, loose scarf, hat and trainers completed his identity. Was it convincing? He thought it was and decided to walk around the town and visit various places of interest. But before embarking on an inquisitive foray, he concluded that moving tomorrow was the best bet. Three days was enough of this place. Besides, after the almighty mistake of showing his passport to the bank worker, it had made him vulnerable to being arrested. Time was now of the essence. He would withdraw all his money early tomorrow morning and immediately take the express train to Peshawar. As he didn't speak the native language, which was predominantly Pashto, he very much hoped that people would communicate in English. The journey would take about seven hours by express train. His mind was set on which direction to take.

Except for a small group of girls sitting outside the hostel laughing, the streets were still quiet and hot. He felt confident that he hadn't yet encountered any other residents. The last thing he needed was to explain another story to a stranger about his presence in Johar Town. That would project all sorts of problems that Pathan didn't want to experience. Anonymously, he walked down the road the opposite way to the restaurant, passing cheap but smart and tidy terraced houses and small blocks of flats. A few women dressed in colourful saris tended their gardens. There they knelt, all of them perfectly quiet, industriously concentrating on the tasks in front of them. Who knew, perhaps their minds were focused on loftier ideas such as religion? Anyhow, none of them appeared aware of the Englishman in their presence.

After ambling about for a mile, Pathan was soaked with perspiration and decided to seek shade in a nearby park. Upon entering, a few people gestured their presence to him. One - a middle-aged man - said good morning in a local dialect which Pathan understood. Sitting on a wooden bench under a large peach tree, Pathan surveyed the place. Most of the park's occupants were mothers playing with their babies. Some of them wore various coloured head scarves. Older children fed seeds to a flock of ravenous teal ducks from the nearby wetlands. The little birds fought each other like savages as their beaks devoured the food. It reminded him of many awful experiences at borstal.

What was uppermost in his mind right now was the incessant desire to speak with someone, anyone that could offer a few words of comfort and friendliness. Perhaps that desire was undeserving for a man who had broken the golden rule. But surely even Pathan, despite being hunted like a dog, deserved some compassion. He was a human being; he had feelings and still retained those qualities that his parents had instilled in him from childhood. He wished for someone to love him right now, to hold his hand and kiss him with honest intent. Pathan wasn't beyond developing a loving relationship again. Most of us could recover, he told himself, he was no different.

The only sources that could provide emotional nourishment were his uncle and family, but he had declined to contact them. His uncle, Saad Passi, was aged about 67 and lived somewhere in Johar, but he didn't have the address. By looking in the local phone book, verbal contact could have been possible, even desirable for Pathan. It would have given him much needed stability at a time when his inner resources were being stretched to their limits. It was also an ideal opportunity to confess to his uncle what he had done to Henrietta Marlow. He could seek forgiveness from the whole Passi family, which was what he desperately needed. They wouldn't condemn or condone but try and understand his distorted motives. Above all else, they could support him later at the police station. His uncle would see to it that nothing untoward happened to him while in Pakistani custody. He could also have contacted Pathan's suffering parents back in England. It was the ideal opportunity for him to end his own painful plight. He needed to be brave, to give himself up to the police and return to his country of origin to face justice. Being ever vigilant was obviously wearing him down. Unsurprisingly, it was gradually undermining his mental and physical health. Since being on the run from the police, his sleep had been interrupted by constant disruptive and violent dreams. The dreams had one major theme: he was being hunted by demons - distorted, three headed, ugly fanged animals all trying to devour him.

But, no, Pathan wouldn't dream of voluntarily giving himself up to the police. His last chance had gone when he denied the opportunity his uncle could have given him. Ultimately, he was now on his own and left to his own devices.

Depressed by these intense feelings, Pathan walked back out of the park and continued walking along the road, head bowed, until he reached a bar just off the high street. It was a small nondescript place which was ideal. He didn't require conversation at this moment, just a few beers in a dull dive. There were only a few older men talking, drinking and smoking inside the bar. They wore long robes, and their black, lined faces gave the impression of years of back breaking work under intense heat. It wasn't surprising, therefore, that their thin bodies relished the cool air as they sat underneath the ceiling fan.

'Yes sir, what would you like to drink?' asked a middle-aged man wearing horned rimmed spectacles and a large bushy moustache.

This was another person who had spontaneously addressed him in English. Pathan was becoming more anxious and self-conscious about his appearance. He thought he looked the part, dressed just like any other local young man - but obviously not if the perception of others was anything to go by. What was the point of wearing national dress when western clothes were more comfortable? Communities the world over are aware when a stranger enters their town. One could wear all manner of subterfuge, but people have a vested interest in making a living, feeding their families and keeping others safe from potential harm.

'Large beer please. That will be fine,' Pathan pointed towards an American lager he had not tasted before. After paying the bartender, he walked out of the bar and found a table and three chairs under a cool fig tree. Placing the cold drink upon the wooden table, off came his shirt, scarf and the pricy trainers he had purchased in Pimlico, to combat the sweltering heat. He was conscious of the Muslim tradition of not having bare shoulders or legs in public. A slight welcoming breeze blew against his white cotton t-shirt.

'You on holiday sir?' asked the bartender who had walked outside to collect empty glasses.

'Yea, that's right. Just travelling round a bit. I'm living with my parents in Quetta,' he replied, although he wished the bloke hadn't asked him the question. He didn't know who these people were, or what they might say to others. He was pre-occupied with thoughts of survival.

'Well that's a coincidence sir, my grandfather was born and lived in Quetta most of his miserable life. When he was about nine, a lorry knocked him down smashing one of his legs to pieces, may Allah bless him. He's now dead,' explained the friendly worker, who wore western style clothes. Pathan noticed with some confusion, and at the same time relief, that it wasn't important to be so self-conscious about wearing national dress.

'How long have your parents been living in Quetta sir?' he enthusiastically asked.

'Not long, about five years I think,' Pathan reluctantly replied. The questions were becoming too personal. What could be done about it? He thought about just walking away, but that would be rather suspicious. Alternatively, he could go to the toilet and wait ten minutes until the worker was back in the bar, or buy another beer, or tell him to fuck off. Or he could just engage with the worker, have a very brief chat and then go. That was balanced, friendly and showed respect, he thought.

'Ah, very good sir. By the way, my name is Yasir. I own this small bar. Hefty bloody repayments. It's bloody hard sometimes, but there you are. Would you like to visit me and my family? We only live ten minutes from here. Here's my phone number. Do phone and let me know if you can come round,' he said in a reassuring voice.

'I certainly shall, Yasir. All the best to you and your family,' said Pathan.

Mightily relieved to have escaped the sincere clutches of the bar owner; Pathan walked briskly away from the premises. He had no intention of phoning him, or anyone else for that matter. The thought of sitting with his family, all chatting like sheep and asking questions about his life, would feel like being interrogated by security services. The feelings conjured up many painful experiences of younger days in Bradford, visiting various family members with his parents and siblings. Fat bosomed aunts, all of whom without fail would wear their Sunday best saris and smother him with kisses. That was one of the reasons he had to leave Bradford. Although he loved his parents, their background was far too prescriptive for him. With all the best intentions for their children, their lifestyle imposed restraint upon them, especially when they were young. They couldn't do this or that without explaining in detail before they were let loose to play with friends. But at least when it came to Muslim study, prayer or visiting the Iman, his parents relented somewhat.

As he kept walking along the now busy street, head down and anonymous, the realisation dawned on him that many people were leaving the local mosque after prayer. The men left the holy place on their own, only to be followed by the women five minutes later. Due to custom, the women's heads when entering a mosque or church were covered by a dupatta, which he had observed earlier on travelling with his foul landlord. This was a familiar sight back home. He himself had not been in a mosque for many years. Neither had he prayed, read holy books or had anything to do with his inherited religion - something he regretted now that secular life had taken an untoward grip over him.

Interested by a local paper advertising varied financial services, Pathan decided that his hunger couldn't be suppressed any more. The name Chicken Shack appealed to his western mind and starving appetite. Three hundred yards away, neon lights flashed and buzzed encouraging people to spend their money. It was now late afternoon, and as this was his last day in Johar he needed to remember to phone for a taxi reservation tonight to pick him up early tomorrow morning. He needed to be on the doorstep of that bank early in Lahore to collect his cash and return the key to Mr Barr. The latter didn't deserve such kind consideration, but there was no other choice.

Having looked at the restaurant from the roadside for several minutes, he decided to enter. He was no doubt motivated by the hot delicious chicken, but also by an attractive white woman with long blond hair sitting on her own. She momentarily reminded him of Henrietta. It was like a huge magnet had drawn this obsessional man into her sexual clutches. At that moment in time everything else ceased to exist. It appeared that white girls were his plaything. And yet, he acknowledged the destruction this particular preoccupation had caused!

He entered the restaurant and made a beeline for the woman sitting in the corner reading a magazine. She didn't look up, even though Pathan was an imposing figure intruding on her personal space. She was aware of his presence but did not pay any attention to what she thought was another young, virile male looking for sex. He was attracted by her slender western style presence. She had shiny hair, a face full of enchanting cosmetics, a short dress and high heeled shoes. Could any young man have denied such beauty?

'Hi there, how are you? Are you English?' asked Pathan, who had by now sat down opposite her. A rather threatening move.

'Hello. Yes, I'm British,' she hesitatingly replied.

'Where you from in the UK?' he asked.

'London,' she reluctantly answered.

'What is your name?' said Pathan.

'Look. Please leave me alone. I want to be on my own. Do you understand?' she told him in no uncertain manner.

'Can I buy you a coffee or anything?' She didn't answer.

'I'm from London. Don't be so standoffish,' Pathan was now becoming a nuisance to the woman. He wouldn't take no for an answer.

'If you don't leave me alone this minute, I shall inform the manager that you are harassing me,' she angrily replied.

He had an overwhelming desire to strangle the bitch. Who did she think she was? As far as he was concerned, women were inferior to men in every way. On such occasions, when feeling undermined, his rationale was to elevate male scientists who had improved the lives of countless people - not that he could name one invention to prove his assertion. Those men saved humanity wholesale from the precipice of war, disease and poverty. He had carried this stereotypical defence around with him since becoming aware of the sexual power that women had over him.

By this time, many people back home in England would have shaken their heads in disbelief at the terrifying revelations unfolding about Pathan's life - especially given that this was not the first time he had inflicted horrendous violence on Henrietta. Even though she told no one of that wounding, she had written it down in her diary, recorded for all of time! A few, no doubt, would sympathise with him. They would understand that human violence could lurk in all of us. But most people would by now be outraged by a person who had demonstrated his guilt trying to outsmart the police and fleeing the country.

They must have felt for his children, who would no doubt be mortified by the national and international news coverage about their father. That wasn't the father that kissed and cuddled them in bed, who took them to the local playground where they all had great fun and laughter. This wasn't the same man who took them to visit their doting grandparents for lunch most weekends. He was so kind, funny, generous and happy. He wasn't the father they had either forgiven or forgotten, that flogged them without little sympathy.

Inwardly incandescent with rage by the outrageous behaviour of the woman in the restaurant, Pathan quickly, and without unwanted attention, ordered a large takeaway and slid unnoticed out of the front door. That bulk of food would sustain him for hours. He decided to walk back to his flat and stay there until the taxi came tomorrow morning at about 7am. For the first time in weeks, rain fell in buckets upon the people of Johar. It cleared the stifling air and the roads of its accumulated rubbish. One could breathe with more depth and vigour. Tariq felt delighted as the rain lashed down, soaking him. At one stage he just stood and allowed himself to be completely saturated. His trainers overflowed with water.

Before retiring to his flat for the next twelve hours, there was one last thing to be done which was most important for his security. He bought yet another phone from a shop not far from where he was staying. Just like the other phones, the old one was immediately discarded into a large rubbish container, but the sim card he threw away separately. He was constantly aware that phone calls could be traced, but he was determined the police weren't going to find him.

Pathan woke at around 5am after a most turbulent night of disturbing dreams. He imagined himself incarcerated in a prison cell on a deserted island, miles from humanity - for the rest of his life he was deprived of hope.

Still there was no presence of any other residents in the block of flats. An occasional faint sound of a television or radio could be heard next door. Other than that, it appeared that the place was almost empty. That pleased Tariq, for no one had seen him and he was now leaving for a comfortable family life, he hoped, with a new wife in Peshawar. This was the delusion he carried. But, nonetheless, in about twelve hours he was convinced that life would begin anew.

Feeling spruced all over by a shower, enhanced by a change back into western clothes and full after stuffing himself with the last of the cold chicken, Pathan cheerfully entered the battered old taxi that drove him the ten miles to Lahore. During the first mile he kept looking back at Johar Town, trying to convince himself that it really existed. What an odd place. The driver was a local man, aged about 25 years. He wasn't very well dressed, his shifty eyes said much about his incorrigibility. No doubt he would be open to anything illegal if money was involved. This was understandable in the chronic social circumstances in which most lived. It appeared that the taxi hadn't been cleaned for some time if all the empty cigarette packets and newspapers that were strewn around were any guide.

'You on holiday sir?' the driver asked.

'Just travelling around for a few days,' Pathan replied half-heartedly. Once again, conversation wasn't on the agenda but being trapped in this old banger there was no other possibility - other than getting out and finding another driver, which he was most reluctant to do considering the time factor and his early appearance at the bank being imperative.

'You live in London sir?' came the next personal question.

He needed to keep to the same story, he thought to himself, just in case by some quirk of fate that all those he had met so far were questioned about him. He hadn't forgotten that he informed the woman in the Johar restaurant that he came from London. But other lies had completely escaped his memory. Being constantly anxious, it was not surprising that confusion clouded his judgement.

'No, I'm living with my parents in Quetta,' came the predictable reply. Pathan had to take the attention off himself and back onto the driver.

'What about yourself. How long you been living in Johar and do you own this taxi?' he asked.

'Yes, I was born not far from where I picked you up earlier. I live with my wife and three children. Life is hard here, but we manage. Other than driving this taxi, which I rent from a local company, I make money from other things to pay my way. I've got a lot of mouths to feed sir, which sometimes means I won't ask questions about certain things I'm asked to do,' he said with a broad grin.

Suspecting that the driver was about to suggest some kind of criminal negotiation, Pathan was mightily relieved when the taxi pulled up outside Mr Barr's address. Beggars lined the street. He quickly paid the driver in rupees, got out of the car with the case by his side, banged the door closed and hurried upstairs to put the flat key under his door. Within five minutes he was back downstairs. As it was past 8am, he knew the bank should now be open. This was the most anxious he had felt since leaving Heathrow. Like a bloody stupid imbecile he had given the cashier his passport details so that he could leave his cash in a secure place for a while - not thinking that the police could well have by now traced him to Western United Bank. Pathan looked around for several minutes anticipating anything suspicious. The police could be waiting for him inside the bank, like snakes in the grass ready to pounce. There was nothing else he could do but walk calmly into the foyer and withdraw his money. It could all be over for the wandering fugitive. A part of him was resigned to his fate.

The bank was no different to a few days ago. Bright lights, plush decorations, and well-trained smartly dressed staff filled the place with professionalism. It resembled a hotel, he thought. He stood in a small queue of businessmen waiting to be served. The young woman that had dealt with him the other day sat behind the same counter. She still had that honest smile on her face. Who knew where she came from, or what hand of cards she had been dealt in the human jungle?

'Good morning sir. How can I help?' she asked Pathan, who had the key to his strongbox ready in his sweating right hand - which was visibly shaking.

He looked slowly to the left and right, there was no sign of police around unless they were waiting downstairs ready to pounce when the cash was about to be taken out of the safety deposit box.

'Good morning. I've come to withdraw my money from downstairs. I have the key with me,' said Pathan.

'As you are the first customer this morning, I will have to open the main security door for you. Then you can open the second door with your own key,' she explained.

Minutes later she walked ahead of him downstairs to the security room. For a few seconds his prying eyes were fixed on her small round bottom. The woman opened the main door for him and he walked in unassisted. Once inside he opened the deposit box, withdrew the money and placed it into a body belt he had bought in Johar. The belt was tied secure and evenly around his waist so that it didn't show once he had put his shirt and jacket back on.

After letting himself out of the security room, his heart was pounding like a hydraulic piston, he walked back up the stairs and handed the key to the young female worker. She asked him to sign a piece of paper and then calmly - although inside his anxiety was rising fast - walked out of the door. He hailed a taxi immediately, and drove off at pace to Lahore railway station.

CHAPTER EIGHT

Lahore railway station, opened in 1860, was packed with customers walking and running in all directions. It looked as though pandemonium had broken out, but Pathan was aware of the intensity of Pakistani cities. Armed police and army personnel added to the mass anxiety that oozed from the growing throng. Porters pulled large trolleys at full speed, carrying first class customers' baggage to the waiting trains. Street traders, who were selling anything from boot laces to cooked rice, shouted at and cajoled people into buying their cheap wares. Station bars and cafés were packed into every other inch of space that covered the large turreted station. Even the birds fought each other over scraps of rotten discarded food - something that even the poor beggars would not entertain.

This was the mayhem that greeted the fugitive. Without delay Pathan bought a first class, single accommodation ticket for the express train that would be departing in thirty minutes for Peshawar. The accommodation comprised of a bed, sitting space with small armchair, toilet and sink. It was ideal for the needs of a man who needed time and space to gather his thoughts. One thing was for sure - his money belt would stay tightly secured around his body at all times until he could find a secure place, possibly a hotel, where he could relax somewhat. As there were tea and coffee facilities, and having bought food at the station, there was no need to leave the comfortable environment throughout the journey. It was just like a small self-contained bedsit.

Opening up his case he reckoned a check was in order to find out what, if anything, needed to be added to his existing, sparse chattels. Upon opening the case, a disgusting smell shot out across the room. His clothes needed to be washed as soon as possible. Other than the clothes he was wearing: a shirt, jumper, warm jacket, trousers, socks and an expensive pair of pig skin shoes, the remainder didn't add up to much. Besides his Pakistani clothes, which he would wear when appropriate, he had trainers, three pairs of socks, two shirts, two pairs of trousers, another jumper, vests, another pair of good quality shoes, a mohair jacket and the usual toiletries. An A4 plastic wallet contained his passport and insignificant papers. All other personal identification had been destroyed, including credit and debit cards, his driving license and birth certificate. At some stage the ten year passport would also have to be destroyed. Other than the cash, that was all Pathan owned. If the passport was discarded, then he really would become a man with no identity. Rudderless and set adrift in an ocean without a map, his existence was fast becoming devoid of purpose.

He took off all his clothes, except his pants and cash belt. He sat down, made coffee and relaxed as the modern express train, non-stop to Peshawar, travelled at great speeds through the huge barren countryside. It was crucial that he found a decent, impersonal hotel and, soon thereafter bought a false identity. The latter was imperative if he was to survive without detection.

His next experience of consciousness came when his wrist watch was ringing for him to get up out of bed. He had slept peacefully for at least five hours. An hour of the journey remained, and he needed to wash, dress and have coffee along with the derisory pastries freely offered by the train company.

'Would you like breakfast, sir?' asked a whispered female voice knocking on his door.

'No thank you,' he replied.

Tariq Pathan sat still and thought deeply about the potential problems that lay ahead in Peshawar. He was full of apprehension. There didn't appear to be any sort of police danger at Lahore station. He hadn't noticed any boarding the train there either. If they were onto him, then surely they wouldn't wait until he had travelled all the way to Peshawar to make the arrest.

Minutes later, an intercom announcement informed passengers that Peshawar station was near, and that they should collect their personal belongings and make their way to the exit. That message sparked danger levels.

The train manager thanked Pathan goodbye as he stepped down onto the tarmac platform. Loud speakers wailed everywhere. Porters asked if he needed someone to carry his case. No, was his abrupt response. After walking along the platform, down an escalator and out of the station, he was suddenly accosted by poor street kids all begging for money in Saddar Road. A station worker told them to fuck off, otherwise he would call the police. That was no deterrent to the homeless children who were some of the most poverty-stricken people in a city of over three million inhabitants. Indeed, it was estimated that Peshawar had one of the highest incidences of poverty in Pakistan.

Though aware of the new, frequent bus services around the city, Pathan preferred to take a taxi to Khyber road where several hotels were available. The Iranian refugee driver, who was smoking a cigarette and smelling like horse shit, dropped him off at a large, rather pretentious looking place. The larger the better – it was impersonal, he thought. Before entering the Intercontinental, he needed to get his mind straight if that was possible at this stage. He would think up a different name and stick to it while staying there. He would pay in cash at all times and would never show his passport to anyone. His cover story was that he was on holiday from Islamabad. He was desperate for a drink by now, preferably several large brandies. They would calm his nerves, which felt like they had been in trench warfare.

In Pathan walked, with a rather nonchalant air of super confidence. No police force, as of yet, had arrested the boy from Bradford. At reception the young lady worker dressed in a purple sari stood smiling at her newest customer.

'Good evening, sir. How can I help you?' she asked.

'Good evening my dear. I would like a single room, preferably at the back of the hotel where it appears to be quieter,' he said politely. He hadn't felt so friendly since way back in Bath. He had also realised that nearly everyone he had met so far had addressed him as sir - not because they had to, but because they wanted to. They had all been genuinely friendly. It was about time the gesture was returned. Be that as it may, he thought, where was the bar? He needed to sort himself out so that he once again resembled an intelligent, if superficial, man.

'Of course, sir. We have a lovely, colourful single room on the fourth floor overlooking the polo ground. Firstly, you must sign this form stating your name, address and method of payment for me. By the way, polo is a big sporting occasion here in Peshawar. British teams play here sometimes. Beyond that sir, just for your information as you may want to visit these places, is the Kabul River canal. The army stadium is to the north-west and the British cemetery to the west. Here is your key to room 55 and your written guide to the city, sir. Now if you follow me, I will ask a porter to carry your case into the lift for you,' the plump, long haired employee explained in a most helpful manner.

'I've signed the form. No need for the porter. I shall carry it,' replied Pathan.

In this establishment he registered himself as Saad Dogar from Islamabad. He hadn't given the name or address much thought. Any old spiel would do. An inspired insight suddenly dawned on him. What if he was never apprehended by police? What if he was in Pakistan for the rest of his life? That would be most wonderful. In fact, the thought of having another family of his own was all that kept him motivated. The first marriage had been an unmitigated failure due to Pathan's violent behaviour. By now, he had rather reluctantly accepted it as an unequivocal fact. Given the opportunity, he wanted to atone for past misdeeds and live a decent life with another woman who was prepared to give him a chance. This was all rather sentimental considering the serious questions he would need to address sooner or later. But once he had found himself a young – ideally teenage -wife, she would soon be forgotten for another fallen Greek goddess, willing to fulfil his impulsive, perverted fantasies.

'Very well, sir. The lift is just over there,' she said helpfully.

The fugitive thanked her and marched into the lift. Within a minute or so, modern technology had hurtled him up to the fourth floor. The hotel, he thought, resembled Caesar's Palace in Las Vegas. The foyer, ceilings, walls, floors, carpets, nearly everything inanimate was painted or papered in a sort of yellow-cream-peach colour. Were they all on drugs?

Pathan walked fifty feet along the landing, found his room, unlocked the teak door and immediately locked it again. Some security at last - he breathed a heavy sigh of relief. He took off his clothes and jumped onto the bed intending to have a sleep. But intrusive thoughts wouldn't allow it. He needed to get that new fake identification, wash his clothes and change pounds into rupees. All these tasks needed urgent attention tomorrow, but the ID was the most important. Without this, things were hopeless, especially if he was stopped by the police on a routine check. He knew from family members that this was a regular occurrence in Pakistani cities due to extra security being enforced to combat crime.

His bedroom was just as colourful as the rest of the hotel he had seen. There was a large, soft bed covered with a red cotton duvet and a comfortable armchair covered in blue mohair. He had access to all the latest technologies: a colour television, DVD player and other musical gadgets. There was a large tiled bathroom, and several soft drinks of his choice. What more could one wish for? It wasn't too dissimilar to the decadent hotels in Western Europe.

Drinking a bottle of chilled water, he surveyed the hotel below. The manicured lawn was surrounded by gardens full of various and colourful plants. Red collared doves sat peacefully, sleeping in the shade of Bakiyan trees, while cats sat hopefully with their mouths open waiting for a potential meal. It was all such a contrast to the apartment he had rented for a short while back in Johar. Looking beyond the hotel grounds, the polo ground was easily spotted. There appeared to be two small seated enclosures, but the place was empty. There was no match today being fought out by the great and good and affluent, where players would whack the brains out of each other with startling ferocity.

Right, he thought, after changing his shirt and trousers - a positive attitude was certainly needed downstairs in the bar. He needed to be discreet, but at the same time to find someone to put some business his way. He would take his time, being careful not to stand out or push for attention on his search for a corrupt man looking to make money. It was the oldest incentive in history. Illegality and money were universal bedfellows, there was no doubt about it. Tariq had known this all his life. From the time he sold stolen school sports equipment to friends at the age of ten, he knew what people were like. All he needed was to do something on the cheap and droves would stampede - experience had taught him.

'Hello,' Pathan said to the young female receptionist.

'Hello sir. How is your room? To your expectations I hope?' she asked.

'Excellent. Could the hotel wash clothes for me, and can you exchange pounds for rupees?' asked Pathan.

'Yes of course, sir. Please bring the clothes down tomorrow and I can exchange the currencies for you now, although there is a limit of £100 per day. We pay slightly less than banks, but it's still a good deal,' she explained.

That was great news, he concluded, he may not have to use the banks after all. Although if a deal was struck over a bent identification, he would need to use one unless the person accepted pounds – he was hoping this would be the case.

'That's fine. So, £100 exchange for rupees now please?' he confirmed.

'Yes sir. We pay about 80 rupees to £1 sterling,' she informed him.

Pathan didn't know whether that was correct or not, but it sounded about right. There was no way of knowing. She was probably making some money herself, but what the heck, he thought. He didn't want to cash too many £50 notes in the hotel, but it was handy if it came to using rupees outside the hotel. Tariq handed over the cash and she paid him accordingly. All seemed as well as could be expected at this stage.

He walked slowly and cautiously yet confidently to the large bar. He sat on a stool and was immediately served by a smartly dressed, tall young man. As usual, the man spoke perfect English. Pathan was pleased and reminded himself that he understood very little of the local language, Pashto.

'Yes sir, what would you like?' he asked, with an alarmingly broad grin. The barman was just being friendly, of course, but Pathan wasn't so assured by the powerful gaze that penetrated his interior.

'Large brandy and soda.'

'Yes....'

'And a large sheesh kebab and naan. Thank you,' said Pathan, who was rather hesitant after the barman's eye contact had somehow made him feel uneasy.

'Yes, of course, sir.'

He took his drink and sat twenty feet from the bar. After several small gulps the power of the brandy hit his brain with an almighty thud. It was just what he needed to help him relax. Already his perception of the immediate environment was changing. The barman didn't mean any harm. It was just his own fucked up feelings that needed calming from time to time, Pathan thought to himself. Most chemicals did the trick, his brain informed him. Business was in the air, whether that was bent I.D, sex or alcohol.

'Your meal, sir. Shall I charge the bill to your room number?' he asked.

'No, I'll sort it out later with cash. Another large brandy, but no ice please,' Pathan politely asked. His paranoid personality had changed within minutes from confusion to conformity. It was as though a different person had taken over his body since consuming the alcohol. He was aware of the various odd, bizarre thoughts and feelings that entered him. But try as he did, he was unable to make sense of them, or to remain in control to any large degree – although the alcohol and drugs helped.

It was as a young boy at school, and later on at the young offenders' institution, that Pathan had belatedly remembered those who had power over him. That caused him great consternation. Many professionals had tried to discuss his problems. It was only during the latter part of a prison sentence that he was considered unsuitable for therapy, to address the excitable, violent and impulsive behaviour that took him to the edge of normal reality. But nothing came of the support he desperately needed to overcome those demons that were now out of control. Whether by nature or nurture, his hypervigilance had deteriorated into chronic dangerousness. If only someone could have directed Pathan to find a modern-day Juno to restore him to the vigour of his youth. He could have been helped with decision making, emotional intelligence and empathy. But, due to various causes and conditions - he was probably beyond recovery.

He forcefully repressed those menacing thoughts no sooner than they had appeared. Consuming his second large drink did the trick. With food in his guts, the alcohol was now leading his thoughts to darker realms where anything was possible in a mind with such confused emotional boundaries. Relaxed and full of confidence, he looked round and weighed up the possibilities for illegal activity. There were only about twenty customers. Most of them were couples, eating, drinking and socialising. That was no good. He spotted an older male who was sat on his own drinking, using a laptop computer. He was well dressed and looked decent and respectable. This could be a possibility, he thought – this man might be open to making some money. Another male, much younger, caught his eye. Fuck it, Pathan thought, I'll give him a try. He was suited and booted in expensive western clothes that shouted money mania. Well, he wouldn't know unless he asked!

'One large brandy please,' Pathan chirped to the barman. 'Put it on the bill and I'll sort it out later, thanks,' he said as he walked over to the table opposite him.

'Hello, how are you?' he asked the young slim man he had been sizing up for the past ten minutes. He was gradually losing all inhibitions.

'Hello. Good evening. I'm well thank you. And how are you? What brings you to this neck of the woods may I ask?'

'I'm just travelling around for a few weeks. I'm residing here for the next few days,' said Pathan, unconvincingly.

'Please join me. My name is Said Wali. I live not far from here, but I enjoy using this hotel bar unlike most of the other inferior places. Good food, drink and service,' he explained.

Pathan was already impressed by his whole demeanour. Up close he could tell his suit was the latest London design and that his shoes were made of genuine leather. A pink shirt and tie completed the picture of a man full of himself and aware of what he needed. This could be the bloke who could start changing things for someone in a desperate predicament.

'Good to meet you. What do you do for a living?' he asked the look-a-like film star in front of him.

'My parents are Pakistani. They live in France but have businesses here in Peshawar that I manage for them. I was born in London at a time when my parents owned a large hotel there. But most Pakistan cities are cosmopolitan,' he glibly, yet convincingly explained. 'What is your name?' asked Said.

'I'm Saad,' was his response, as the men shook hands

- though Pathan had his mind on other, more important matters right now.

'How do you earn a living Saad, or is some loving aunt keeping you in luxury while you gallivant around the world enjoying yourself?' smiled Said Wali.

'Would you like a drink?' What a flash bastard, Pathan thought.

'Thank you, Saad. I'll have a small lager,' came the response from the younger man who was intrigued by the handsome man in front of him. Was he playing games with him, or in trouble of some kind? Maybe he was just being straight like most tourists.

Pathan avoided the question of employment. It was too intrusive for his liking. He detached himself immediately and walked to the bar for more brandy. He needed to keep his brain topped up with powerful ammunition unless he was to be undermined by the flash businessman who might just make a fool of him. Paranoia was never far from his mind.

'Another large brandy and a small lager please. Put it on the bill. Cheers,' he said, trying to draw attention from himself so he could ask Said Wali some searching questions. He needed to make a breakthrough towards asking about false identification. It was pointless wasting invaluable time fucking around with meaningless small talk, he needed to put the big question to him.

After another hour of superficial questions; sport, fashion and family – which clearly neither men relished - Pathan had passed the point of no return. It was now or never!

'Look this sounds rather far-fetched, and I'm sorry if I have misread the situation, but could you, or do you know of someone who could help me buy false identification?' he blurted out across the table without any prior build up to the subject. Danger! Was that too abrupt, even after consuming several brandies, to a person he had just met. He could be anyone, Pathan realised. Had he shot himself many times in both feet?

'Well that is a loaded question Saad. Be more specific will you? Is it for you, or someone else?' was his straightforward reply.

'Yes, it is for me. I can't go into detail about why I need a new Pakistani I.D, but I'll pay in cash and with used sterling notes. Would a new ID require a photograph? Let me reassure you I am not a wanted murderer, or gun runner or International terrorist!'

'Why you need new ID is your personal business. A photograph will probably be required. You could use it in banks and other places that require security clearance. OK. The card will have a special number, of course, and must be issued by the local ministry. That will cost you, my friend,' he explained to Pathan, who now realised, or rather hoped that he was heading in the right direction. 'I have to leave in a few minutes. Meet me tomorrow at midday in a bar called Freetown on Yakatut Road. It's only a ten minute walk from here. OK?' said Said.

'OK. Thank you,' Pathan said, with feelings of relief and trepidation. This bloke, he thought, could be a police officer or informant. On reflection, the whole brief business seemed rather surreal. Upon his arrival at the bar tomorrow he might well be arrested and taken into custody for deportation. But what could he now do? There was no alternative, other than making a run for it tonight, or facing the music. The vibes the local guy had given out provided encouragement to sleep another night in a warm cosy bed until the morning came, when he would know the outcome.

Two more large brandies were enough for the lonely Englishman sitting on his own. Anxiety, fatigue and booze had brought about early retirement to his bedroom. The warmth and sexual desire for a woman right now was overwhelming. He was desperate for human comfort - someone, anyone, of any age to kiss and cuddle him. He would give all his diminishing wealth for a woman to spend the night with him and make him feel wanted again. All animals had that overwhelming urge for kinship. If only his much-desired fantasy and hoped for Pakistani wife was there to offer unconditional love!

But indifference wasn't far from his feelings towards women. Within minutes his hostility grew towards what he perceived to be the immoral behaviour of westernised women. The influence of his parents' background had gone deeper into his psyche than he had ever realised before, even though they themselves were liberal minded people. Henrietta Marlow symbolised that western female moral emptiness which was so prevalent in Britain. Pathan had made his contribution to further hammering home its shallow and depressing impact.

Unsurprisingly, Pathan's emotions continued to swing violently in all directions. Was he still relatively sane? Or had he at last descended into the depths from which there was no rational return? He had been through a physical and emotional roller coaster journey without any viable destination in sight. One might have sympathised with a certain amount of compassion for his unenviable tragic existence.

Pathan woke early at around 6am. He found himself on top of the bed, without clothes and bathed in sweat. He looked up at the bright ceiling for some time, thinking about the momentous day ahead. Today could make or break him. There could be a trap waiting for him in the bar suggested by that young, arrogant look-a-like film star he met last night.

After showering and changing into the few remaining clean clothes that he possessed, he walked down to reception and handed over his stinking laundry. Reassured that he was smart and presentable, he was shown to his breakfast table. No one else was there. Large ruby coloured chandeliers adorned the high ceiling. Soft orange whirls lined the papered walls, and local gypsy music filled the room as clean cool air filtered in through half-opened windows. A young, most attractive, woman handed him a menu. She carried herself well - tall, upright, skilfully dressed, but not loud, boastful or embarrassing. He could tell she was educated and self-aware.

'Good morning sir, would you like tea, coffee or any other drink?' she asked courteously.

'Strong coffee and orange juice, toast, butter and jam please,' was his sharp response. He was totally preoccupied with the villains he was meeting within the next few hours. It hadn't escaped his notice that he needed to have his hair shaved and beard trimmed. It was important that he looked the part in front of people who were going to scrutinise him from top to toe as a potential security risk. After breakfast he would have a few drinks in another hotel to sort out his anxiety, which was never far away. It gripped his mind, his body, his soul, giving little respite.

Then there was the problem of the cash belt stuck firmly round the waist. If he left it in the hotel room it could easily be stolen. If taken along to the meeting, he was vulnerable to being robbed. The latter was the lesser of two evils. Besides, he might well need the cash. By now he had disposed of all personal identification, including his mobile phone and passport - but if suddenly arrested, explaining the large amount of £50 notes could be incriminating. He would take the chance.

After an hour of intermittent rain, hot sun shone on the streets of Peshawar as a group of Great egrets flew gracefully overhead. The white birds reminded him of the few times he had sauntered the short distance from his flat to watch them on the Thames. Swans, Canadian geese, oyster catchers and many other birds fought each other for the scarce food in the clear shallow waters. The tough looking London boys', fishing, smoking and drinking alcohol, evoked memories of his teenage days. He would swim in the local Victorian canal which was full of old bicycles, supermarket trolleys, milk crates and blocks of concrete.

Trimmed and shorn, he was now relaxed and more aware after several quick brandies. Next, Pathan entered Freetown bar. It was just after midday and the place was already full of young men drinking, smoking and playing pool. He immediately recognised hustlers, gangsters and all manner of humans devoid of conscience. He felt like a minnow in shark infested waters. One false move and he would be devoured. Would it be safest to walk out now while the opportunity was still an option?

'Hello my friend. How are you?' asked Said Wali, who was waiting for him to arrive. 'I discussed with my friend what you asked for last night. After many searching questions about your nationality, security and other requirements and, as they trust me and my family, they are prepared to provide you with a new ID. The man in question should be here soon. One word of warning though, don't ask any questions,' he explained.

'Will you be with us during negotiations?' Pathan asked, concerned for his safety.

'Yes, don't worry Saad,' he said, reassuringly.

Thirty minutes later the man himself arrived. Middle aged, fat and wearing an expensive dark suit, he shook hands with the two men. Pathan was really trapped and had nowhere to go. Fear shook his body. The effects of the alcohol had evaporated. They could easily skin him alive and eight billion people would be none the wiser. My time is up - he thought - these bastards are going to kill me. He was convinced they ha d read all about his crimes in England and were prepared to inform the police right now. They would all share Pathan's money, the bastards.

Although he was petrified, he was ready to go down fighting. With a knife hidden inside his jacket, he would injure someone badly. Intense fear had given him a rush of adrenaline: the kit for survival. Steel could quickly slit open the fat gut in front of him.

Led by the fat man, they walked single file to a small office at the back of the bar.

'Hello my friend,' said the fat man, Said Wali has explained what you need. I can arrange the fake I.D for you. It will cost £2000 cash. If you want to continue, I need to take a photograph of you to attach to the fake document. Or do you want to leave and think it over?

The choice is yours. If you continue now I need £1000 up front,' he said bluntly in a slightly frightening tone. As if to clearly emphasize his point, he raised his thick, bushy eyebrows. The man leading the deal did not intend to divulge any more information. To ask would be suicidal.

He thought for a moment but agreed to pay the £1000 up front and take a chance that the big man leading the proceedings wouldn't fleece him. When the deal was concluded, the hefty financial outlay would replete his resources considerably. The three of them agreed to meet in two days' time, when the new documents would be handed over to Pathan. Said Wali would contact his hotel to let him know the time and place. What an almighty risk he was taking in a business full of danger, deceit and death!

As Pathan walked around the city trying to enjoy the colourful sights and sounds that bombarded his senses from all angles, the shadow of death still followed him. To shake off its grip was near impossible. The only temporary solution was to find a small bar - any dive that sold spirits - and get legless. Paying for sex had crossed his mind many times. Drugs, along with any kind of chemical crap, had also fought with the former craving for similar status. He knew he had to be careful in these places, especially when he wasn't known. He spotted strangers from some distance away. No need to worry, he thought. He looked just like a local man going about his business - but he dared not attract attention while carrying his worldly possessions.

Inhabiting a self-imposed world that even a street dog would have found painful, he walked into a side street bar. It was small, dirty and full of hustlers - a risky place to be with a money belt. But what did it matter when his life felt meaningless?

'Hi there, large brandy and soda. Thanks,' Pathan said to the female barmaid, aged about thirty.

'Of course, sir,' she instinctively knew he wasn't local. 'Are you on holiday sir?'

'Please call me Saad. Yes, I'm travelling around for a few days. My father lives in Lahore,' he told her. Once again he gave a different story. Pathan was becoming so confused by the many lies he had given people that at times he didn't remember who he was, or where he was going.

'How about yourself. What is your name and do you live locally?' he asked the short, slim woman as he immediately knocked back the brandy in one gulp. Manna for the brain.

'Another large brandy, please,' he paid in rupees.

'My name is Anam. Yes, I live about three miles from here. It is beyond the outer ring road going that way,' she said, pointing south. 'I live in two rooms with my two daughters. The area is very poor and dirty. Most people there don't have jobs, but beg, steal or pick stuff off the garbage tips. They do whatever they can to eat,' she quietly explained, as though resigned to a loathsome life of poverty.

Asking for another drink, he was aware that as he spoke to the woman serving him he had drawn the attention of two young men, who were no doubt sizing up the stranger for his goods. Street scum smelling the goods.

'What does your husband do for a living?' he asked her.

'He left me to fight in another country. I don't know who he is fighting. I didn't ask. He hasn't contacted me since the day he left. Without the money I earn here, things would be desperate for me, just like my neighbours. I'm very fortunate that I can provide some medical support for my disabled parents. I left school at twelve and got married at fifteen, so you see I don't have any qualifications or skills to get a better paid job,' she explained.

Fuelled by alcohol and diminishing inhibition, Pathan had started to fancy Anam somewhat. She was quite well presented and spoke good English - this was essential so that Pathan could communicate effectively. She had a small place where he could hide away for a while, even though it would probably not be what he was used to. People there probably hated the police. Two children being around wouldn't be a problem either, although the thought of a husband who could return at any time did make him rather apprehensive about the fantasy he was conjuring up in his mind.

In recent years there had been an ever-growing number of local young men leaving their homes and families to fight abroad in a war that local people didn't question. Their daily lives were totally preoccupied with finding enough food to survive, yet alone using their energies to figure out something that was happening in distant lands.

Pathan arranged to meet Anam in two days' time in the evening at the hotel. By that time, he hoped he would have in his possession a new identity. Meanwhile, he ate all his meals at the hotel trying to keep a low profile. Alcohol, of course, was on the agenda, but kept to a minimum as he wanted to try and clear his mind for the meeting that could offer him safety from the police. He ventured out on several occasions for brief walks around the British cemetery and Peshawar university. Many British soldiers and civilians, thousands of miles from home, were buried in the immaculately maintained area of peace. Shady trees such as neem and rose wood stood like tall sturdy obelisks, lining the perimeter fence. He sat for a few minutes on a wooden bench dedicated to a former Welsh army captain buried nearby. Who was he and what was he doing here? Pathan thought, wondering whether family or friends ever visited the white granite grave. For the first time in ages he felt a rare joy of gratitude and peace while thinking of his precious parents.

The phone call he had been desperately waiting for arrived from Said Wali. With £1000 cash ready to do business in his body belt, he took a chance and hid the rest in his room. The young man arrived at midday and drove them to a rubble strewn car park next to a deserted building, occupied by homeless people and wild cats on the edge of town. Pathan didn't know where he was. His life was in the hands of Said Wali. There they sat for the next fifteen minutes waiting for someone to turn up. Nothing was said between the two men. Both were very anxious for this momentous occasion to be concluded. Pathan was sweating profusely as fear surged through his body. All he needed right now was a chemical that could change his consciousness. Waiting felt as though a lifetime had passed.

All of a sudden, a large dark blue car drove into the car park. The driver beckoned them to join him in his car.

'Jump in the back,' the man said.

Pathan realised that it was a different man to the one he first met in the bar two days ago. Trembling, he thought the driver might pull out a gun, shoot him, steal his money and dump his body. Who would know that he ever existed? Said Wali had probably instigated it. Pathan's mind was near out of control. Why did he go to Heatherslade? Why did he take drugs, beat people and live a terrible existence? Why did he hate himself?

'Here is your new identification. Your photograph name is now Yasir Shirani. And you have a serial number unique to your name,' the man handed the new ID to Pathan, who looked at it for a minute or so. It was completely different to his previous, now discarded, ten year passport photograph. No one would recognise him now. He was satisfied that it was genuine, as was Said Wali.

'Have you got the £1000 in cash?' demanded the driver, who had kept his face partly hidden throughout their exchange by wearing dark sunglasses. The cash was handed to the driver who counted it. The two men got out of the car and it sped away leaving a plume of dust and grit in its wake.

On the drive back to the city centre, Said Wali declined Pathan's offer of £100 cash for supporting him during the dreadful ordeal over the last few days. Pathan was truly sorry that he had doubted the man's sincere wishes to help him buy a new identification. But why? He didn't know.

'I really appreciate your help and support. Without you being there during the two meetings with the fraudsters, I doubt whether I would have had the confidence to have dealt with them on my own,' he said to Said Wali as they shook hands on the busy pavement while walking from his hotel. They parted on good terms. Pathan realised that not all people were sharks, not everyone was after what they could steal, beg or borrow from you!

As he walked through the attractive grounds of the municipal gardens, which were filled with exotic trees and flowers he had not seen before, his eyes were suddenly drawn to a golden coloured figure twenty yards or so in front of him. The life sized figure was a Buddha, with black plaited hair covered in jewels, sitting on a large pink lotus and with snakes coiled around his legs. The figure sat in the front window of a Thai restaurant with a beautiful serene smile on his lips. It was most enchanting and inspiring for Pathan. He had not seen anything like it before. There were many, of course, in London, but not with the kind of spiritual powers this one had. Pathan was deeply moved by how the Buddha penetrated his soul, looking down from his heavenly throne with such force that Pathan felt overwhelmed by its compassion for him.

Spontaneously he fell to his knees sobbing uncontrollably in front of the figure. At that moment, his life suddenly flashed in front of him - all the good and bad things that only he was accountable for. It was a tragic, yet mesmerising view of someone on the edge of life. After everything he had done to other people, Buddha knew of his immense suffering. Shakyamuni, the name of the enlightened one enthroned in front of him, offered a ray of light, a vision that could lead to salvation, according to the inscription.

He had been kneeling for fifteen minutes when an older man came up to ask if he needed assistance. He had been watching him, intrigued by the young man's behaviour. Only with great reluctance did he intervene.

'Are you OK young man?' the gentleman asked kindly, placing his frail hand gently upon Pathan's shoulder.

'Yes, yes, I'm fine thank you,' he said. His conscience was being confronted by the suffering he had inflicted upon the Marlow family.

The men embraced and went their separate ways. Pathan was clearly moved by what he had just experienced. Nothing like that had happened to him before, so profound was the impact.

He stood up and made his way to the hotel to meet Anam. Her attractive face, it looked so radiant, full of life and hope. Change was in the air after the extraordinary encounter with Buddha, he felt so happy for the first time in ages. Now was the right time to express the inspired thoughts and feelings that had been circulating in his head, not just for the last few days, but ever since his incarceration in the depressing Bath bedsit.

'Hello Anam. How lovely to see you. I'm so pleased to see your smiling face. I didn't think you would turn up knowing that your children are at home alone,' he said, smiling from ear to ear. After everything he had experienced since leaving Britain, all the dreadful negotiations with various people, his heart began to feel for another person. Guilt lay heavily on his conscience, but perhaps in time he could explain to Anam what lead to that unforgivable crime. He sincerely wanted to live a normal family existence where he could provide for others for the first time in his life. Where others could love and depend on him for their nourishment. Were they mere dreams of a desperate man whose time had nearly run its course, or a realistic achievement given honesty, acceptance and commitment?

'Hello, how are you?' she asked. She was mildly optimistic that a better life was ahead for her and the family.

'I feel well, Anam. I've been thinking that I am so pleased to have met you. I admire what you are doing for your children and parents. Have you found it difficult to cope with little money yet carrying out heavy responsibilities?' he asked.

'I manage,' she responded. 'There are many people, even where I live, who have nothing. They wear rags, eat rotten food and sleep in sheds. It could be a lot worse for me,' she smiled.

After ordering their food, they sat quietly eating and drinking together, enjoying the peace and quiet of the hotel restaurant. It was probably the first time that Anam had ever been in this kind of environment, being waited upon by well dressed, friendly staff. A young woman from her social background would not have been here on her own, not without the presence of a man. She felt good and confident about herself. She also thought that the man opposite her was a decent person, who was kind and thoughtful. Less than a handful of men had ever taken her to a cheap roadside cafe before. Yet here she was in this expensive hotel, sitting close to middle-class, educated men with money and influence.

Pathan ordered another large brandy. He was not sure he was sufficiently confident enough to ask Anam a very personal question.

'Anam, I have been thinking about this question ever since we met, and that hasn't been very long, I know. But, erm, please forgive my arrogance, if that is what it sounds like, would you consider it proper, the right thing to do, if I could live with you? So soon, I do understand. I've not had successful relations with women over the years. Why? I don't, erm, know. It's taking a big risk. I mean, I could be a dangerous person for all you know. We all have our secret histories. I'm sure you do. Perhaps we could try it for a few weeks and see if things work out. But, of course, there are your daughters to think about and, living together, they might potentially be placed in harm's way. They have already lost their father and I know he could well return home at any time, which makes things that much more difficult for them. But I could help you out with money to buy food for the time I am around. Of course, you may be against us living together on religious grounds and I would of course understand,' said Pathan cautiously. It was either that, or he would need to move on again. But the new I.D. at least gave him more time to think about his next move if he failed to convince Anam of his sincere desire to live with her.

'Well you have really shocked me. As I've told you, my home is only two rooms. But they are comfortable,' she said. No doubt, and understandably, the mention of money outshone all other considerations. That could mean healthier food for all the family, perhaps clothes for the children and medicines for her disabled parents. 'But Saad, you are on holiday. How long do you expect to stay with me?' she asked, beginning to realise what Pathan was asking, and trying to think out the potential implications of her actions. Did she actually believe him? Was she convinced that his intentions were genuine? Again, her mind, understandably, returned to how Pathan's money could improve her family's quality of life. She thought of the hundreds living close to her whose lives were painful and short. Anam needed to grab this opportunity with both hands.

'I don't really know. If things go well, then perhaps many months, or years. The rest of our lives even. You could teach me Pashto so that I am be able to talk with local people. It is very important to earn money, isn't it? Is that all right with you?' he asked. Why fork out £2000 for a new I.D? he kept thinking confusedly to himself. If he was stopped by police now, how would he explain a Peshawari identity with an English accent if he was unable to communicate in the local dialect? Big problem!

'When did you want to move in?' Anam asked.

'Is it worth waiting weeks or months? I'm not, em, sure. How about tomorrow? Please let's try sweetheart, or otherwise we will never know what we could have achieved together. I could meet you outside the station and then we can take a taxi to your home. I only have one largish case. Or would you rather wait until you have discussed this move with your family?' Pathan sounded as if he was at a crossroads, and with the right conditions, his dream, mixed with delusion, could come true.

'OK. That's fine. What time? I finish work around seven,' Anam smiled, reassured by Pathan's apparent motive to develop something good, kind and worthwhile. But was that his only motive? Living anonymously, hidden away from those who sought his capture had, no doubt, crossed his mind many times.

'I realise all this change won't be easy for you, but we can make it. Seven thirty outside the taxi rank. How are you getting back home today?' Pathan asked enthusiastically.

'I'll take one of the cheap, frequent buses directly to where I live,' she replied.

They held hands as they left the hotel bar. Both of

them were pleased that tomorrow might change their lives for the better. Pathan certainly hoped so. His growing apprehension, however, was that she might be leading him up a blind dark alley for one reason or other. Perhaps her husband was at home, or didn't even exist. The I.D fraudsters could have used her to look into his background, thinking he could have been a detective or army officer brought in under disguise to break the institutional fraud that was, apparently, rife within public life. Pathan could be a marked man, in danger of being snuffed out by ruthless bastards who ran the underworld of violence. They could even have set him up so that the police, rather than Anam, were waiting at the station to capture him. What a terrible predicament he had potentially placed himself in.

Fuck it, he thought, should he depart at once while the going was safe, or hang around and take a chance? Pathan didn't know anyone in Peshawar he could trust. Asking too many questions of strangers might well have been his undoing. And visiting the club where he met the big boss was next to signing his death certificate. He needed to be extra mindful that he was an outsider, and to keep in mind that making waves against others might well mean finding his body in the canal north of the polo club - minus his last £2700, or so. He would be just another piece of flotsam, like so many others, floating downstream to obscurity.

The following morning, he slept until late, missed his breakfast so that he could prepare himself for the momentous day ahead. He showered, changed into clean clothing and packed his case with the few worn out clothes he possessed. He spread his cash over the multi-coloured bed cover and counted it for a third time, making sure all was correct. It wasn't surprising that his anxiety levels were once again rising. How much more torment could a human being take? Rupees, the new I.D and a money belt was all he owned. Everything else had been thrown away, including the new mobile phone. Nothing remained of his former identity.

He compulsively looked into drawers, on shelves, under the bed and in the bathroom, he searched the apartment until he was convinced that he had left nothing behind. His money belt sat securely around his waist; Pathan locked the bedroom for the last time. Carrying his case, he slowly walked downstairs to the reception. Before settling the bill, he needed to eat and have a few drinks. He would approach the world with a relaxed mental attitude, fuelled by the chemicals his body craved.

'Good morning. I'll leave my case here and have a meal. When I return, I will pay my bill,' he explained to the young male receptionist.

'Of course, sir,' came his response.

Pathan made his way into the bar and found a single table overlooking the garden. He ordered a small beer, large brandy and fried chicken. As he stared at the attractive garden, various birds flew around preening each other. A hotel employee was feeding them fruit and nuts. Some of them were so tame they pecked food from his hand. The sight moved him somewhat. There was mutual trust between the characters before him. How the world needed trust to heal itself! Pathan desperately craved trust from anyone willing enough to have faith in him. He felt that the Buddha he had seen a few days ago trusted him, and wanted the best for his well-being regardless of his past actions. But he had a moral mountain to confront before most people could try and bring themselves to understand the actions of a person who had slain another. Pathan knew that most people were unforgiving when serious legal codes were breached. Somehow, he thought the Buddha figure had showed him compassion for his heinous crime.

With his brain once again deadened by the harmful effects of several brandies, he paid his outstanding bill, tipped the receptionist and walked out into the afternoon sunshine full of a glimmering of hope. Having a few hours to spare before meeting Anam, although still not totally committed, Pathan walked to the park where he had first set his eyes on the distinctive Buddha figure. So strong was the feeling that he felt drawn, like a magnet, towards seeing it once again, before the gravitational pull took him elsewhere. Parked on the soft lawn some twenty feet away and directly facing the figure that so inspired him, Pathan was overcome with emotion. A tear fell down his left cheek., most likely due to the deep remorse he felt for the suffering he had caused so many people. He did not take his eyes off the shining golden figure, made more intense by the sun, for more than thirty minutes. Diners must have wondered, unaware of his intentions, why this young man was staring at the restaurant.

Only with great reluctance did the young man thrust himself away from the park. To have stayed would have caused further personal suffering. He walked slowly along the hot crowded pavement, pulling his only possession behind him. Street vendors sold their cheap goods and beggars prayed for alms. Waves of compassion flooded through Pathan's body for the ragged street children's terrible lives. Overwhelmed by the miserable sight, he gave at least twenty children a few rupees each. Many others flocked to him, but unable to handle the situation he fled across the road - still being pursued - and into a bar. The usual place of refuge.

'Hi. A large brandy please,' he requested of the barman, a rather disgruntled, middle aged man with a grey beard and rotten teeth.

'Yes sir,' the man said in Pashto. Pathan recognised a few Pashto words that he had overheard elsewhere. 'You from Britain sir and on holiday?' he asked Pathan, in English, who wasn't eager to have a personal conversation.

'That's right,' he replied, quickly seizing his drink and walking to the other side of the small, dreary bar. There were several groups, mainly young men, sitting around drinking, smoking, playing cards and talking. Local music played quietly in the background. He had been in worse bars in London, where prices were more expensive. Due to his physical appearance he thought he fitted into his surroundings, so wasn't unduly worried about armed security personnel walking the streets. If they spoke to him, of course, shit would hit the fan. His immediate anxiety was the meeting with Anam in about two hours, he wasn't sure whether to go. Could he trust her, or would she turn him in for a fat reward? Remember Bradford boy, everyone has their price.

'Another large brandy, please?' he said to the barman.

'There we go sir. Where are you from in England sir? My brother once lived in a place called Hackney, where he washed dishes. The bastard owner of the cafe gave him

207

only £2 an hour. He worked twelve hours a day and slept upstairs in a filthy room with five other men,' the barman said, becoming angrier and increasingly animated the more he spoke.

'Sorry to hear that my friend,' said Pathan as he paid his dues and walked briskly away, this time to a seat outside on the pavement. Only feet away the street kids followed his every move. They were like lions, ready to pounce on their next meal.

The bar was stifling with thick smoke and sweaty bodies. He felt uncomfortable sitting next to men he didn't know, or how they might react to a stranger in their bar. From on the ground underneath his chair he picked up a British newspaper which was a few days old. There was nothing on the front page about an Englishman wanted for questioning about a murder committed in his own country. He was relieved that all the other pages carried no mention of him. No news was good news as far as Pathan was concerned. Although, he obviously realised by now, or should have done, that modern surveillance methods had, at some stage, picked up his trail.

Within minutes he was joined by an older customer, a man who had caught his eye when he first entered the bar. He looked tough, weather beaten, and had a pronounced stoop and a lined face. A man of the land, whose face spoke a thousand stories. Most of them honest and powerful. Had he been educated, his words could have entranced the rich and privileged. He wasn't too dissimilar to a few of his parents' older friends.

The old man spoke in Pashto and Punjabi to Pathan. The latter explained that his mother tongue was Punjabi.

'Where are you from? Are you English or Pakistani?' the man asked.

'I'm from England, but of Pakistani parents. They live in Quetta after working many years in the English textile business,' Pathan said, once again using another fictitious story. The chap couldn't have given a damn if Pathan had originated from the moon.

'Good for them. I admire those early pioneers who moved from Pakistan to Europe to earn a better living. I wish I had done that, but I had many young mouths to feed from the age of eleven, working in the fields fifteen hours a day. Not long after partition there was turmoil in Pakistan and India. Some of my family were killed,' the old man spoke and gesticulated in rapid succession, characteristic of a tick-tack man at the races.

'Yea, my parents and their generation worked incredibly hard. I have a lot to thank them for,' Pathan humbly commented.

'Don't be afraid to talk my friend. I won't say anything to anyone. I've seen a great deal of crime in my time, I have enough stories to keep you occupied for a year,' the old man assured him.

'Would you like a beer?' Pathan asked the man, whose clothes, like his body, had seen better days.

'Would love one, young man,' he replied.

After a few minutes Pathan returned with two large brandies and two beers. His face lit up when he saw the brandy being placed in front of him. In monetary terms, that represented a few days of rice for him and his ageing wife.

'Thank you, thank you,' he said, with a smiling face

that summed up a thousand words. 'My name is Nur Wali. What is your name?' he asked.

'I'm Saad. I'm on holiday for a few weeks travelling around Pakistan visiting palaces, restaurants and other grand places. I visited family in Lahore last week,' Pathan said, mindful not to mention his other name: Yasir Shirani.

'Good. Good. It's very good to visit our families,' the old man said as he stood to shake Pathan's hand. 'It's important to remember the responsibility they had to shoulder when working so hard to feed us,' he continued, gesticulating to make his point understood. The two men continued talking about their forebear's lives.

'It was good meeting you Nur Wali. Please accept this small gift of two hundred rupees for you and your wife,' Pathan stood, handed the money over and shook his hand goodbye. The money would keep the old man and his wife supplied with food for several weeks. Looking deeper into Nur Wali's weary, bloodshot eyes he saw a world of knowledge unknown to the educated. His inner world had experienced a life of being undisturbed by superficial modernity. A body near broken understood the way of solitude during planting, digging and harvesting. He couldn't read or write, yet intuition informed his actions in a world of silence.

In their late teens, Nur Wali's two young brothers had left home with few possessions to seek their fortunes elsewhere in Pakistan and India. They found various labouring jobs on large building sites. Long hours, filthy conditions and poor pay: yet the brothers nearly always managed to send home a little money to help their family escape the widening jaws of starvation. The occasional letter, read to them by the local teacher, reassured the parents that the boys were doing their best to survive in an alien world of cities they had never seen before. Poverty levels, they wrote, were similar to those in the village they had lived in for eighteen years, but on a much larger scale. The homeless were attacked by rats the size of domestic cats.

Both brothers were now deceased. Long backbreaking hours and working in thick mud and rat-infested poisoned water had probably brought about their premature demise. They tried to raise themselves up from slum village life by travelling anywhere, working hard, but all to no avail. They found the same experiences wherever their weary bodies took them. They were treated like feral animals. Both men had children and grandchildren who occasionally visited Nur Wali.

It was possible that the former intrepid naval travellers Robert Fox-Rice and Herbert Tate sailed into the same docks at which the brothers had grafted for many months. The former had certainly disembarked at most of the subcontinent ports equipped to take large ships of the kind he sailed in. The photographs and letters that both former sailors had sent home to their respective families vividly demonstrated the degradation that squalor reduced people to. Information that forebears would, no doubt, have been aware of during colonial assignments by various British governments. From the luxury surroundings of their ships, both men ventured beyond those ports to experience a world of unimaginable hell.

Although used to a comfortable lifestyle, Pathan had to adapt to a poorer way of life. He must if things were to succeed. He was now self-assured - although taking a mighty risk - that he would meet her at the station. He needed to keep the money belt tightly strapped to his waist at all times. Her home and surroundings were dire, but his money would buy them decent food and clothes. He would make life bearable for the unfortunate dregs forgotten by society. He walked into a bar for a drink before making his way by taxi to Peshawar station. He needed the last few brandies to top up his flagging confidence before the point of no return was breached.

The taxi dropped Pathan off outside the crowded station at around 7pm. Many street children rushed to accost him for money. He fled into the safe confines of the station cafe. From there he had sight of the metal gates where the meeting with Anam was due at 7.30pm. He would wait there until she arrived. If any other people looked like they could be accompanying or shadowing her - like gangsters or police - he would immediately leave the station by the back entrance. He already had an escape plan sorted out.

His anxiety levels had outgrown the alcohol consumption. He now had high expectations of having a new family of his own. With Anam that might be possible. He had a burning desire to find out who he really was, and what impelled him to carry out such insane behaviour. But, unbeknown to Pathan, the legal grip of justice wasn't far behind. Sadly, it was too late to begin fantasising about the future with several police forces now breathing down his neck.

It was 7.40pm and she had not yet arrived. In panic, he rushed to the bar and bought a large brandy to steady his trembling hands. He wouldn't wait much longer. They must have set me up – he thought to himself - the bastards! As soon as he finished his drink, he was going. He wouldn't waste a second more waiting on some woman from the slums.

Five minutes later Anam arrived on her own. She waited at the gates and looked around several times, presumably trying to find Pathan. He waited a few more minutes just to make sure no one was following her. Pulling his suitcase, he walked around the back of her, partly hidden by huge concrete columns to reassure himself that it was safe to approach. He was now less than fifty feet behind Anam, who was pleasantly dressed in a long dark blue jacket, trousers and headscarf with a black bag hung across her slim shoulders.

Pathan walked slowly and cautiously towards the woman who could fundamentally change his life. Two middle aged men were talking together not ten feet from her. But they were amongst the many people who entered and exited the heaving platforms intermittently as trains arrived. It was now 7.55pm. He was late, but for good reason. It wasn't surprising that since the murder, and the treacherous path subsequently journeyed, his mental state was near rock bottom. He was in danger of collapse and committing suicide! Anyone who had been through the torment he had, although personally induced, would surely have surrendered himself to the police. But he wasn't prepared to give up fighting. When just feet from the woman who could set him free, loud thunder, followed by warm torrential rain fell on the dirty, dusty streets which gave the city fresh air once again.

'Hello. I'm sorry I'm late. Hope you haven't been waiting long. How are you?' he said, hugging her as he spoke.

'Hello Saad. I'm very well thank you,' she replied, smiling, praying that she was making the right decision.

They sat in silence, both preoccupied with personal thoughts as the taxi threaded its way out of the teeming city centre towards Anam's village. It seemed that the barren countryside, except for scant vegetation where a few women earned a meagre living on a large rubbish tip, was devoid of life. No one had spoken since departing from the station. The middle-aged driver, wearing a black shirt and trousers, smoked contentedly. He had driven in this area for years. He hadn't seen Anam before though, which wasn't surprising. But he knew, even though he was given scant directions of three miles south, where they were heading for. There was only one place and that was the tiny village of Ameen: meaning the faithful and trustworthy. No one knew how the village acquired that name, but if there was any justice in the world it would be recognition to the downtrodden inhabitants.

'Ameen is coming up sir. Whereabouts shall I drop you off?' he asked in English. The driver was another person who obviously and instinctively knew where Pathan was from. His appearance: a shaven head and long thick black beard wasn't convincing, thought the driver. He didn't resemble a local man.

They alighted from the taxi that had transported Pathan from one world to a completely different one. As it drove off, a crusted dust cloud had temporarily covered his vision of everything in sight. He and Anam were covered in minute flakes of mud, vegetation and cow dung. The road where he stood was meant to be the main thoroughfare through the village. It was a ten foot wide dirt track, with large potholes made by vehicles in muddy conditions. It reminded him of a war zone that was used by tanks in battle. Either side of the road, as far as he could see, were small single-story houses and shacks. Children, cattle and other animals roamed where they liked. There were no fences or brick walls or any other kind of physical obstacles stopping people from walking where they chose to. People in Ameen didn't give a damn who sat on their doorstep, or walked across their land, or even urinated on their shack. They were too preoccupied trying to earn a few rupees to buy food. Most travelled by foot to the outskirts of Peshawar where food and other necessities could be scavenged from the garbage tips. It was unlike anything he had witnessed before. What had Pathan done agreeing to come to this place? At least the police wouldn't bother him, or anyone else, in this place long forgotten by mankind. The only animals to visit this place were the occasional wild animals like deer, goat and fox, foraging on the grassy plains before heading back to higher, safer ground.

'Well here we are Saad. Nothing like Peshawar is it?' Anam said, still smiling and optimistic. 'I live about ten minutes up there on the left.' She had strong nagging feelings as to whether it could contain Tariq Pathan for long. But she remained cautiously optimistic.

After a hundred yards of walking over earth as hard as concrete, they turned left into a narrower track. Small prefab-like houses and dilapidated sheds lined the place. The old buildings reminded Pathan of his father's rundown allotment in Bradford. There were more children and animals, the occasional burnt out old car, and a rusting, decaying lorry. A few people walked wearily with bundles of clothes and bags of food balanced on their heads. Most of the carriers were women whose heads were covered with scarves. Men followed wearing the traditional red tarboosh hats. Some way behind they were followed by children covered in rags, and dogs diseased with mange – a gruesome sight, even in the failing evening light.

If the Marlows, and the whole of Heatherslade, could have seen Pathan now, suffering in the hell-hole called Ameen, it would have probably made them all ecstatic with delight. He fully deserved it. They didn't realise, of course, as no one else had at that time, that there was a lot more pain and suffering yet for Pathan to endure. If Karma existed, then the young man from Bradford could not escape its consequences.

Despite the poverty and deprivation of Ameen, there were still a few local scrawny pink and blue flowers still shining, like scarce jewels, on the ground - though most had been devoured by the donkeys and dogs. Small banyan, neem and rosewood trees clung onto life, as Pathan found this reassuring presence in such a desolate place. Due to nearby marshland and productive farming land a mile to the north, crake, egret and ibis were attracted in their thousands to the various edible insects and cereal that was plentiful here. Feathered war invariably broke out. Given rifles, the starving locals would have been provided with plenty of fresh meat.

People acknowledged Anam as she and Pathan, his faithful case still trailing behind, walked across a bare patch of ground and into her home. It was built using timber with a corrugated roof. There were two brightly decorated largish rooms. They were separated by plaster boards. One was for sleeping, two large beds covered the room, the other for cooking, eating and everything else. A communal latrine sat fifty feet to the rear. Small photographs of her late grandparents, parents and children gave the place a colourful and interesting history. Anam had done her best to give the children a decent, comfortable home against overwhelming odds.

'Saad, meet my two daughters,' she kissed and hugged them, and felt so pleased to be back home after leaving early this morning to work in Peshawar. Due to the roads being so poor, and the buses' refusal to travel through Ameen, she had to walk a mile every morning to a recognised road where there were frequent buses.

'Hello girls. I'm so pleased to meet you. Your mum has told me so much about you. She loves you so much,' he said. He intended to help the girls, aged 12 and 14, as much as possible. His money could buy them better clothes and more books for school, which they attended nearby. The girls were tall, slim and pretty with long raven hair. Their dark, piercing eyes suggested a hunger for knowledge. But their old, frayed clothes suggested another story. Anam had nurtured them to be confident and considerate.

'Your mother told me you enjoy education. That could give you a better life,' he said, remembering how fortunate he had been in his own country, where he took free schooling for granted.

'Yes, we do very much,' said Uzma, who spoke very good English, and was the older of the two sisters.

'As I left school at 12 years of age, I always insist they read, write and attend school. Their teacher knows they are intelligent and have the ability to go to college,' said Anam enthusiastically. No doubt she wanted them to achieve something and to make it better than her own upbringing. Anam had married young and would graft in the fields for a grateful few rupees.

For the next few days Pathan doted on the two girls. He said and did all the right things, but what was going on? He gave money to Anam to buy healthier food for them all, and new clothes for her daughters while she was working in the City. Pathan realised that a part of his actions were artificial: in essence a sham. Yet fear was again taking over his feelings. He had realised during the flight from England, in fact years before, that fear had dominated his life. It was the reason why drugs became so dominant from an early age. He was over compensating for inadequacies when unable to cope. Anticipating the worst exacerbated the emotions that racked his inner life. Could love and support from Anam help him recover somewhat, help put down roots and be mature enough to live with a family that appeared, provisionally, to accept him?

On the fourth day, Sunday - the only day of the week when Anam didn't work - the four of them made the short journey to her parents' home. Upon entering a dark, gloomy shack, he saw two frail people sitting on dilapidated chairs in the corner. Few possessions could be seen. They looked eighty years old, yet they were only about fifty. A hard life of scavenging and begging had torn their souls to shreds. Due to physical disabilities from birth, they had not been able to earn a decent living. In their earlier lives they had made a few rupees a day dyeing cloth, washing latrines, milking cows and collecting fire wood for various local farmers. Now it was all too much for them.

Anam and her daughters hugged and kissed the poor wrecks in front of them. They held them for some time, it was sincere and very moving. Tears flowed down the smooth cheeks of Anam's young but pained face. She gave her parents both a new set of warm clothes bought by Pathan. He was so thrilled that he was able to replace the rags they had been wearing for years. He also bought them new sandals to replace their old ones, bags of rice, fruit and vegetables. So moved was he by the pathetic lives in front of him, that tears of genuine sorrow fell from his clouded eyes.

'Meet my dear parents, Saad. I love them dearly. As I told you, at least I can help them with the money I earn in that wretched bar,' she said, smiling and crying at the same time.

Pathan spontaneously put his arms around them and kissed their prematurely aged faces.

'Hello. My name is Saad. I am honoured to meet you,' he said, overwhelmed by compassion for them.

Anam's father, Abdul-Wahaad (Servant of the Giver), spoke to Pathan in Pashto.

'My wife and I are also honoured to have you here. Thank you for buying us the great gifts before us. May you enjoy your time here with our beautiful daughter and grandchildren. May you be blessed by the great one,' he said quietly and courteously.

Regardless of his own precarious position, Pathan had to act now to assist them. What good was the money strapped around his waist going to do for him? He was resigned to his inevitable fate. Before that happened, he must help somehow to improve the lives of two crippled people before he departed from this world. His money could buy an artificial right arm for the father, who could then, perhaps, find some menial paid work to help alleviate dire poverty.

Anam's mother had a neurological problem that affected her movement. She had always found it difficult to walk due to the growing pain that racked her body. She had been given a diagnosis many years ago at a hospital in Peshawar but had now forgotten its name. Her left leg was three inches shorter than the other. Various supports for her sandals had been tried, nearly all of them hopeless for her needs. He wanted to send her to see a specialist in Peshawar for an up-to-date diagnosis, treatment and long-term medication for both of them. Anam's meagre income was too limited to meet the growing medical needs of her parents. Abdul-Wahaad also suffered from debilitating pains to the neck, shoulders and chest. X-rays could diagnose his problem and medication could be administered. Private healthcare, the father explained, had made life difficult for them. Local government services had been withdrawn, which meant they had been virtually housebound for years and were unable to go out for a walk and meet friends.

Ever since Pathan had read the Buddha figure inscription 'actions have consequences' he had been preoccupied trying to understand its meaning. He had not read those words before yet found them powerfully provocative. He began to realise more clearly that those words were looking at him, pointing the finger and talking to him. They were his own actions and he needed to take responsibility for himself now before it was too late. That inscription, like an inverted mirror, kept reminding him to support Anam's family, especially the parents now, while he had the chance, before his departure - whenever that may be!

Trying to keep true to his inner convictions - and to the financial promises made to Anam, it pleased him that he could provide a better quality of life for the whole family. In the city she could buy anything relatively cheaply. Many knew her, from the many flourishing street markets to the expensive tourist's shops.

Anam had been able to make two appointments for her parents to consult private doctors in Peshawar hospital. She was delighted, thrilled that at last her parents would get the treatment that had been denied for many years. That medical opportunity was due to the compassion that Pathan had for them. There was goodness in all people, and Tariq Pathan was no different. He just didn't care any more about keeping bundles of money around his waist for his wellbeing only. He sincerely wanted to help others. A spiritual transformation was taking place within a person who, hitherto, had disdain for nearly everything that moved.

After a week of flourishing activity, the family met in Anam's parents' house for a meal to celebrate recent developments.

'Thank you my son, for the great deeds you have bestowed upon me and my wife. We are most fortunate to have met you. May the Gods treat you with special kindness,' said Abdul-Wahaad. He was so moved that he placed his only silk scarf around the young man's neck and kissed him several times.

'You are a most wonderful man Saad. God must have sent you to us,' Anam said, embracing her new partner and hoping that he remained in her household. Not just because he had greatly supported all her family, although she didn't expect it to last long term, but because she sought a committed, loving relationship. If only things were that straightforward!

'No, I'm not a wonderful man. You and your parents are the good, honest people. Your parents have suffered for most of their lives, yet I do not hear or see them complain,' Pathan humbly murmured. But a part of him was proud of what had been achieved for those less fortunate. Whether or not he was going to stay here and try to make a home with Anam was out of his control. He realised after just a few days that this life of rural poverty and silence was for him - but others, of course, had different ideas. His money wouldn't last for ever. But Pathan had enough to provide for several people for some time, until his Pashto was fluent enough for him to find work in the city. With he and Anam both working, they could afford a decent way of life. Good food, reasonably priced clothes and medication for the old folks. Pathan would settle for that peasant existence, if only life wasn't so precarious. If only he could turn back the clock, re-write history, but all that was pie-in-the-sky.

No bars, drugs, loose women or other detrimental influences would distract his attention. He was becoming really excited about his long-term prospects living with Anam. In fact, why was working in the city even on his mind? He was in the financial position to buy a lorry, a few cows and tools. He and Abdul-Wahaad, when he was able, could make a living working together. The latter, he surmised, must know local people and farmers who hired labour. For all his physical, painful disabilities he was nonetheless a resourceful man - similar to his wife.

They had scratched the planets' surface and found some sustenance. They never thought of self-pity. Besides, with a vehicle and the right equipment, they would have the opportunity to impress those with land and money. They could rear their own meat and vegetables. A good life beckoned for those who helped themselves.

The day with Anam's family had been a success. Lots of good, healthy food and group singing warmed the hearts of all those present. Just before they were about to return home, a police car and van parked quietly not fifty feet down the road. Only a little dust blew around. Two dogs barked, while several children ran out from their shacks and surrounded the police, asking them numerous questions. The police ignored them. They viewed them as vermin.

'Don't worry Saad. The police make occasional trips down here to Ameen from the city looking for gangsters, guns and whatever. They never find anything but harass those they don't like. We don't co-operate with them. They might ask you for your passport or other identification. Have you got any on you? They know all of us, so won't bother to ask,' Anam explained to Pathan, who was panicking and full of fear.

'Anam can I talk to you outside now, quickly. I've got to explain something to you,' he said fretfully. They walked around the back of the shack where Pathan now had no choice but to be honest with her. 'Anam, I will explain everything to you later. Please inform the police that I am deaf, but I do have local I.D that I recently bought'.

'Show me the I.D'' she demanded.

Pathan handed her the small wallet from his back pocket, containing his new fraudulent credentials with photograph. This was the situation he had been anticipating and dreading ever since leaving England.

'Yasir Shirani. Who is he? Who are you? What is going on Saad? I don't suppose that is your real name. I will try and convince the police that you are deaf. At least you have an official I.D stamped by the ministry. As soon as they have left, that's if they don't take you with them, I need a full explanation, otherwise you must leave my home immediately, taking your things with you,' she was in no mood to waste her time, even though Pathan had been most supportive.

The armed police began checking each home for whatever they were looking for. Perhaps who or what they were seeking was only feet from them! Officers were friendly when asking permission to enter each house. Eventually they entered the home of Abdul-Wahaad.

'Hello sir. You know me by now. Just a routine check. Have you seen anyone you don't know recently? Any strangers around here?' asked the young male officer, who smiled to all the other occupants. 'I've not seen this gentleman before. Who are you sir?' he asked Pathan.

'This is my friend. He is deaf sir, but here is his local identification,' Anam passed it to the officer.

'That's fine madam. By the way next week a couple of young local university students will be coming around doing research. Please help them. Thank you,' he said. 'Thank you for your time sir,' said the officer, nodding to Abdul-Wahaad. They left, convinced by Pathan's identification.

He had made it on this occasion, but knew he needed to learn Pashto as a priority. It would be imperative to be able to communicate effectively with local people in order to find work. If the same officer came around again he would have to play the deaf friend again. This was another problem he had fallen into without much thought.

Back at Anam's home, all was silent while they waited for the children to fall asleep in the bedroom. Now in the kitchen, she needed clear explanations about Pathan's real presence in Peshawar. She was not going to be used by any more men. Her days of being the scapegoat for others' misdemeanours were over, she thought angrily.

'Right, Saad or Yasir, or whoever you are, please explain what is happening right now. I'm so outraged by some of your behaviour. In other ways you have been so kind to me and my family that I can't thank you enough, but I'm so confused,' she demanded.

'I'm so sorry to have misled you, I lied to you. I had no choice when I first met you as I genuinely enjoyed your presence and thought we might have a future together. My real name is Tariq Pathan and I am from London, England. I am on the run from the police for supplying drugs and being in possession of an illegal loaded gun. I've fled my flat in London with just a case of clothes, withdrew all my money - hence the money belt tied to my waist - hid in a bedsit for a week and took a flight to Lahore, where my parents hail from. As I can speak fluent Punjabi, had my head shaved and grew a beard, no one suspected me of anything. I fitted into the scenery,' was his plausible, persuasive, yet insincere story. 'I didn't want to burden you with my problems, but of course now that the police have been here, it has also become your problem. I'm sorry, Anam. It's not the end of the world is it? We can still make things work out together,' he said, holding her hands with an element of reassurance and manipulation.

'OK. Thank you for telling me the truth. That's not so bad - lots of youngsters around here are mixed up with drugs and other illegality. Should I call you Tariq from now on?' she asked, with a voice bordering on utter frustration.

'As the children and parents know me as Saad, lets continue with that familiar name, thereby not adding to the confusion,' he said.

As expected, several days later, two well-dressed youngsters, a male and female, around 25 years of age stood knocking on Anam's door. Both had small rucksacks on their backs and identification pinned to their jackets, looking more like war refugees than students. As more than 80% of Pakistanis spoke English as a second language – with the percentage even higher in the younger generation - they automatically spoke to Pathan in English. Besides, they were Anglo-English, having been born in London of parents originally from Peshawar. The students were from London University where they were studying for a masters-degree in rural poverty in Pakistan. There clearly weren't any money problems, with parents digging deep into their pockets so their kids could become middle-class professionals, unlike their forebears. Pathan knew it was very important for future generations to help their mother country out of poverty.

'Good afternoon sir. We are students from the local university. We asked the police, prior to visiting you, if we could carry out research around the estate, and they gave us permission,' the young man explained to Pathan, who was on his own. The family were elsewhere, at work and school.

'Please come in both of you. Take a seat over there while I fetch my coffee. Would you like a cup?' he asked. Pathan felt exposed and vulnerable here on his own without Anam to supply the correct information about her life in the village. One wrong word and he could be in big trouble. They were from the local university and in touch with news from around the world. Had they seen his photograph on the local television news or in newspapers? What was he to do without support? Perhaps he should ask them back another time when Anam was there.

'No thank you sir,' they replied in unison.

'So, what are you researching and how can I help you?' he asked the attentive pair in front of him. Pathan had noticed, however, from the corner of his eye when reaching for his coffee on a small table nearby, that both students scanned their surroundings several times. Pathan put that down to finding out the quality and quantity of household goods. Unlike most hovels on the estate, Anam's home was relatively well equipped, clean and tidy.

'We are researching the extent of poverty on various estates. How many of you live here sir, and how many are working full or part-time?' the short slim woman asked.

Pathan's anxiety levels began to rise immediately after he heard that question. Fuck it, he thought, he shouldn't have let the nosey spoilt bastards into his only secure world. He would give them any old shit and tell them to leave as soon as possible.

'My wife and I are both in full-time work. Just two of us live here,' he quickly replied.

'How long have you and your wife worked at your present employment?' the tall, well-built young man, wearing spectacles and a greenish suit asked.

'Not very long,' Pathan abruptly replied.

As the questions continued for about twenty minutes, both students were glued to their laptops recording every word on questionnaires; Pathan brought their presence to an abrupt end. Their pre-set questions covered most aspects of employment, incomes, people per household, education and so on. They thanked him for participating and went next door to interview another tenant. Pathan was angry and livid when he realised their computers had the potential to expose his whereabouts. What a fool he was to discuss London life with two people he didn't know at all. That was ego taking over again. He needed to act quickly. It was not possible to talk to Anam about it until she arrived home from work. That monumental gaff could really jeopardise his future plans. Should he run now or wait?

At the end of a successful day, the students were pleased with the positive response and friendliness they received from people whose lives were completely different to their own. The locals were used to being bombarded by young middle-class students and other do-gooders, all seeking answers to help solve the poverty crisis that afflicted many Peshwari inhabitants. But nothing ever changed for them! The students might just have learned something important, if only the authorities allowed them to live with village families for a few weeks. Picking up useless items on rubbish tips, human and animal shit everywhere, poor food, and lack of most infrastructure locals - it would have been far more educational for young students to have experienced it rather than filling in statistical questionnaires.

At 7pm the two students joined their fellow workers, all littered with rucksacks and laptops, and clambered aboard the university van that took them back to the lodging house where most had bed and breakfast residence. No doubt, all were pleased with their scientific work. Self-praise and large egos fed their dreams. Good food, hot water, clean clothes and a secure bed awaited. It was a palace compared to those living in Ameen. Other than the students receiving a degree, and their useless statistics sent to gather dust at the local government offices, all the information would probably be forgotten within weeks.

However, the two sharp eyed students who had interviewed Pathan had remembered, with clarity, that his face, accent, and knowledge of various London places and clothes had, somehow, stood out. Both were suspicions of his unusual presence and demeanour, which looked out of place in such a deprived area and required further investigation. These were western educated youngsters, taught to delve below the visual presence of something obvious. Extensions of the ubiquitous CCTV! Underneath Pathan's rough clothes they were aware he was wearing an expensive T-shirt available only in up-market British shops. The male student recognised his expensive trainers, and an unusual small gold ring, which he remembered had been for sale online in Hatton Garden, London. Oh yes, the eagle eyed, smart arsed students were ready to serve their state-run security

229

services. Stanley Milgram had, indeed, prepared the millions to obey authority.

After scrutinising their computers several times, they were both convinced that the man they had interviewed back in Ameen was, indeed, Pathan. They were shocked to find that an extradition warrant for his arrest for murder had been enacted by the British government. There were photographs of him before he had his head shaved and grew a long black beard. Somehow the police had found a recent photograph of his somewhat changed appearance. It wasn't stated when and where this had been obtained; but the students, no doubt out of duty, immediately contacted the local police. Their rare chance to become heroes, in front of students, teachers and parents alike, would not be denied.

CHAPTER NINE

Meanwhile, the local police had given regular support to the Marlow family, updating them with regards to the extensive nationwide search of Pathan's whereabouts. Nearly all the local and national television and newspaper companies had published information on his old and new identity. The internet had carried Henrietta's case to a worldwide audience. His infamous face had become a household name. Wherever they went, people spoke of the gruesome case in which he was implicated. Even though he had not been charged with Henrietta Marlow's murder, there was ever growing evidence that the police were hunting the right person. A warrant for his arrest had even been received by the Pakistani authorities. The police were aware he had made only one substantial cash withdrawal from his bank account, and that no further attempts had been made to access the small amount of money that remained in his officially frozen account. Pathan's various activities had by now been carefully detected: residence in Bath, attendance at Heathrow, and subsequent flight out of Britain.

Led by superintendent Pearce, there had been a further press interview outside Maysbridge police station. He informed the demanding press that damning forensic evidence had concluded that the tyre marks found in

Slindon woods car park belonged to the type of car owned by Pathan. Furthermore, the suspects' finger prints had been found on a supermarket receipt which had been recovered by police searching the same car park. Various minute particles of detritus from Slindon wood had been found in the Marlow home. Large male shoe imprints, matching the prints found in the same car park, had also been found in two of the rooms.

'And to conclude with another piece of overwhelming evidence,' Pearce's tough, stern voice expressed to the many seasoned hacks in front of him, all anticipating the final nail in the suspects coffin, 'the empty brandy bottle, found by a local dog walker in Heatherslade village, had Pathan's fingerprints all over it,' he said, with a rare smile all over his face. Some of the evidence had been known, to a few hacks, for some time, but the police had been tight-lipped. Even in the superintendent's secure castle at the station, leaks had escaped through the walls, windows and doors. He suspected someone was taking backhanders, but who was the culprit?

The jigsaw was coming together very nicely indeed, thought Pearce as he walked back into the station, accompanied by Tamworth and Thomas. He was pleased with the way he had handled the well-oiled doom merchants. He knew his professional manner in delivering the information to some of the most smart, astute and manipulative hacks had been first class. His colleagues had congratulated him. Even the chief constable, mindful that an extradition was out for Pathan, phoned to deliver his half-hearted praise to the colleague he once worked with on the front line. Then, as now, their professional relationship, at best, was never beyond lukewarm. At other times it was downright hostile. That was the nature of any such institution. Most officers accepted this in turn for a career with decent pay, supportive colleagues and a stable family life - officers such as Childs and Tamworth. But there were a few like Pearce, whose sole purpose was unrestrained, unremitting, unrelenting determination to get to that top position regardless of who or what stood in his way. The superintendent had so far done a most thorough professional job. It was now the responsibility of the Pakistani police to apprehend and return him to Britain to face justice. The final piece of the jigsaw would be complete, surmised Pearce.

During his time on the run in Pakistan, the entire Pathan family had co-operated with the various British authorities. Other than his mother, who was most reluctant, the rest had been interviewed by various news media, where they pleaded for their loved one to go immediately to the police. Journalists, and many other interested parties, had all enticed the Pathans with money for telling their family story. But steadfastly they had declined, in a most sensitive way, against aggressive tactics used by devious means. They appeared to be a proud, hard-working family and certainly unused to media manipulation. Front page headlines carried news about Pathan's parents, along with several other family members. They had worked long hours at unskilled jobs manufacturing carpets, rugs and silk cloth for the those with the means to purchase such luxuries. Sympathetic journalists had praised how the parents had saved, regardless of their own needs, to buy a small terraced home for their three children. They had tried to give them a better life than they had themselves. To those ends, they had succeeded.

As decent, religious people, Mr and Mrs Pathan were both confused, bewildered and saddened by the disappearance and allegations against their son. But they had made a significant contribution to British life and were always trying to help others less fortunate.

Mr Pathan and superintendent Pearce were interviewed together by the local news media. Sitting in their new suburban family home, not ten miles east of Bradford, where they had recently moved to live with older relatives, both tried to answer difficult and personal questions about the case in a most intense atmosphere.

'Mr Pathan, where do you think your son is?' asked a young brusque man from the Daily Token.

'I've no idea. If I did know, I would tell him to give himself up at once,' replied Mr Pathan humbly. Now 67 years old, short, slim and with a sunken worn-out face, Mr Pathan wore a colourful, traditional Pakistani dress. He came across as a placid, thoughtful and sincere man. It was terrible, almost humiliating, that he had had to endure the ugly imposition from professional people trained to extract the last ounce of juice from the article in front of them. To his credit, Pearce had tried to deflect some of the questions away from Mr Pathan. The former soon cottoned on to the intrusive questions and, with his usual guile and panache, made mincemeat of the younger, less experienced journalists. When he realised where the questioning were heading, the superintendent abruptly brought proceedings to an end, resembling a field marshal dictating to his underlings.

Similar unethical behaviour was applied to the

Marlow family, who had been approached on numerous occasions by the international media aggressively begging, cajoling and offering large sums of money for a successful coup. Five figure sums were offered for a family photograph, so intense was the worldwide frenzy that had accumulated around this murder case. Marlow's money had hired the most expensive lawyers around, yet they too were impotent to stop the continuing onslaught that could bring down a family still in mourning. The wolves were baying for blood.

Around the time of this unacceptable family intrusion, Toby Marlow received a rather disturbing letter which was delivered to his legal chambers in Chelmsford where he practised as a criminal barrister. Now 28 years old, Toby was the youngest of his six male colleagues. With two experienced Queens Counsel leading the law firm, St Charles Chambers had grown to become one of the most successful in the area. Young Marlow had played his part particularly well in that development. He had won most of his cases in a convincing, not to say, decisive professional manner. He was being noticed in court by his opponents for his sharp, powerful legal arguments - even when the prosecuting counsel were many years his senior. There appeared a promising and prosperous career ahead of him. If he held his cool, strong, confident nerve, which his father had done with utmost skill, then he was assured of reaching the top. That was indisputable - according to his experienced colleagues.

Tony Marlow was most proud of his son, especially when he observed him arguing vociferously for defendants in the local Crown Court. If only, Tony thought to himself many times, his grandfather could have witnessed Toby standing in court wearing his black gown and wig. A gladiator trained to fight in a modern arena. He would have realised that those powerful Marlow genes had not been wasted.

After looking apprehensively at the typed and recorded letter sent from Sharpethorne, a small town not twenty miles from Heatherslade, he gingerly opened it. He pulled out four neatly hand-written pages. Toby was initially shocked by the content of the letter. It transpired that his sister had had a female lover for several years. Her name was Susan Tudor. After reading the letter twice and trying to assimilate the nature of it, he realised that the author of the letter and Henrietta had been very much in love with each other. It appeared that the two women had met casually in a wine bar somewhere in Maysbridge. According to Susan Tudor's letter, over time they became lovers and spent as much time as possible at her cheap bedsit above a small supermarket in the town. She explained that she had come from a troubled background, having been socialised in children's homes in another part of the country and fostered by several families. She emphasized how much she loved Henrietta and was devastated by her death. At the time of such family grief, her only way of showing that love was by anonymously sending flowers to her funeral.

Re-reading the letter again, tears fell down Toby's cheeks thinking of the deep love his sister had found. Yet she had felt unable to share this with her family and friends. He thought how Susan must have been heartbroken by events. How was Susan now coping? What was the quality of her life and what did she do for a living? All he knew about her, a unique individual human being, was written on four pages of white A4 paper.

From his privileged background, how could Toby have the faintest idea about the nature of Susan Tudor's personal background? The nearest he came to understanding that sort of background was when he met his clients in the cells below the courts. Most of them were recidivists, uneducated, suffered from mental ill-health, were homeless and addicted. A sub-world far removed from the middle-class, secure life from which he himself had always benefited from. In the earliest days, when visiting clients in such painful surroundings, he had very little empathy for those he viewed as useless and a drain on resources. But during the last years defending the faceless people very few would even look at, let alone speak to, he had come to realise that life was most unfair. He, of course, realised that the occasional client was middle class. Most of their criminal charges were domestic problems – most frequently the cases were of husbands who had inflicted physical harm upon either their spouse or their lovers. The reasons varied, but usually involved, sex and money.

Thanks to his parents' generosity, he had been educated at various private schools from the age of 4. Money was no object for a father who wanted only the best for his son. Sadly though, when it came to education and success, Henrietta wasn't included in her father's plan. That exclusion could explain her subsequent behaviour, which became a problem when she was still young. She knew, at some level, that her father didn't value her as much as her sibling. She always felt inferior to Toby. She outright refused to attend her brother's dinners.

These were professional, formal occasions in honour of a person or event. But they didn't impress Henrietta, who told the family, when such occasions arose, that she would rather eat at the local chippie. You can stuff yourself with your Cambridge mob if you like, she used to tell Toby in no uncertain terms, but leave me out – such was her ungracious attitude.

Therefore, Toby was categorised along with his growing cohort as rich and selfish whose only interest was self-preservation. Who could blame him for that? It was only with great reluctance that Susan Tudor had written to Toby in the first place. She was motivated by the desire to understand what held Henrietta back from committing herself to an open relationship with her. She was aware that she came from a wealthy background and assumed that if her family found out she was cavorting with her they would disown her. Of course, Susan didn't realise Tony Marlow had working-class origins. He wasn't class conscious and would probably have enjoyed meeting her.

Susan Tudor had to somehow quell the burning curiosity she had about her former lover's family - in particular the anger and resentment that Henrietta had felt towards them. After considerable bouts of drinking, Henrietta used to express passionate, virulent, hostility against her parents for the unfair way they had treated her. Even rage at times! She told Susan that she felt second best, and had been denied, unlike her brother, an opportunity to lead a more self-fulfilling life. These vicious claims had pre-occupied Susan's thoughts from the earliest days of meeting Henrietta Marlow. She wondered whether she was a spoilt daughter and looked to blame her parents to justify her own failings. After all, Susan knew what hardship was all about and inwardly accused her lover of theatrics. It also crossed her mind many times that Henrietta was in denial about her sexuality. Perhaps in actuality, she preferred sex with men, but sex with women gave her a rational reason to be hostile towards her parents. It was a kind of blackmail; aware that her brother was gay, she could afford to play emotional games knowing that her parents craved grandchildren.

However, at the bottom of the letter there was a heartfelt plea from Susan Tudor requesting to meet Toby. There were many unanswered questions she would like to put before him which could clear up some of the lingering doubt she carried around with her. Susan knew she was treading potentially dangerous water. As was common in most families, the Marlow family were no different when it came to defending each other. All things considered, Toby thought it was the decent thing to meet Susan. After all, she had made the effort to contact him. She claimed to have had a relationship with his sister, and, if that were true, then her story deserved to be heard.

Toby wasn't a heartless, high flying barrister who only thought about himself. No; he did good deeds for others. He donated money to various charities and gave his professional services for free at a local monthly drop-in centre. He realised that privilege and profession had been paramount in helping him achieve what he had achieved so far, but there were many others ready to pounce and hack his career to pieces. He needed to make the best of what he had now.

At Toby's suggestion, he met Susan Tudor three

weeks later at a small, quiet bar in West Kensington. As she had made the longish journey from Sharpethorne, he felt it proper that he should also make the effort by taking the train to central London. He knew the Coach and Horses public house well. It was down a tree lined, small residential road of expensive town houses. Anyone looking to maintain such opulence would need to earn a more substantial income than Toby. New limousines filled the streets which were paved with gold! Even the few chattering birds appeared to have their own superior language. Toby's loose connection with the pub related to a former lover whom he used to meet there weekly, but briefly, before they flew off to his rich apartment in Chelsea for a night of sex and alcohol. Fresh out of law school at Cambridge, he used to fabricate various fictitious stories for his concerned parents. The usual story was that he was meeting with fellow graduates to discuss law, or staying with his girlfriend, Sandra, in Battersea. Of course, his parents at that time didn't know he was gay. But he had known since attending a private school for young boys, where he indulged his sensual pleasures with many other like-minded nymphs. Once hooked, he explained years later to his supportive parents that there was no looking back. There had been a succession of different lovers over the years. Here and there, his parents had met a few of the more presentable ones. One of Toby's current colleagues was gay, but as yet he hadn't had the pleasure of Toby taking down his shiny pin-striped trousers. The Marlows were always apprehensive for their dear son Toby: smart, educated Toby, socialising in dark hellish corners of seedy London.

'Hello, you must be Susan?' he asked a smiling,

attractive woman who was sitting in a discreet corner of the pub. She had short brown hair, wore just a little lipstick which barely covered her small lips and sported a very bright blue trouser suit. Her brown leather shoulder bag was on the floor between her high heeled shoes. She had a large dimple on her right cheek. On the surface, Toby thought she was a well presented, appealing woman. 'I'm Toby Marlow,' he said.

'Hello Toby. Thank you for meeting me today,' she said, almost apologetically.

'Not at all. Thank you for the letter you sent me. Of course, I had no idea that you and Henrietta knew each other,' he diplomatically replied, aware that he was wearing his metaphorical barrister's hat. At this stage he thought he should let his guard down. He wasn't in court. He needed to be social. For God's sake he was about to discuss his late sister's brutal murder. He needed to do all he could to remember her; and one of the most productive ways was to open up to Susan Tudor. Come on Toby, pull yourself together, he thought to himself.

'Yes, as I wrote several times in my letter, I loved Henrietta very much,' said Susan. Tears rolled down her soft pink face as she felt the pain of losing her partner. Toby felt embarrassed, yet so sad, not only for his own loss, but for the suffering of the woman in front of him.

'How did you first meet Henrietta?' he asked, as they both self-consciously sipped their wine.

'Oh, it was in a crummy wine bar, frequented by a few lessies, sorry lesbians, in Maysbridge. You could hold hands with other women, kiss and cuddle. Neither the owner, nor the customers took offence. Henny was always funny, gregarious, generous, loud and friendly.

Everyone liked her, you know. She was that kind of girl,' Susan explained, singing the praises of the woman that motivated her to feel alive at times.

'It's wonderful to hear about the many good qualities my sister had. It's strange for me to hear about a person I really didn't know anything about. It's as though we are talking about two different people,' said Toby. He was hearing things about his sister that were alien to his experience. He felt confused. Perhaps it was right to assume that he had been the privileged son, and his sister, justifiably, had rebelled.

'There were times when Henny was really secretive about her background. I found that very hard to stomach. Sometimes I felt second best, especially when she had nothing else to do and would visit me as a last resort. There was a sort of divide in her life. But she was an adult, it was her life and if she didn't want to let her family know what she did, where she went and all that. Well that was her prerogative, wasn't it?' Yet Susan and Toby were both aware, to some extent, of their own lives, and similarly to many others, appreciated the various patterns of openness and deception that could present to people.

'Of course, it was Henrietta's prerogative. What she did with her life had nothing to do with her family,' Toby responded. In essence, he thought, he had never really known his sister. As children they had played together, but as the years went by they became increasingly separated by different schools and friends. In their teens, Toby had spent the occasional social meeting with his sister around the local bars, but from university onwards their contact was rare. He had to admit he was hearing most things about his sister for the first time. Perhaps that happened in most families, he thought.

'Due to my own emotionally starved background, it was most wonderful when Henrietta used to come and stay with me in my bedsit. On my own, I often felt so alone, so bleak. It was all I could afford, but Henny helped me decorate it. She helped me buy new or decent second-hand furniture. She hung prints on the walls by Picasso, Turner, Reynolds, and many other painters that she informed me about. She bought me books about various artists. One day, she insisted we would visit the Tate Gallery together. We never did. But it felt like paradise on earth when she was around. Henny was very intelligent you know,' Susan enthusiastically explained to Toby, who listened with great intent. He observed Susan's whole body radiating as she spoke about Henrietta with such deep passion and gratitude.

'Yes, I can imagine, Susan. I can't help repeating myself again. All this interesting, creative information about my sister is so enjoyable to hear. It is, without doubt, a wonderful learning curve. It shall stay with me for the rest of my life,' he sighed. 'Your letter also hinted at the difficult background you had.'

'That's right. It was fucking hard. I was deprived of so many things, especially in children's homes, although staff did their best for us and tried to throw us a birthday and Christmas party. For whatever reason, my mum couldn't look after me so the Catholic Church placed me in a children's home near Manchester. After several years I moved onto another home for teenage girls where we had lots of fun, and were allowed out to cafés, the pictures and that sort of thing. We met older men who gave us fags, for you know what. But it was never like a real home where people do different things together. That's what I thought when I was a kid anyway, and some of the older children who had been in real homes told me what it was really like, you know. Henny brought some of that real family life into my life. It sort of filled my bedsit with goodness, kindness and love. She breathed energy into the sad old place and brought it alive.'

'I'm very sorry to hear about your life Susan. I realise how very fortunate I have been,' he said, rather hesitatingly, but sincerely. He felt so moved, he pretended to use the toilet but actually he just needed to go and compose himself. What an amazing woman Susan was to have survived, he thought. His body shook in response. 'Do you have any family, Susan?' he asked, as her large dark brown eyes appeared to penetrate his inner being searching for the unknown.

'The Salvation Army found my sister for me about five years ago in Scotland. She's married with three children. I've visited her once. Being younger, mum was able to look after her at home, but we don't know who our father is. He was never around. He was a bit of a scoundrel by all accounts. The Salvation Army also found my mum, but she didn't want to meet me so I've left it at that. Sod her!' was Susan's angry response. 'Mind you, she did send one Christmas card, with a small letter of apology to me, via the Army. The Army have been bloody good to me you know.'

'What happened when you left the home for teenagers?' Toby asked.

'I was 16. I didn't have any qualifications and was only fit to carry out unskilled work. I worked here and there for a while. Couldn't settle anywhere for long. I was homeless for two years until a charity found me a small flat. But I fucked that up drinking and taking drugs. I tried several live-in jobs. None of them paid well, but it was a roof over my head. About five years ago I saw a grocery assistant vacancy advertised in Sharpethorne with a small self-contained bedsit available. I've been there ever since. It's an old established family business – it's over a hundred years old apparently. The family are really decent people, and they're good to me, even though the bedsit was dowdy and dirty when I first moved in. I'm now 33 years old and maturing at last,' Susan explained, at times smiling, then frowning, but always looking Toby straight in the eyes as if to say - I wish I had your privileged background and worked as a barrister. It was a world that Susan could only read about in the novels that she enjoyed so much. Fantasy helped her cope. Occasionally her jacket lifted to reveal a tattoo of a colourful bird just below her wrist.

'Henrietta loved that tattoo and was thinking of having one done on the top of her arm. It's a little more discreet than my bird of paradise,' she said. With great anticipation and excitement, Susan was looking forward to visiting Henrietta at her new flat in London. Sadly, she never had the opportunity.

After four long, arduous hours of personal discussions about Susan Tudor's life, Toby Marlow suggested they go for a walk around two local parks to get some much much-needed exercise. These were the parks that he himself had walked around many times before when visiting London.

The two of them walked slowly down to the end of

a quiet peaceful cul-de-sac. Toby looked so tall next to Susan, who was no more than five feet two inches. He looked very suave and debonair in his man about town attire, which consisted of a cashmere overcoat, grey trousers and brown brogues. Most people would have assumed they were husband and wife going out for an afternoon stroll or heading for one of the many local cosmopolitan coffee houses. Fifteen minutes later they were walking around Platchett Gardens on a warm spring day. They both hoped that it would be a happier year than the trauma of the previous one. It was encouraging for both of them to watch young children running, jumping and laughing without a care in the world as they played among themselves in the playground, watched by their attentive parents. Grey squirrels hopped and jumped over the spring flowers, searching for the nuts they had buried a few months before.

They continued walking to the far end of the park, crossed the road and walked into a smaller park known as Glover Heights. This was another park familiar to Toby's social exploits. The scene was similar to the one they had just experienced in Platchett Gardens. Hornbeam and Beech had started their yearly growing cycles. The sun shone on the delicate mauve, yellow and red bulbs which were dwarfed by everything around.

'Are there many parks in Sharpethorne, Susan?' asked Toby.

'There are two small parks, much smaller than these two, where young families take their children. I enjoy sitting on one of the benches reading novels or magazines. There, I can dwell amongst clouds of my own making, and think of Henny. Local unemployed lads use the parks to drink cider and smoke some shit,' she replied. What was uppermost in her mind and flooding her tormented feelings was watching the children enjoying themselves, being loved and cared for by parents. One day, she thought, she would like to have a baby herself. How that could happen was another matter; perhaps by artificial insemination, or a sperm donor. She thought those options rather distasteful. She didn't fancy a one-off sexual encounter in a pub or club either. None of those options appealed to her most intense emotional needs. She felt so focused on those beautiful children in front of her; she would smother them with, love and support. Her child would receive a good start in life, given the opportunity. Susan knew she was capable. But that was not possible in her current financial position. Besides, Susan herself had to grow up, mature and take responsibility. This wasn't an easy task when the world appeared to be constantly pushing down on her shoulders. Give her a break!

Susan was crying inside, feeling so starved of the love she desperately missed from Henrietta. How she adored her reassuring cuddles, the warmth that told her she was somebody – not alone in a harsh world. Susan felt like exploding her anger was so great. She kept a tight lid on her emotions as she didn't want to embarrass Toby.

'I forgot to tell you that when I left the home I was only 16 years old; the council had to legally find me a foster home. Well they found me four foster homes. They were decent people, but all had their own children. They were kind enough to me, but I suppose they did it for the money. It's understandable. I wasn't the easiest of teenagers. I used to get drunk, take drugs and have sex with anyone who cared to chat up a young slapper'.

As they walked slowly, Susan wanted to explain about her former foster homes. She wanted Toby to realise what a home really meant to her if only for short periods. Subconsciously, though, she was trying to make him feel guilty because of his privileged upbringing, whereby he didn't have to worry about anything. Money was no object. Susan thought it didn't really matter what she told him, he wouldn't understand and would only pay lip service to what she had to say. To a certain point this was true enough; but she couldn't blame Toby for her life's ills.

'Those foster families were better than any large children's home I had been in,' she nearly spat the words at him. 'I had my own bedroom for the first time, a luxury where I could fantasize about Christmas dinner and presents. I could look at myself in the mirror with nothing on for the first time, without the painful intrusion from damaged girls ridiculing me, or taking away my personal possessions and trashing everything,' she sighed.

They continued walking around the park. Silence fell between them. They were both emotionally exhausted from hours of conversation and had by this stage ran out of words. Only their inner thoughts and feelings remained. Did he like her? She was a decent woman, thought Toby, it was sad that Henrietta didn't live to spend more time with her! He must earn a good living, thought Susan -the rich, lucky bastard. Susan came across as a tough cookie, he surmised. He could only imagine the many unanswered questions that would remain in both of their lives for a long time.

They were about fifty yards from the park exit when

Toby bent down and picked a small narcissus from a flower bed and placed it in Susan's jacket lapel.

'A flower fit for a most wonderful woman,' he said. They hugged and kissed each other on the cheek. A truly fitting end to a momentous day.

Toby reflected on his sisters' short, yet eventful life. He thought that his parents, similar to most other people who knew her, would, no doubt, have thought that a character from a novel was being portrayed. But Toby had to be honest with himself about aspects of his sister's tragic life which was being revealed. We are all faceless ghosts at times, floating through space and time, seemingly unseen and unheard by the many, he thought. Most people lived different, yet parallel lives at the same time. Even though he thought he knew Henrietta, he didn't. Like everyone else, he had assumed, presumed, projected, introspected, and believed what he had been told by fickle others. Freud had warned humanity about the powerful effects of inner defences to survive outer attacks. Some of those old women from Heatherslade village were wise enough to have realised that. Toby knew he still had a lot to learn about himself.

Besides, who would ever know what really motivated Henrietta Marlow to act as she did? Perhaps she didn't even understand her own impulses, drives and destructive instincts enough to alter or change the direction of her own life. No one would ever know what was really happening to this young woman, who presumably on the face of things had a good life in front of her.

If Toby himself was honest about his own life, he accepted, he knew that at times he wore many different, multi-faceted professional and social hats. Each hat represented a small element of his complex personality. If known, there would be those colleagues, friends, even family perhaps, who might condemn his behaviour as: irrelevant, irresponsible, inappropriate, immoral and so on. There would be many judgements from different quarters, all depending on the vested interests of a certain individual. However, the world needed go-getters. It would soon decline if a culture of bread-and-circuses were to prevail.

After trying to clarify some of the hectic and confusing day's events in his mind, Toby reluctantly phoned his parents. They knew of Toby's planned visit to meet Susan Tudor after he told them about her letter. But he held back on some of the content of the letter as he did not want to add further suffering to their already grieving existence.

'Hi, Dad. I met Susan Tudor. We conversed for several hours about many things. It was pretty arduous. I won't go into detail over the phone. After we left the pub, we walked around two parks in the warm sunshine for much needed exercise. That was most enjoyable,' he half-heartedly explained to his parents.

It wouldn't be until a week later when seated in front of his parents with a heavy heart, that he would have the confidence to reveal most of the details of Henrietta's former life. Even at that stage, he would be flexible with the factual details.

'I'm pleased you met with her, son. It is important to learn and understand about Henny's life. As they say, parents tend to know the least about their children,' Tony Marlow, slowly and quietly muttered, still feeling unsure of himself. For the moment, all his energy, confidence and drive had evaporated. He and his wife needed time, space and peace from everyday life.

'Susan appeared a decent person dad. She's had a hard life, but she's trying to get things back in order. Drugs and that sort of thing apparently. She enjoyed Henrietta's company very much,' said Toby, but his father didn't sound convinced his daughter would have known someone like Susan socially. He was becoming stressed again, anticipating more untimely news about his late daughter.

'Where was she from?' asked Marlow, who was rather sceptical about the whole story and thought he could smell a hoax being played out by some crank craving publicity. But Toby didn't want to be drawn into explaining details over the phone.

'Dad, it's a rather long and complex story. I will explain things to you and mum when I visit very soon,' was all Toby would divulge. Marlow pursed his dry, swollen lips, unconvinced by the authenticity of the letter his son had received.

During their conversation, Tony Marlow explained that two days earlier at the parish meeting he had resigned due to business expansion and the ongoing investigations into Pathan's disappearance. He also explained, briefly, that the local council was even more cash strapped than it was two months ago and therefore unable to find the finances for the new road scheme. The proposed community centre had also been shelved indefinitely - only the most urgent of problems would be addressed.

But he went on to explain to Toby that he appreciated that he had been given the opportunity to represent his especially considering he was relatively unknown to the village, and also politically wet between the ears. It added another dimension to his already challenging life, yet he had learnt so much about himself, his family, the frailty of existence, and the fact that without co-operation - everything was meaningless.

'I've put up a large reward, £50,000 in fact for any information that leads to the arrest and conviction of Pathan,' he explained to his son, who had preferred to remain silent during most of their phone conversation. Furthermore, he explained, 'Several newspapers, including two local papers, have also come forward with varying amounts of rewards. So, I'm hoping that cash - we all have our price - will motivate those who know Pathan, or saw anything and have reason to come forward,' he revealed. His voice began to rise in anticipation of anything that could lead to the arrest of his daughter's murderer. He was grasping at any straw that might achieve his obsessively desired outcome.

Totally driven by his hatred for Pathan and motivated by his son's recent experience meeting with Susan Tudor, he knew he had to talk to the one person who, it appeared, knew his daughter quite well. But he was rather sceptical about the nature of their so-called relationship. Susan could hold the potential key in unlocking the vital hidden clues that Marlow desperately needed to know about Henrietta's short, but mysterious life. But doubts clouded his rational thoughts on the whole affair.

But how was Tony Marlow to approach Miss Tudor not long after her meeting with his son? This must already have been an arduous experience for her. With justification, she could complain to the police citing harassment. She'd discussed a lot of her own life's problems with Toby. Henrietta's death had been most painful to her at a time when she thought of stability, friendship and a potential long-term loving relationship. All those dreams had been blown sky high by Pathan, thought Susan. She had to try and pick herself up from the emotional ashes and forage for new shoots of recovery. That process, she informed Toby, had tentatively begun.

With his emotions understandably so raw and not knowing where to turn, Tony Marlow had to try to find out more information about his daughter's short, tragic life. He entertained just a few embers of hope that he might gain an understanding of what motivated a futile life, which seemed irrational to Marlow. But confusion kept hammering away at his fragile inner life.

Tony Marlow couldn't hold back the tide any longer. He wrote a brief letter to Susan Tudor requesting they meet, explaining his purpose for writing and hoped she understood his utter grief. He apologised if he had upset her and said he would understand if she refused to meet him.

Within a few days Susan Tudor had written to Marlow expressing her concern about the terrible plight he must be in and consented to meet him at her flat.

Marlow was flabbergasted at the quick response, and yet excited at the prospect of meeting the one woman who could help further his overwhelming desire to learn more. If she had spent a considerable time and given so much information to Toby: he wondered if there was any more to give. Were Marlow's prospects of squeezing _ _ _ _listic? He hoped not, but a part of him thought he was barking up the wrong tree. Perhaps the information he sought resided in the head of only one person: his daughter. Nonetheless, he immediately phoned to confirm he would meet her.

A new Daimler, a symbol of class and wealth, pulled up outside Susan Tudor's flat around midday. Several heads were attracted by the shining new dark green car that looked out of place in an area so predominantly poor and shabby compared to Heatherslade. Marlow was apprehensive about the meeting, which had preoccupied his thoughts ever since receiving the letter. He walked up to flat 2 carrying flowers - the front door was rather shabbily painted - and rang the bell. He could hear faint pop music being played. It was the Rolling Stones, he remembered. A strong aroma of scent wafted from the building. Two minutes later a young smiling woman dressed in a smart green trouser suit opened the door.

'Hello, Susan. I'm Tony Marlow. Nice to meet you,' he said, as they shook hands standing on either side of the door. His first projected impressions were what he had expected. She was young, white, attractive and with loud cosmetics and appeared friendly. She might well give him a hard time if he ventured out of her comfort zone, he thought – but it was early days.

'Hello, Mr Marlow. Please come upstairs to my flat,' she said, leading the way past walls that were covered in light blue striped wallpaper and a low white flaking ceiling. The flat was small but bright with a few decent pieces of furniture. Marlow instantly recognised Henrietta's presence by the various wall prints that Toby had told him about. Various art history books lined the small, tattered cabinets. But it was home, he thought. Her home and a place of warmth and safety. That comforted

Marlow after what his son had briefly explained about Susan Tudor's rather difficult life.

'I've bought you flowers Susan. I hope you like lilies?' he asked rather tentatively.

'Thanks a lot, I rather...'

'Yes, Henrietta always bought lilies for her mother. That was her favourite flower, you know,' he anxiously interrupted.

'Were they? I didn't know that,' she replied. 'Fancy a coffee or tea?'

'Black coffee, Susan. Thanks,' he said.

'Any biscuits or cake?'

'No thanks'.

Both were rather tense. Things were awkward for both of them. Who was going to break the ice and ask that first question? Dredging it all up again from the past was on both of their minds.

'Fancy some sugar Mr Marlow?'

'Please call me Tony. No thanks'.

'You of course know I met with Toby the other...'

'Yes, he told me,' he said, once again interrupting her. Marlow knew that he now had to ask Susan questions about her relationship with Henrietta, or continue with the facade - which was painful and counterproductive.

'Susan, I appreciate you met with Toby not long ago, and he asked you many personal questions about your relationship with Henrietta. I apologise if I ask the same or similar questions. It can't be easy I know, but...'

'That's all right Tony. I loved Henny, please ask me anything you need to while you have the opportunity,' she responded simply.

'Look Susan if any of my questions are...'

'Don't fucking worry about that. Just ask, and if I want to, I will answer them,' she didn't mince her words.

'Yes sorry. Obviously Toby told me a few things. Do you have any personal effects that belong to Henrietta, and if you do, can I buy them off you please?'

'For fuck sake Tony, even if I did have her things, I wouldn't give them to you or anyone else. Look...'

'Apologies Susan. I didn't mean you are hiding anything intentionally of hers. They are yours, of course. But I'm willing to give you a few thousand pounds if you do have anything that would remind us of...'

'Look, I don't want your fucking money. I have a few personal mementoes that will stay with me forever,' she furiously shouted at Marlow. The intensity made things worse between them.

'Sorry. I was out of order. I was only thinking about my own feelings'.

'What I didn't tell Toby about were the years of intense self-loathing which lead to cutting my arms, legs and tits with various sharp objects. I attempted suicide many times. And on top of that, which I did inform Toby about, was my drug taking and excessive alcohol abuse. I'm now over the worst of it. Various people have helped me settle into my little flat. It isn't much, but it's my home. And I have a regular job downstairs. Thanks for the offer of money, but some things cannot be bought no matter how much you offer. Henny was a good person. She took me seriously, and I enjoyed her company so much. You have your memories of her; I have mine. I think it's best we call it a day don't you?

'Yes, you are right Susan. I wish you...'

'Goodbye Tony'.

Tony Marlow, looking a forlorn figure, walked slowly back to his car. He sat there for a few minutes trying to assimilate what he had just experienced. This had to be the end of the matter. He had tried his best. He thought of trying to find his daughter's former colleagues and friends in London but thought it a bad idea. He had even toiled with the idea of hiring a private investigator to delve into her past. Don't even go there - he kept reminding himself. Information could come to light that might damage him, and his cherished memories of Henny, for the rest of his life. That would be unbearable for him and his family. No, no, no, he needed to leave things to history. Enough was enough.

It was the inevitable closure on the painful life of Henrietta Marlow. Her parents had accepted that they had done all they could to try and understand why their daughter had suffered so much during her short, tragic life. No doubt, there were times when mental ill-health ruled her confused mind. Due to the nature of her social activities, how could it have been otherwise? Wherever they go, whatever the Marlows endeavours might be in the future, the unforgettable memory of their beloved daughter's shadow would always be there as a constant reminder that she made an impact.

However, Tony and Eleanor had no justifiable grounds to reproach themselves because of her premature death. Neither were from a privileged background, as young people they both worked diligently for years so that they could provide their children with a secure home and good start in life. The Marlows were socialised into a fundamentally different generation from the one children experienced today.

Young people today live in a culture of the self. The traditional supports provided by religion, school, community, neighbours and extended family has all but disappeared. Many are left to their own despairing, alienated self-abused cocoons, where anything goes and boundaries are set by the world of social media, among other mediums of control. That leads to a tyranny that binds and stagnates young, vulnerable people, not just the underclass or working class, into a rootless, shocking waste of life. Henrietta Marlow, Tariq Pathan and countless others lived a cruel, victimized and contemptuous existence. Devoid of anything spiritual.

Nevertheless, Tony and Eleanor Marlow had to move on from their deep sadness. To have dwelt indefinitely on their overwhelming sorrow would have caused their fragile happiness to collapse and turn into deep a depression. Both agreed unequivocally, they were going forward, even if that meant at some stage moving from the village where they enjoyed living.

Tony, with a new found resurgence of energy, took on more lucrative contracts. Foolhardy, some thought. The last thing he needed was to be overwhelmed due to his family loss, or because of it, by work. But this time further arduous work carried with it an important proviso: an insistence stipulated by his supportive family. He employed a long-standing, trustworthy friend, with many years of civil engineering experience, to run the business for him. Although Tony would still be around to oversee the crucial aspects of construction. He was still relatively young by today's standards, therefore he, along with his wife, wanted to enjoy the fruits of their life-long labours.

As his passion to help nurture a grandchild did not

materialize, and he and his wife had now also changed their minds about adopting; he was inspired to help young people, financially and practically, overcome drug and mental ill-health issues. There were two charities where he volunteered his services. One was a drop-in centre based in Maysbridge and another ten miles west near Alchester. In both charities he made tea, food and gave advice to youngsters based on his own personal experiences. He also listened and learned about the fragile world many of them experienced. He found labouring work for several young men in his own business and placed others with colleagues willing to give them a chance. There were failures, not surprisingly, but on the whole most found work fulfilling and character building. A wage packet of their own gave choice and opportunities.

Tony Marlow anonymously donated a hefty sum of money to both charities so they could make building repairs, buy computers and other equipment to help users develop new skills. But all the while he never sought any kind of recognition for his volunteering. Many other volunteers, who had very little compared to Marlow, were the real unsung heroes, he concluded. They had been beavering away without praise or reward for many years to help and support youngsters to grow, develop, mature and live a worthwhile life.

After several months of fruitful volunteering at Maysbridge, a face from the past entered the small, brick-built premises. It was the governor himself, former chief superintendent Pearce. He looked relaxed, smart, heavier and wore a noticeable wry smile.

'Well hello dear stranger. What a pleasant surprise seeing you here,' said Tony Marlow, as they shook hands. He hadn't lost his immense energy, thought Marlow.

'Likewise Tony. How are you? It's marvellous that you are helping youngsters onto the straight and narrow. How is the family?' asked Pearce.

'We are all well. I'm really enjoying volunteering here. Great people to be with. I've learned a lot, not just from my colleagues, but from these youngsters in front of us. Some of them are rather resourceful and given the opportunity could lead productive and useful lives,' he enthusiastically explained to the man in front of him, who had experienced the other end of the criminal process. No doubt, the governor had imprisoned some of the fathers of those youngsters now in front of him.

'Well done, Tony. As you know, I have had a long career in the police force. Seen some terrible and tragic individuals. Many of them should never have been given custodial sentences, let alone appeared in courts. I realised after a few years as a detective that there was a succession of problem families ending up in prisons. There were no preventative agencies to help them when I was younger. It's somewhat different now thanks to these places,' he said.

'What you doing with yourself these days? Retired to the Cayman Islands or found a young wife?' he laughed.

'Well, I'm in Maysbridge visiting a former colleague for a chat and a scotch or two. Hence my growing bulk. I live on my own in a new bungalow I had built a few years ago. About six miles from here. I enjoy gardening but no sooner have I mowed the lawn the damn thing grows again. Shall have to look into investing a few bob on a plastic lawn Tony,' he said as both men laughed at the suggestion. 'Mind you it allows more time for golf, which I took up after retirement, and a few bevvies with former colleagues. We are drinking more now than we ever did when in the force. Perhaps their wives have accepted that the old reprobates won't, can't, change,' scoffed Pearce. 'Thank god, I'm single,' he said, cynically. 'Mind you Tony, no woman could ever suffer my dictatorial presence.'

'I nearly forgot to ask, how is your business?' asked Pearce.

'It's progressing well, thanks. It gives me great satisfaction to visit schools to talk to children about the dangers of taking illegal drugs. It's all informal, I'm no expert. No preaching to the kids. Headteachers help me approach and talk to children. Of course, I was motivated by the subject for obvious reasons'.

'That's very decent of you Tony. You're busier now than ever before. You must have amazing energy and drive. It's not surprising you are a successful businessman,' commented Pearce, who cautiously reminded himself not to mention Tony's personal loss.

'What I most enjoy is when the kids cheer and clap me. They never fail. Sometimes I imagine Henny is sitting among the children smiling at me. On one occasion I just spontaneously started crying. Immediately one little girl, with long blond hair and blue eyes, ran up and gave me a handkerchief. I was so moved,' he said, with a radiant smile that seemed to express that he had moved on with his life.

After titanic struggles with bereavement and grief, ... months of therapy, Eleanor decided to retrain as a social worker. For various ...

she trained for two years at a London University. Age, travel and the mayhem of the large metropolis meant she regularly struggled to engage. Being away from her husband was at times unbearable. They phoned each other every day and messaged innumerable times. Tony wanted to live with Eleanor, but she insisted that must not happen - although she drove home every fortnight for a weekend of peace and happiness. Early every other Monday morning at around 5am for two years she fought off her demons when it was time to drive back to London. Although with great reluctance, she never failed to arrive for the first Monday lecture or placement.

She had the money to rent a flat in nearby fashionable Richmond. She ate in local restaurants, attended lectures, dedicated herself to academic research. She was used to that environment and easily fitted in. But most importantly, she felt anticipated excitement, even at times in trepidation at attending two practical placements she was allocated. They were drug rehabilitation centres. To begin with, both very were challenging and frequently frightening. Centre users were often observed ingesting illegal drugs on the premises. At first Eleanor didn't have the confidence to challenge them, but eventually she bit the bullet, realising it was her responsibility. She often felt like leaving the course and driving back to her husband and secure home. But she persisted. It was the young, rootless addicts that made the most impact on her. Eleanor had experienced only the outer limits of a sub-culture, which she vaguely understood from her daughter's detrimental behaviour.

Family, many friends, some villagers and former colleagues attended Eleanor's graduation. What a day to remember - she regularly thought about that special occasion. Walking across the catwalk holding her deserved degree, witnessed by several thousand appreciative attendees, tears fell as she thought about her daughter. An array of emotions surged through her shivering body when she looked at countless eyes witnessing her success. That powerful word 'witness' had been uppermost in her mind for some considerable time. Eleanor, her family, and others were not given the opportunity - conditions hadn't allowed it - to witness the immense suffering her daughter had experienced by taking drugs, and her eventual death. But conditions had given her the opportunity to travel thus far.

'Congratulations, darling,' said Tony Marlow as he hugged his relieved partner.

'Well done mum. Wonderful achievement by someone special,' Toby proudly praised his mother.

She was mobbed, kissed and congratulated by so many different people. Eleanor was so pleased to have moved on after so much upheaval. It would have been unachievable without her family. Thousands had given their time, money and energy for her to graduate. She was mightily grateful.

Eleanor built on that success. Two months later she successfully applied for the care manager position at a residential home not far from Heatherslade. Her humility and compassion for all others became infectious. She had the occasional bout of depression, which was difficult to handle, but kept it confidential, except for her family. She had grown, taken off into a world of unknown horizons that could change the direction, quality and purpose of her life.

The Marlow family had grown closer in certain ways. Of course, there had always been a strong bond, but they now spent more time together whenever possible. Although Toby had been promoted to undertake more serious criminal cases, and on occasions supported a QC, he wanted to change direction and train to practise civil action cases instead. Although the financial rewards, he thought, were potentially higher than his current position, he felt it more interesting and challenging. Besides, it suited his personality.

Given any opportunity, Tony used to drive down to Essex Crown Court to observe his son, donned in gladiatorial black garments, engaged in intellectual battle against his legal adversary. In the legal arena, a modern-day Roman amphitheatre, Toby didn't hold back from the metaphorical rampaging bulls, who were focused on destroying his defence. He appeared to relish being seen and heard in one of the most demanding and combative public places to make a living. Without his legal armour and sword, Toby was socially quiet, mild mannered, and at times diffident. But he was also observant, crafty and insightful.

None more so than when his father used to phone early on Saturday mornings suggesting lunch in a small cafe in the Portobello Road. Toby realised that an hour or two later the venue would change to an expensive Hotel in Knightsbridge. His parents always immaculately dressed for a most luxurious lunch fit for Royalty. In anticipation, Toby always dressed accordingly and was mindful not to forget to take a huge bouquet of his mother's favourite red roses. They used to eat, drink, talk and laugh for hours. Tony excelled after several glasses of brandy. It was great fun. At the end of the day, Tony invariably pulled out of his pocket an expensive gift for his son. However, these were the occasions when he felt intensely guilty. He put that down to irrationality, and he quickly suppressed it. He had to move on from constantly beating himself up.

Another tragedy soon struck beleaguered Heatherslade village. Still mournful and recovering from the loss of their village daughter, William Hetherington, lover of all little animals, died suddenly in his sleep aged 67. His mother, Celia, was naturally inconsolable. Her son had spent every day of his waking life with a mother who worshipped him. William was known to everyone. The many people who drove through the village came to know him as that smiling little chap who was always smoking. His bright, chubby face always wore a smile that positively affected the hardest of villagers. Although mentally handicapped from birth, and also deaf, William had a profound instinct for understanding the decent, spiritual side of people. These were Christian qualities that many others had observed, including Reverend Bullchat who spoke of his committed faith, rare simplicity and innocence.

Most villagers attended his funeral at All Angels church. Many others, even people from his former school, were there to pay their respects to a friend who threw worms at them, laughed, and then reburied them back under the earth. William was convinced that all life was a spiritual journey. He used to feed the tits and finches, usually alone, that visited his garden as he constantly read his bible. He so loved to wander about looking for his favourite frog called Bob.

The Elizabethan music of Thomas Tallis echoed

through the old church as four pallbearers carried William's coffin, draped with silks bearing pictures of various animals, and placed it in front of his almighty friend. Councillor Pringleton, Brigadier Dowdeswell and Anne Woodhouse all gave brief eulogies praising the life of a village son who touched many hearts with goodness. Celia Hetherington stood in the pulpit for several minutes in silent prayer. She spoke of the gratitude she had for her son and the happy life they had together. Finally, Reverend Bullchat gave a talk about William's Christian qualities, and the way he applied them to his everyday life.

'His heart was truly touched by the hand of the almighty,' he informed the congregation.

William was buried next to his maternal grandparents in the local cemetery. It was a way of recognising that he was now one of the family. When he was young, William wasn't fully accepted by some of his family due to the stigma in those days of having no father and being mentally handicapped. His deafness further exacerbated his alienation from everyday life activities, but his mother always included him in everything she did. He grew in every way possible, just like a sweet smelling rose that flowered from a young bud, according to Anne Woodthorne he was a life-long friend. For Celia, William was an intelligent man, and unique; given the opportunity he could fully participate in life along with others.

Parked outside his house, Tony Marlow was greeted sitting in his car by councillor Barnes-Jowell. He stood there on the pavement smiling and gesturing to his former colleague. To what did he owe this surprise visit from a person he hadn't personally spoken to for some time?

'Hello Tony old chap. How are you? Well I hope?' he said, rather pleasantly.

'Hi Peter. How nice to see you. I'm well thanks. And yourself? How are you and the dear old council farts?'

'Bearing up. Look is it possible I could talk to you for a few minutes?' he asked, sounding rather upbeat.

'Of course, Peter come in and have a drink'.

'What's your poison?' he asked the tall, thin, stooped figure of Barnes-Jowell, who was as usual well dressed in a suit. He had been a diligent and active councillor for at least six years and earned a living as an accountant in Cooksley, some twelve miles south of Heatherslade. He was always beavering away at something, digging below the surface hoping to unearth gems of extraordinary political significance. He was ever optimistic in a village where presidents, spies, despots and oligarchs never seemed to venture.

'By the way Peter, are you still involved with the Quakers?'

'White wine, thanks. Oh yes. I've been involved since my early days at college. It was either attend geometry or an informal talk about Quakerism. I was so pleased that I chose the latter. No sacraments or ordained ministry, just inner light based on pacifism and silence. The elders there didn't stuff anything down your throat Tony'.

'You've lost me already Peter, I'm afraid. You must try and convert Fox-Rice, it sounds right up his street. No, I'll stick to a large glass of red wine instead. By the way didn't you at some stage used to drive Celia and William to Quaker meetings held at Cowfield?'

'I did Tony. They both loved those evenings, William in particular. He was a lovely lost soul. Tony the main reason I foisted myself upon you was to inform you that the council, after dithering for many months, have adopted most of your road proposals. It is a cheaper scheme and it will, according to the council, relieve long suffering Heatherslade of its historic traffic problems. I brought the plans over for you to scrutinise. Keep them for a while, but please don't mention it to anyone, otherwise they'll lop my bollocks off,' said Barnes-Jowell.

'Thanks Peter. That's very generous of you. Well, well, who would have thought that they would cough up the money to sort out the traffic flow problem,' Tony remarked.

'Mainly thanks to you. Most of the locals are also thankful for your tenacious attitude in getting things done,' he muttered, shaking Tony's hand.

'Have another drink'.

CHAPTER TEN

After the students had departed Anam's home, Pathan sat for a while realising that he had made one almighty, stupid mistake that could cost him dearly. What a bloody fool he was to have been so naive in front of educated people, wielding computers that could disclose everything. Wearing his expensive trainers and ring in their presence – undoubtedly they would contact the police. Speaking in fluent English with a slight northern accent and briefly discussing clubs in London, but wearing Pakistani dress, was asking for trouble. You bloody fool! He thought to himself. He now understood how odd and out of place he must have come across to them in such a poverty-stricken place. Panic had set in again. Anxiety tormented his thoughts. By now the British police would have almost certainly found overwhelming, incriminating evidence against Pathan that would lead them to contact the Pakistani authorities requesting his arrest. He had to act fast and decisively.

It was nearly 5pm. Anam wouldn't return home from work until later. After school, her children would visit their grandparents for food and security. Alone, Pathan first wrote a brief letter to his girlfriend explaining his abrupt departure. He outlined the student interviews and how he had let slip various information about himself. He told her that the students were from London on a secondment; he had inadvertently been wearing expensive items which looked out of place, and that they had computers which could incriminate him. All that meant to him, he wrote, was that the students would no doubt, sooner or later, find out all about him and contact the police. She would, no doubt, think his actions rather irrational for someone wanted for dealing illegal drugs and owning an unlicensed gun.

He informed her he was travelling to Islamabad, but his intended destination was Quetta. He deliberately wanted to mislead the police when they arrived hoping to arrest him at Anam's home. Besides, it cleared Anam from any collaboration with him. It pained him to think that she might be arrested and held in custody, interrogated by insensitive brutes, miles from her daughters.

He hurriedly forced a few of his clothes and toiletries into Uzma's small rucksack. Just enough for a few days. Nothing he would be carrying could identify who he was or where he came from. Clothes, shoes and other items he left in the suitcase, requesting that she destroy it all immediately, including the trainers, but that the ring was left for her eternal possession. This needed to be safely hidden until such time as all police activity stopped. Otherwise she should sell it and keep the proceeds, he hurriedly wrote. He left nearly all his cash to the woman who he thought one day could have been his wife. That would now never materialise. At least, he thought, the money would provide decent food and warmer clothes. His heart was in great turmoil. Tears flowed down his hairy cheeks and into his long thick beard.

Wearing dark glasses, a long robe, scarf, hat, shirt,

trousers and leather shoes, with a rucksack flung over his shoulders and enough rupees for travel in his waist belt, Pathan was ready to walk discreetly back into Peshawar. On the outward journey to Ameen he had seen numerous tracks leading out of the city. Dusk was fast approaching. By the time he had walked about three miles to the train station it would be safe enough to buy a ticket to his destination.

Before setting forth, his conscience impelled him to be utterly honest with Anam. He picked up the pencil he had been using and, digging deep into his soul, he expressed his final regretful words. Pathan didn't hold back any sordid details of the murder. He revealed his real name and background. He hoped she could in time forgive him for such a heinous act of revenge.

Other than a few barking mange infested dogs, no one was on the dirt tracks as he walked out of Ameen for the final time. A few of the shacks were lit by electricity supplied by generators from the back of the buildings. At the back of others a few wood fires flared. Faint talking could be heard. What an unforgettable sight the whole area looked. The one last hope of living a decent existence within Anam's family had gone. There would be no other opportunity, even if he had the motivation to live with anyone again. Pathan had a vague idea where he was eventually heading. The persistent thought had not left him since his arrival in Lahore. Then it was faint - but now it was a roar that had to be obeyed.

Scrambling around in the dark after falling over the baked earth twice, Pathan found one of two tracks that would take him back to the city. He struck out, following his instincts. It was three miles to the station where he escaped. He would go by train to Quetta, north-west of Pakistan. Half way there he came across a huddle of men sitting on the ground, smoking and drinking alcohol. They all looked a terrible sight. They wore dirty, torn clothes, some had bare feet and all appeared drunk on whatever concoction they had brewed amongst the dead vermin, rubbish and rotting vegetables. Two of them garbled something to Pathan but he didn't understand their language. He took out rupees from his pocket and gave them cash. They were half-demented by the money and gave him alcohol and cigarettes. One old man kissed his feet. The fugitive declined and walked on towards his goal.

A half mile before his destination, fresh and upbeat, he sat down to have food and water. It was too early to enter Peshawar because of the large number of police that would be patrolling in and around the station. They had increased their presence considerably due to the escalation in all kinds of criminality. This included the persistent presence of feral street children who were forever milling around trying to steal, beg or sell something worthless to an unsuspecting tourist.

As Pathan had thrown his watch away, he didn't have much of a guide as to when it was safe to enter the station. He knew it was around 10pm - the time the traffic started to thin out. Ever vigilant of the police he nonetheless walked straight up to the booking office and bought a single, first class sleeping accommodation ticket to Quetta: the city known as the garden of Pakistan because of its numerous fruit orchards.

Once through the crowded concourse, a menacing menagerie of degraded humans, gruesome smells and loud piercing noises greeted him. Pathan found some peace and space on the platform from where the modern sixteen carriage train would depart in twenty minutes. He sat there depressed, homeless and unwanted. A tragic figure. A forlorn and broken character whose mind was focused only on one last deed: suicide. There was no way out of his intractable dilemma. His only hopeful motive was to find a sparsely populated area where he could spend a few days on his own and write a final letter to his parents begging for forgiveness. After that, his life would come to an end.

The sleeping accommodation was colourful, warm and comfortable. Restaurant personnel knocked on the door informing him of the availability of supper. He declined. He didn't want to be trapped in a group of people asking him awkward personal questions that could reveal his identity. His only security was to stay in the small compartment throughout the journey. He left the cooked food. Besides, there was coffee, tea and various filled rolls at his fingertips - plus the food he had made in Ameen. He would try to get some sleep during the very long journey to Quetta. He didn't know how long it would take and couldn't be bothered to find out. This wasn't easy when he was so preoccupied by thoughts of being captured by the police, imprisoned and forcibly returned to England to face justice. But he assured himself, confident that this would not happen to him at this late stage.

From his small window all he could see from the speeding train were oceans of empty plains with occasional vehicle lights and village fires burning in the distance. Out in all that vast nothingness lived various animals, including people. How did they live and survive? he asked himself. All were searching for food, some eating each other without any concern. It was a dog eat dog world. People were no different to any other species when it came to power and control over one another. No one gave a damn whether Pathan lived or died; he was way down the pecking order. Who or what was the ultimate arbiter over such grave matters?

The regular stopping, starting and jolting caused Pathan to wake up several times from a deep sleep. He shouted and banged on the door in frustration, but refused to pull the emergency button as he did not want to draw attention to himself. Anonymity was his survival kit. He made coffee, ate the remaining rolls and turned the small television on. The delights of first-class travel. He tried many different television stations until he found one speaking English. It was about 2.30am according to the young female presenter. She reviewed the world's news headlines. Same old garbage, nothing ever changed, he thought. Suddenly: shock, horror, he saw a picture of himself glaring straight back at him. His eyes were transfixed on the shaven head, long black beard and tattered clothes. 'Where did they get that fucking image from?' he angrily shouted. He had met so many people and had been in many places since his arrival in Lahore, it could have come from anyone or anywhere. He knew that everyone had their price, and that some were cheaper than others.

'This man is believed to be Tariq Pathan wanted for murder in Britain. The British police have contacted the Pakistani authorities requesting his extradition...' the young woman sardonically announced.

The fugitive was mortified by what he had just

witnessed. He now knew for sure that it was all over, that the police weren't far away. They were probably on the same train going to Quetta watching his every move. The remainder of the journey he wrote notes, very powerful words that he thought could express his deepest feelings about his family and for bringing shame upon them – which was the main motive for ending his life. There was no escape, only a life behind prison bars awaited if he was apprehended. That prospect filled him with terror, dread and utmost guilt. Judgement would be most harshly inflicted upon him. If he had achieved any merit in his life, he prayed that the money he had left Anam should help her and her suffering, disabled parents. He constantly thought of the family and their meagre possessions in the little slum that would probably be Anam's home until death.

Many hours later the train stopped at Quetta station. It was around 6am. Pathan had dressed himself two hours earlier, prepared for what he knew would be his last steps of freedom. The restaurant staff made him aware that breakfast was being served. He remained in his sleeper cabin looking out onto the station. Rats, mice, feral cats and dogs ran all over the train lines below him. A group of ravenous wild animals were eating anything that didn't move. Carcasses of all descriptions were pounced upon. Nothing was spared from their destructive teeth, craving blood.

'Time to leave the train, sir. It is just after 7am. We shall be cleaning the compartments soon. Please exit the train. Thank you,' a deep male voice boomed at him through the wooden door. He had briefly fallen asleep again, fully clothed, upon the soft mattress of the single bed. He didn't know what day it was. The draft letter to his family and the pencil he was using had fallen onto the floor. This was the last time he would have to experience the intense anxiety of negotiating the security problems of walking past armed and vigilant police. Pathan, understandably, couldn't take any more. The constant anxiety had worn him down to a grovelling, half-witted person.

Other than the oblivious homeless people sleeping on the benches, commuters streamed onto the platforms like armies of ants. The same overpowering station smell instantly hit his senses. It was a kind of sickly sweetish smell - a mixture of toilet waste, rotting food, human odour and dead animals. With his eyes fixed firmly onto the ground, Pathan walked out of Quetta station and into the Zaughan Road outside. The old station, built in 1887, looked tired, dirty and in need of a coat of bright paint.

Due to the television warning and apprehensive of not being able to communicate in Pashto and Balochi Pathan was deterred from spending two nights in a nearby hostel. Instead, he convinced himself to head north-west, out of the city and beyond the suburbs, where he hoped to find a small village or an abandoned shack or cave where he could spend his last hours contemplating his miserable and wasted life. But the hills, and the far distant mountains near the border with Afghanistan, echoed their welcoming presence. He hoped and prayed that the boar, bear, ibex and other animals wouldn't judge him too harshly. After all, he would soon become their prey.

Before that, however, he needed to buy a sturdy pair of boots; his slick city leather shoes would prove useless on tough terrain. He also needed to pick up some essentials for his demise: a large bottle of brandy and several packets of strong painkillers would suffice. The poisonous chemicals were bought in a supermarket close to the station. It was a psychedelic painted place with countless CCTV cameras and flashing buzzing lights. Smart, young, confident students from the local University added to the confusion. He briefly looked at them all laughing and joking. How he wished he too could have once been a student of learning. How he hated the lot of them.

After buying all the items he needed he went to the store toilet, found a cubicle and changed into his new black boots. He threw his old shoes into a waste bin, put the pills and brandy in the rucksack and hastily left the hellish din behind.

It had emotionally exhausted him just to walk around and purchase what was necessary for the journey ahead. He realised that he had had enough of towns and cities. They were all the same: faceless and heartless. They degraded people to mere automatons, with no more value than the concrete that entombed them.

The last thing he needed to do before leaving was post his final heart rendering words of goodbye to his family. He had written several drafts before coming up with a final version in which he had tried to cover the story of events. He hoped the letter would provide them with a clearer, factual picture - unlike the news media stories that sensationalised the terrible sordid details of murder, sex and drugs in a middle-upper class leafy village in rural England. The thought of his suffering parents brought him to his knees for a few minutes.

'A large coffee, chicken kebab and two naans please,' he said to the old man behind the counter of a small cafe he had found after walking four miles out of the city. Here it was quiet. A few old men smoked and drank tea. They spoke occasionally. He still kept his diminishing minds' eye on the hills and mountains. The lofty peaks were never out of his sight, they represented total sanctuary - even though he knew he may never arrive there. Wherever he was right now he didn't know, nor bothered to ask. It was all the same at this stage. Racked by utter confusion, Pathan was hanging onto the last vestiges of life that clung to his frail failing body.

'A large bottle of water. Thanks,' he paid the man, who had large protruding stained yellow teeth resembling those of an ass, one eye and a shock of silver hair. He spoke fluent English.

'You English or Pakistani?' he asked Pathan.

'I'm English, I think, but forgotten really,' was his rambling response.

'What you doing in this deserted place?'

'Looking for wild animals to befriend. Take photographs if I can,' he incoherently answered.

'I wish you well my friend. Be careful of robbers,' he gave the water to Pathan who placed it into his rucksack. Before leaving the cafe he put on several more clothes underneath his shirts and robe. It was sunny most days in March, but in the evenings it could freeze. This part of Pakistan was at high altitude which could leave even the wild animals vulnerable and exposed to starvation. Yet the intrepid wanderer was unconcerned.

'Any buses round here that could take me nearer to the plains and hills?' Pathan asked.

'Just across the road, an old bus will take you to Quenton. It departs in two hours. It's about twenty miles on old dirt roads. That's the end of the line. From there on you have to walk. There's a few small villages from where you can get food, and probably accommodation. But please be careful, you could end up in big trouble on your own,' he explained. Foreboding racked the cafe owners' conscience. He thought he had a duty to express his misgivings about the young man's foolhardy journey.

Dirt track was an understatement. At times it seemed that the old bus – which was on its last legs if sight and sound were any indication - would be swallowed up by gigantic potholes. Passengers and goods regularly fell off seats and overhead storage. The majority who were standing stabilized the clapped-out bus. The bus, which had thirty seats, was carrying at least three times that number. Pathan took no notice, he was preoccupied with more important matters. Those dirt-poor people had no choice but to use the only means available to take them back home. Otherwise they'd need to walk many miles, where the possibility of being robbed, beaten and even killed was a constant threat.

Four hours later, the dilapidated bus, covered in mud, crawled into Quenton. What a great relief this was for his fellow passengers. But most didn't complain, who would listen? They had made the trip many times. He thought Ameen was the end of the world, but this place was just indescribable. A shack opposite the bus stop sold various drinks; it was a lifeline for Pathan as he was dehydrated after nearly suffocating from the stench of human sweat, old food and continuous chain-smoking. Three quick beers jolted his brain into action; he then left in a hurry on a dirt track leading out of the village with no idea where he was heading. That wasn't a problem. He could still see the sweeping plains, hills and mountains many miles in the distance. Although he wouldn't reach that far - he was convinced by his failing mind that it would be another five miles or so until he found secure surroundings where he could then commit suicide.

He continued walking south-west out of Quenton, instinct drove him on towards a remote place. The worn dirt track, used for centuries by people and animals, was ideal as it went through a large Banyan and Peepal forest. It gave cover from unwanted eyes and the biting wind which had descended rapidly. Pathan marched on towards his vague goal, occasionally stopping to listen to the strange sounds of wild animals, aware that dusk was no more than two hours away. After several miles he stopped. All was quiet in the wood. He felt that all the animals were watching and supporting him. They all wanted to witness the last few hours of his life. He felt the wild beasts instinctively congregate, knowing he deserved some recognition.

Half a mile off the main dirt track Pathan found several low-profile berry bushes. He crawled into them and made himself comfortable. This was the end of the line. He ate the remainder of his food. Being hunted like a dog was over. For many minutes he just sat still thinking of nothing in particular. Just before he reached for the rucksack to pull out the pills and bottle of brandy, a shining Buddha figure flashed vividly before him. He then eagerly swallowed all the contents of the small white packets - at least one hundred pills - and took large swigs of brandy until the bottle was empty. Very quickly he became unconscious. His carcass would thereafter supply wild scavenging animals, who were watching in anticipation, with fresh meat for several days. No one with a heart could deny it was the end to a tragic life. Tariq Pathan had died in the land of his heritage. He was permanently back home.

ACKNOWLEDGEMENTS

I am eternally grateful to Lis Bird who, over two years, has diligently and skilfully corrected three manuscripts of this book. Her support has been beyond the call of duty. Thank you so much.

My thanks to Tony Green for correcting my earlier work and suggesting various ideas to further this book.

Many thanks to the friendly and helpful staff at Woodingdean Library.

ABOUT THE AUTHOR

Barry Merchant was born in West Ewell, Surrey, in 1947. He was one of thirteen children from a working class background. After leaving school without qualifications, his life thereafter for many years was life-enhancing tramping and unskilled, frustrating work. Realising that he was woefully underdeveloped, he worked hard to gain BA (Hons) and MSc qualifications which led to a more fulfilling life. Buddhist practise empowered his personal growth and development. To date, he has written four books:

Seeking a New Voice (2013)

A Working Class Saga (2014)

A Quest for Self-discovery (2016)

A Web of Delusion (2019)